CW00929145

DANCE OF DEATH

HELEN MCCLOY

AGORA BOOKS

ABOUT THE AUTHOR

Helen McCloy was born in New York City in 1904 to writer Helen Worrell McCloy and managing editor William McCloy. After discovering a love for Sherlock Holmes as young girl, McCloy began writing her own mystery novels in the 1930s. In 1933, she introduced her psychiatrist-detective Dr Basil Willing in her first novel, *Dance of Death*. Dr Basil Willing features in 12 of McCloy's novels as well as several short stories; however, both are best known from McCloy's 1955 supernatural mystery *Through a Glass, Darkly* — hailed as her masterpiece and likened to John Dickson Carr.

McCloy went on in the 1950s and 1960s to co-author a review column a Connecticut newspaper. In 1950, she became the first female president of Mystery Writers of America and in 1953, she was honoured with an Edgar Award from the MWA for her critiques.

Better Off Dead

He Never Came Back

The Slayer and the Slain

Before I Die

Surprise, Surprise

The Further Side of Fear

Question of Time

A Change of Heart

The Sleepwalker

Minotaur Country

Cruel as the Grave

The Imposter

The Smoking Mirror

A DR BASIL WILLING MYSTERY

DANCE OF DEATH

HELEN MCCLOY

This edition published in 2020 by Agora Books

First published in 1938 by Heinemann

Agora Books is a division of Peters Fraser + Dunlop Ltd

55 New Oxford Street, London WC1A 1BS

To my mother

Persons of Interest in this **MYSTERY**...

KATHERINE JOCELYN

…slim, dark-eyed debutante, stepdaughter of Mrs Gerald Jocelyn, who has spent her life preparing for her debut — looking out for her complexion and figure, learning just enough French, dancing, and music to make her civilised without the taint of intellect.

RHODA JOCELYN

…Katherine's attractive, young-looking, beautifully dressed stepmother with a low, dulcet voice and crisp brown hair flecked with grey, whose general appearance of kindliness is spoiled when her face is turned and the obstinate line of her morbid mouth and shapeless lips is seen.

ANN JOCELYN CLAUDE

…grey-eyed, hollow-cheeked niece of Edgar Jocelyn, now secretary to Rhoda Jocelyn (Ann's mother had been a Jocelyn but was disowned when she married against the family's wishes).

EDGAR JOCELYN

…Katherine Jocelyn's tall, grey-haired uncle, her nearest relative, who has the pale Jocelyn eyes under black brows.

LUIS PASQUALE

…a South American artist who looks like a middle-aged faun who has forsaken Arcady for an air-conditioned drawing room, and has acquired a gloss and paunch in the process.

MRS JOWETT

…the popular social secretary for coming-out parties. She doesn't look clever but seems capable and reminds one of the motherly type of woman who inhabits sunny farm kitchens and hands out slices of freshly baked bread.

NICHOLAS DANINE

…the fantastically rich director of a German explosives company. He is of either Russian or Prussian descent but looks and talks like an Englishman.

PHILIP LEACH

…writer of a gossip column under the name of Lowell Cabot. He spent some time in Europe and returned to America on the same boat as the Jocelyns.

DR BASIL WILLING

...psychiatrist attached to the district attorney's office, has a thin-skinned temperament, is unusually sympathetic and living proof that a doctor to the mad must be slightly mad himself to understand his patients.

INSPECTOR FOYLE

...a small, compact, resilient man who regards the entire universe with the alert scepticism of a wire-haired terrier.

Objects of Interest in this **MYSTERY**...

- A black COAT from Paris
- Two engraved MENU cards
- A red chalk DRAWING
- A diamond RING
- A smelling-salts PHIAL
- An old khaki RAINCOAT
- An ADVERTISEMENT for a reducing treatment
- A sapphire-studded CIGARETTE CASE
- A signed CHEQUE
- A Bronx COCKTAIL

AUTHOR NOTE

All the human characters in this book are fictitious. But the most important character, thermol, or 2, 4 di-nitro-phenol, is taken from real life. No scientific knowledge is needed for the solution of the crime, beyond that which is given in the course of the narrative before the solution is reached.

ELSIE: how dark it grows! What are these paintings on the walls around?

PRINCE HENRY: The Dance of Death. All that go to and fro must look upon it.

—The Golden Legend

1

FRONTISPIECE

The snow began to fall Tuesday, about cocktail time — huge flakes whirling spirally in a north wind. By six o'clock the next morning, in the middle of the street the snow was packed hard and stamped with interlacing tire patterns. On the pavement it was fine and powdery, piled in smooth drifts by the wind. On roofs and cars it had hardened to a crusty, white glaze. And it was still falling.

It was only natural that Butch and Buddy should be on the list of men "available for snow removal". They had been working on a street-repair project that was held up by the storm.

Earlier that morning a plough had pushed most of the snow into gutters. But the wind had blown fresh snow on top of this, until it towered in mounds. Their job was to shovel it into the truck, for there were not enough loading machines. The north wind cut like a knife. Buddy shivered and paused in his shovelling. He began to dig again, and his shovel struck something solid. He frowned and tried another place. Again the shovel stuck. There was no scraping sound. It couldn't be asphalt. It was something hot as well as solid. He kicked away the snow — and blinked.

There was no light but the faint radiance of dawn that made everything look unreal. Was he seeing this? He crouched and touched something with his bare fingers — something rigid as a board. Then he screamed.

Butch came running.

"There's a stiff in the snow!" sobbed Buddy.

"Pipe down! Ain't it natural to get froze stiff on a night like this?"

"B-but it ain't froze!" Buddy choked. "It's — *hot*!"

2

GROTESQUE

D r Basil Willing, psychiatrist attached to the district attorney's office, lived in an antiquated house at the unfashionable end of Park Avenue, below Grand Central. After dinner, next evening, he was settled in the living room with General Archer, the Police Commissioner.

Firelight made the glass doors of the bookcases glitter and brought a faint blush to the white panelling. Juniper, a soft-spoken Baltimore man, who has been with Basil Willing since Johns Hopkins days, served the Commissioner with coffee and brandy, murmuring hospitably, "Help yourself, sir, help yourself!"

When he had gone, there was no sound but the whispering of the fire and the distant hooting of motor horns. General Archer twirled his big, bell-shaped glass, frowned, and continued an argument that had flared up at dinner.

"I don't know what you mean — there's no place of psychology in detection. Police work deals with physical facts — nasty facts like dried bloodstains, greasy fingerprints, and

17

microscopic bits of dirt under a dead man's nails. In half our murder cases we have no way of identifying the body at the beginning. It isn't like detective stories where a man gets murdered in his own library while there are a dozen convenient suspects in the house.

"When we start out, we hardly even know who anybody is — murderer, suspects, or victim. We want a biologist or a chemist on the trail — not a psychologist... Why, just this morning — Did the evening papers have anything about a girl's body found in the snow on 78th Street?"

Deliberately, Basil rose and scanned the newspaper on the table. Tall and lean, he moved at a measured pace that was the antithesis of "hustle". His mother had been Russian and that accounted for many things — among them his thin-skinned temperament, more sympathetic, irritable, and intuitive than that of nationalities on whom the shell of civilisation has had time to harden. He was a living proof of the theory that a successful doctor to the mad must be slightly mad himself in order to understand his patients.

"Let me see..." Like most people who speak several other languages, his English was distinct and unslurred. "Three cases of death from exposure last night. An unemployed man. A street walker. And the unidentified body of a girl. No details."

"That's the one. The girl. Only she didn't die from exposure. We kept the details from the papers purposely." Archer finished his brandy. "We have absolutely no clue to her identity and I ask you what good psychology—"

"How did she die?"

Archer was lighting one of Basil's cigarettes. He inhaled deeply before he answered, "Heat stroke."

"But — that's impossible!"

18

"That's the trouble with police work. The impossible is always happening. The body was found about six this morning by men shovelling snow. Remember how cold it was? The body was lying under the snow and there were no footprints, so it must have been there some time. But the men swear it was hot when they found it. Not just warm, but hot as a fever patient. By the time the precinct men got there it was still warm. They call it the 'Red Hot Momma Case'."

"They would!"

"Inspector Foyle got an assistant medical examiner to do an autopsy at once. Just before I left the office this evening, Foyle brought me a preliminary report. A lot of technical gibberish about being unable to assign the exact cause of death, and then he says: '*the condition of the internal organs, especially the lungs, heart and liver, strikingly resembles that in cases of death from heat stroke*'." Archer snorted. "Heat stroke! And it was nine above zero last night! The thing's grotesque!"

"I'm not so sure." Basil picked up the poker unhurriedly and frowned at the logs as he pushed them apart. "You say it was lying *under* the snow? A deep snowdrift conserves heat. Ice forms a thinner layer than usual on a lake protected by snow, because the snow keeps the water warm. Some Inuit build shelters of snow to keep warm. If this dead body were unusually hot to start with the snow might delay its cooling."

"But how could it get unusually hot to start with?" demanded Archer. "People can't get heat stroke on a winter night!"

"I don't suppose your doctor meant to say that the girl died of heat stroke. He was just using the term to describe her condition. What about chemical analysis?"

"No results so far." Archer sighed. "The laboratory fellows can always tell you what a thing isn't. But they can't always tell you what it is."

"Then you'll have to fall back on psychology."

"But psychology couldn't possibly help when we don't even know who the girl is! That's the point."

"Are there no clues at all?"

"Precious few. She was about twenty, the doctors say, and a virgin. Rather unusual face — grey eyes, dark hair and lashes. No one fitting her description is listed at the Missing Persons Bureau. Her fingerprints are not on file. Her teeth have never been filled. Her nails are absolutely clean, except for a trace of soap — it might be any soap. Her clothes are poor quality — the sort of thing that's turned out by the gross. Mass production is the modern detective's biggest handicap. Her coat is poor stuff, too, but it has a French label — *Bazar* something or other. No laundry marks. It's a pity so many police reporters have told the world we keep a file of six thousand laundry marks."

"No signs of violence?"

"None, except two marks made after death — the shovel of the man who found her struck the body in digging."

Basil laid down the poker gently. "I'd like to talk with the fellow who did the autopsy."

Archer's eyes twinkled in the firelight. "I thought you told me your official duties consisted in answering just one question: '*Say, doc, is this guy nuts?*'"

Basil smiled. "Perhaps I might see this man unofficially."

"All right. But remember — one good fingerprint is worth all the psychology in the world!"

"Every criminal leaves psychic fingerprints." Basil was still smiling. "And he can't wear gloves to hide them."

"You're incurable!" Archer rose to go. At the door he paused. "One thing I forgot to mention — if you're really interested. When the medical examiner washed off the girl's make-up, he found the face underneath stained yellow. Not suntan, but a canary yellow. Odd, isn't it?"

3

NUDE

"Dr Wiling? From the district attorney's office? The
Commissioner phoned you'd be here this morning. My
name's Dalton, assistant medical examiner. I did the autopsy."
The brisk, business-like young doctor was chewing gum. He
trotted down a corridor, and Basil ambled after him. The room
they entered was bare and chill, smelling of disinfectant.
"Number seventeen, Sam!" called Dr Dalton.

"Okay," responded the attendant.

"All there but the viscera and the brain." Dalton's jaws
moved rhythmically.

The first thing Basil noticed was the extreme thinness of
the nude girl. The dead face was free of make-up, and a vivid
yellow stain covered it as far as the throat, ending in an irregular line. The rest of the skin was a warm ivory. The vacant
eyes were grey, pale in contrast to feathery black lashes, and
black brows plucked to a diagonal line like the brows of a
Javanese doll. Muslin bands were about the abdomen where
incisions had been made for the autopsy.

Basil began to analyse the face according to the method

originated by Bertillon, through which a French policeman learns to recognise a face he has never seen from a spoken description: "General contour — oval. Profile — rectilinear. Nose — root depth, short; tip, pointed; nostrils, distended; partition, well-defined…"

Suddenly, he paused. In life, this face had been beautiful. The dull grey eyes had been shining. The dry, parted lips had curved deliciously when they smiled.

Why was he so sure? Slowly, there rose in his mind a conviction that he had seen this face before. But where? The girl was too young to be anyone he had known long ago. Yet if he had met recently, why couldn't he recall her?

He lifted one of the limp hands. Long-fingered, narrow at the knuckles, soft and well-kept. Cuticle, unbroken. Nails, oval. Not the hand of a woman who did her own washing. Yet there were no laundry marks.

"Say," broke in Sam, "couldn't that there yeller stain be a kinda disguise-like?"

Dalton shook his head. "It's internal. The conjunctivae are yellow and all the internal secretions. At first I thought it might be jaundice. But some of the other symptoms didn't fit. All the signs of heat stroke were there — congestion and oedema of the lungs, scatter ecchymoses in various organs, separation of liver lobules, renal tubular degeneration, and marked fragmentation of the heart muscle."

"Painful," said Basil. He studied the jaws. "No fillings. No caries. Only the rich care for their teeth like that."

"But her clothes were cheap!" protested Dalton.

"That's just the point. Are they still here?"

"Yes, sir," said Sam. "Shall I get 'em?"

"Please."

Basil studied the shabby, black dress with touches of green

at neck and wrists, the high-heeled papery shoes, and the flimsy rayon under things. There were not in bad taste, but they were all machine-made and shoddy.

"She doesn't look like a girl who would dress like that." He turned to the coat — a coarse, black cloth with no fur. In the lining was a label: *Bazar de l'Hôtel de Ville.* "That's the most inexpensive department store in Paris," he remarked. "I wish I could see your full report."

Dr Dalton shifted his gum to the other cheek. "I'll send you a carbon if you like."

"Thanks. I suppose you're testing the viscera for poison?"

"Not me. Lambert, the city toxicologist, has that job."

Basil looked up. "Not 'Piggy' Lambert?"

"They call him 'Piggy'. Know him?"

"Yes — if he's the 'Piggy' I mean. Where's his lab?"

"Bellevue."

Outside, a pale sun cast light without heat on snow piled two feet high in the gutters. Basil breasted the north wind as he walked the short distance from the mortuary to the hospital. He had not come in contact with the city toxicologist before. His work for the district attorney consisted chiefly in testing the sanity of accused men and the reliability of witnesses. But he recalled vaguely having seen the name "Dr Lambert" in newspaper accounts of murder cases. Could it be the "Piggy" Lambert he had known at Johns Hopkins? Years of study in Paris and Vienna had left Basil out of touch with friends of student days.

"I'm from the district attorney's office. Where can I find Dr Lambert?"

"Fourth floor."

The laboratory wasn't very large or very new. The walls were splashed with acid. Chairs and tables were stained and scarred. The only clean, bright things here were the micro-scopes, scales, separators, and other instruments.

Just then a man at the other end of the laboratory looked up. "Basil Willing! Well, I'll be…"

It was Piggy, all right, looking more like a pink and white hog than ever. Lambert tipped a volume off a kitchen chair onto the floor and pushed the chair toward Basil.

"I read that blasted book of yours," he informed Basil. "You might just as well be an astrologist or a snake doctor. How long were you in Vienna? Six weeks?"

"I was in Paris, London, and Vienna nearly eight years."

"Expatriate, eh? Well, let me tell you the Freudian theory is absolutely repudiated by the medical profession in this coun-try! And don't smoke! Just like a psychologist to pull out matches the minute he gets in a lab!"

"Still the same old Piggy with the same old charm of manner!" Basil put away his cigarette case. "Not so very long ago the medical profession was 'repudiating' the germ theory."

"That's different!"

"Oh, yeah?" returned Basil, proving that he was not an expatriate. "I didn't come in here to talk psychology. I came to get information about one of your cases."

"Which one?"

"Girl whose body was found in the snow — still warm."

"Oh, the 'Red Hot Momma Case'. What do you want to know?"

"Cause of death."

"Frankly, I haven't the remotest idea — yet." Lambert thumbed rapidly through a pile of typewritten reports on the table. "Most poisoners are so conservative. They stick to the old stand-bys — arsenic, morphine, strychnine, cyanide, or hyoscine. So we get in a rut, and when anything new comes along we're stumped. Here's a copy of Dalton's report on the autopsy. What do you make of it?"

Basil glanced at the first page and sighed. "Autopsy reports always remind me of the doctor who said: *'What a beautiful ulcer!'* Just listen: *'Cut section surface of left lung — purplish red… kidney surface smooth, medium reddish brown… liver grass green… spleen a rich, dark purple… bile, pale, golden yellow…'* Who would ever suspect Dalton of such aesthetic enthusiasm? Could it be some liver poison? Chloroform? Or phosphorus?"

"I thought of that. But some things — like the marked destruction of blood cells — aren't in the picture. The anaemia, thinness and enlargement of the spleen rather suggest chronic malaria. But though malaria makes the skin dark and sallow, I never heard of it turning the face canary yellow and leaving the rest of the body a normal colour."

"And though malaria causes high fever it could scarcely account for the extraordinary heat of the body after death," added Basil.

"Nothing I can think of offhand would account for that!" admitted Lambert. "Heat stroke in December! It's just screwy!"

Basil was looking at a photograph of the dead girl clipped to the report. "It's queer, but I've a hunch I've seen this girl somewhere before."

Lambert stared. "That," he said, "is damned queer. Because I have the same hunch myself. She makes me think of surf-riding, and I don't know why. I haven't been to the seashore for years."

.   .   .

DURING HIS SOLITARY DINNER, Basil's thoughts turned to the dead girl's face, with its wide, grey eyes and long, black lashes. As a rule, he could climb through the jungle of associated ideas with the agility of a monkey until he traced a thought or memory to its lair. But tonight he was tired. The memory of that tantalising face seemed always just ahead of him. Then, when he pounced, it slid out of his mental grasp, as if snatched away by a physical force with a will of its own opposed to his. Once again he realised that the unconscious mind is not a mere word or convention, but something living and human.

After dinner, Basil went into the living room and sat down in a wing chair. He closed his eyes and tried to concentrate. At last the word *magazine* floated into his mind. He saw dozens of magazines every week. Mostly scientific journals that had little to do with girls. Or surf-riding. "Juniper! Where is that old magazine you were reading Sunday? The one with the girl riding a surfboard on the cover?"

Juniper stared. "Why, it's in the kitchen, sir."

It was the May number of a sensational fiction magazine. The surf-rider wore a scarlet bathing suit and she was as blonde as a daffodil. She did not resemble the dead girl in any way.

Basil glanced at the illustrations inside. Then, the advertisements. Why should he connect the dead girl's face with this magazine? He turned it over and looked at the advertisement on the back cover. There she was — a photograph in colours showing her just as he had imagined her in life. The wide, grey eyes black-lashed. The diagonal black brows. The hollow cheeks. The smooth waves of dark hair. And the skin a warm ivory with no hint of a yellow stain.

Of course it was difficult to be sure. He was comparing a

dead face with the photograph of a living one. But the picture showed her face at three-quarters — the best angle for identification.

Like all women in advertisements, she was inhumanly sleek and slim. She had been photographed in evening dress — a deep, cream colour that seemed to be satin. Her only ornament was a long rope of pearls — fabulous had they been real. But of course they couldn't be real in an advertisement.

Poor girl! What a rotten life it must have been selling her face and figure and seeing them blazoned on every magazine and billboard. But doubtless she had no choice. At last, Basil read the words printed below the picture:

Miss Catharine Jocelyn, lovely debutante daughter of Mrs Gerald Jocelyn of New York and Paris, whose coming-out party this winter promises to be the most brilliant event of the season. Miss Jocelyn — 'Kitty' to her intimates — is famous for her svelte and willowy figure. Read what she has to say about SVELTIS:

"I like SVELTIS because it's ABSOLUTELY SAFE. Now I've begun to reduce the SVELTIS WAY, I can eat all the chocolates and marshmallows I like without counting calories. And never has my skin had such a rose-petal glow, for SVELTIS is not only harmless, it's a tonic and beautifier as well! (signed) Catharine Jocelyn."

Basil read on, fascinated by the bland, hypnotic insistence of the advertisement copy writer's style:

Why not be modern and keep slim with SVELTIS, the reducing method of the sophisticate? No diet! No massage! No tedious exercises! Just slip a SVELTIS tablet in your *evening cocktail and you'll never have a 'spare-tire-waist' or 'balloon hips!' SVELTIS comes in a luxurious, modernistic bottle. Boudoir Size:--$10.00. Pocket Size:--$7.50.*

At the bottom of the page was a trademark — a smiling, but anonymous young man whose high-necked white overall and binocular microscope proved that he was a scientist. And the mystic rune:

Science Says SVELTIS Is the Sane Way to Reduce!
Based on an Old Persian Beauty Secret!

4

ILLUSTRATION FOR ADVERTISEMENT

The Police Commissioner was glancing through some letters, his cheeks still pink from their morning shave. "Well, what did Dalton say?"

Basil made himself comfortable in an armchair. "Have you seen the body?"

"I saw photographs."

Basil took the Sveltis advertisement out of his briefcase.

"Good Lord! What an extraordinary resemblance! And I never noticed it!"

"Resemblance? It's the same girl."

"But that's impossible."

"Why?"

"Because this Miss Jocelyn is still alive."

The commissioner pressed a key and spoke into the inter-office telephone. "Evarts, have we Wednesday's *Times*?"

When the paper came, Archer turned to the social page, folded it, and handed it across the desk to Basil. There was another photograph — black and white this time:

Miss Katherine Jocelyn, who made her debut last evening at a dance given by her stepmother, Mrs Gerald Jocelyn... Most brilliant party of the year... nothing like it since 1929... white velvet with the Jocelyn pearls... lavish decorations in an original colour scheme of pink and mauve including roses, sweet peas, violets and branches of lilac blossom... two famous dance orchestras... three supper rooms and a bar...

There followed a long list of guests.

Basil handed the paper back to Archer. "So this girl's party took place the night the body was found?"

"Exactly. The body was found just before dawn Wednesday while Kitty Jocelyn was dancing at her coming-out party. I know because my own niece was there. You see, Willing—" Archer's indulgence was almost patronising "—you've been working hard since you came back to America, and you've been living like a hermit. I don't suppose you ever read fashion magazines or gossip columns, do you?"

Basil smiled faintly. "I can't say I do."

"If you did, you'd know all about Kitty Jocelyn."

The Commissioner relaxed like a lecturer sure of his subject. "Rhoda Jocelyn, her stepmother, is a widow. Until now they've lived abroad. Paris, Rome, Cannes and so forth. But last spring pictures began appearing in newspapers and magazines over here: '*Miss Jocelyn wearing a hat from So-and-So... Miss Jocelyn wearing a Tel-à-Tel dress.*' You couldn't turn round without seeing her. It was epidemic."

"No wonder Lambert thought the face familiar! When did she reach this country?"

"Oh, she and her stepmother arrived this autumn — just a few weeks ago and opened the old Jocelyn house in the Sixties where the party was held. That was her first public appearance and I have it on the authority of my niece Isobel that she is an eyeful. Of course there can't be any connection between that poor, little weed who was found in the snow, and a hothouse flower like Kitty Jocelyn."

"Why not?"

"My dear fellow!" Archer was shocked. "You know as well as I do that people of — er — well, wealth and standing and education don't get mixed up in murder cases!"

"Don't they?" Basil's slow smile was charged with meaning. "Ever hear of Prince Youssoupoff, Madame Caillaux, Count Bocarme, Lord Ferrers or the Marquise de Brinvilliers?"

"All foreigners," muttered Archer.

"Then what about Professor Webster of Harvard? And Harry Thaw? And Edward S Stokes? Murder is a quite irrepressible gate-crasher."

"But this Miss Jocelyn is still alive!" repeated Archer.

"Then why not question her? The dead girl may be a relative."

Archer's fingers drummed a tattoo on the desk. He shook his head. "Willing, you know we can't question a girl as carefully guarded as that on the strength of a chance resemblance!"

"Carefully guarded? From what you say, she sounds like a well-advertised commodity."

"And if the dead girl were a relative of the Jocelyns, they would have come to us already and reported her missing. I can't bother people like that unless I have something more tangible to go on."

Basil rose with a sigh. "There's one rather curious name in that list of guests at the party. Nicholas Danine."

"He arrived on the Queen Mary three weeks ago."

"On business?"

"Oh, no! His secretary told the ship news reporters that his visit to America was strictly personal and had nothing to do with finance or politics."

"And the reporters, like good boys, believed everything the secretary told them?"

"We-ell." Archer moved restlessly under Basil's gaze. "Come to think of it, there is an absurd rumour that he's going to marry Kitty Jocelyn. Probably nothing in it, and yet — he was at the dance and he's a bit old for debutante parties. Between forty and fifty, I should say."

"Old?" Basil laughed. "I'm between forty and fifty myself, Archer. We dodderers do get these senile caprices for very young girls sometimes. And when there's a scheming mother in the background — or a stepmother..." He finished the sentence with a shrug.

"Well, it has nothing to do with me!" cried Archer, impatiently. "If you like you can see Inspector Foyle and show him that Sveltis advertisement. But I warn you, we can't do anything without more evidence."

"And how are you going to get more evidence if you don't do anything?" asked Basil sweetly.

ASSISTANT CHIEF INSPECTOR Patrick Foyle was the officer in command of the Detective Division at this time. A small, compact, resilient man, he regarded the entire universe with the alert scepticism of a wire-haired terrier. Though he and Basil disagreed on many subjects, they were friends.

"Huh!" exclaimed Foyle when he saw the Sveltis advertisement. "I've seen lots of queer things in my life. But that's about the queerest yet."

"What are you going to do about it?"

"What can I do if the Commissioner says, 'Hands off'? You can't question people like the Jocelyns unless you have a strong case, and a resemblance isn't evidence. Of course if this Jocelyn dame were missing it would be different. As it is, we've just got to wait and see what the men who're trying to trace the body can pick up."

"Did you make inquiries where the body was found?"

Foyle grinned expansively. "We may not be psychologists here in Centre Street, doc, but we thought of that one, too! A private watchman in the neighbourhood saw a 1936 Buick sedan parked at 79th and Fifth around 3:30 am. But — well — how many 1936 Buick sedans do you suppose there are in this country? Sergeant Samson questioned the watchman. Of course he didn't get the license number. Said he couldn't see it because the snow was falling. He only noticed the car because the lights were turned off and he couldn't understand anyone parking a car outdoors at 3 am in such a blizzard. At first, he thought it was empty. Then he saw someone moving inside the car. He said he thought it was one of those necking parties. Not being a cop, he let it alone, and a few minutes later the car drove away."

Basil made one more effort.

In the Criminal Courts annex he found Morris Sobel, the district attorney, indulging in a press conference. The big, shabby office was filled with irreverent young men, who wore their hats on the back of their heads. Some of them carried cameras and knelt on the floor to get the Sobel profile at the most effective angle. At a little distance, the scene looked like a religious ritual. Though not religious, it was a ritual. Every few months Sobel received the press and told them racke-teering was a thing of the past. And a week or so later, the press would announce that racketeers had entered a new field. Sobel was always in a blithe humour after one of these press conferences. But his face lengthened as he listened to Basil's story.

"My dear Willing, stick to your last, and leave detecting to the detectives! I'm certainly not going to badger a very charming heiress just because she happens to look like a little waif on a slab in the mortuary!"

Basil had a small office of his own in the district attorney's suite. He sat down at his desk trying to concentrate on the analysis of an association test he had made a few days before in another case. But that pale face with the wide, grey eyes and black lashes came between him and the calculations he was making.

He threw down his pen and stared at the dreary walls beyond his window without seeing them. A dim recollection was stirring in his mind. He reached for the telephone and gave the number of the hospital where he was chief of the psychiatric clinic.

"Dr Bartlett, please... Hello, Fred? What was that new drug you mentioned as a possible cure for schizophrenia? Something that increases the rate of basal metabolism. You said it was sometimes used as a basis for reducing medicines... I see. I suppose it's fatal in large doses? ... Thanks."

He replaced the receiver for a moment, and then called Lambert. "Piggy, I've an idea about that case we talked over yesterday. I haven't time to explain now but look up the *Annales de Physiologie Physico-Chimie Biologiques* for 1932 and you'll get the idea. Volume 8, page 117."

.   .   .

35

FRIDAY EVENING A PERFORMANCE of *Sadko* tempted Basil into the extravagance of an orchestra seat, for he loved the music of his mother's heritage. Only three rows in front of him sat General Archer with his wife and niece. The General looked as if he would rather have been dozing over his evening paper, Mrs Archer looked as if she would rather have been playing contract, and Isobel Archer, thin and nervous, looked as if she would rather have been at a Harlem night club. But Mrs Archer was "bringing out" this niece from Boston in New York that winter and opera was part of the "bringing out" process. They sat through it as they sat through the sermon on Sundays — the General half asleep, Mrs Archer planning her new winter wardrobe, and Isobel — well, even a psychiatrist cannot be absolutely sure what a girl of Isobel's age and character thinks about. But without being unduly Freudian, Basil was prepared to hazard that her thoughts were not wholly unrelated to the opposite sex.

During the first intermission, he spoke to them, slipping into a temporarily vacant seat beside Isobel.

"I wish you'd take me to Harlem when this is over," she said, promptly, and Basil smiled at finding his diagnosis correct in one particular anyway. "Those people have the right idea!" she went on. "They're leaving already. I wonder who they are? Fourth box from this end. Why, I do believe it's Kitty Jocelyn!"

"Where?" Basil turned with a celerity unusual in him, but the box was empty.

"That Dr Willing asked me something awfully queer," chattered Isobel as the Archers were driving home. "He wanted to know if anything out of the ordinary happened at Kitty Jocelyn's dance the other evening. As if anything out of the ordinary could happen at a coming-out party!"

. . .

WHEN BASIL ENTERED his office Saturday morning, he found the district attorney inquiring for him. There was a shade of embarrassment in Morris Sobel's manner.

"Hello!" He grinned self-consciously. "You win! Remember that body found in the snow? There is some connection with Miss Jocelyn after all. I'd like you to come into my office. There's a — a girl in there. A friend of the Commissioner's niece. I don't know just what to make of her story. It's fantastic. And scandalous, if true. I'm hoping she's mentally unsound, and I want you to do your stuff."

"Hoping?"

"We-ell, not exactly hoping. But it would save me a lot of unpopularity in high places if she were suffering from a 'nervous breakdown'. That's what you call it when they're rich, isn't it?"

Basil followed Sobel down a corridor into his private office. General Archer was already there, and with him was Inspector Foyle. By the big window stood a girl with her back to the room. She was excessively thin, and dressed in black, except for pearl stockings and a ripple of chinchilla on her shoulders.

A tawny little Pekinese spaniel pattered toward Basil. "Kai Lung! Come here!" She spoke with a slightly foreign intonation. The dog paid no attention. As she turned from the window, Basil started.

It was uncanny. The hollow cheeks, the slanting brows, the eyes grey as smoked crystal, and startlingly pale under black lashes — only two days ago he had seen this face at the mortuary, relaxed in death and disfigured by a vivid, yellow stain. Now it was alive, the skin a clear, healthy ivory, the lips painted scarlet.

"This is Dr Willing — Miss Jocelyn," said Sobel.

The girl pouted. "Not Jocelyn! Claude. I've told you at least twenty times that my name is Ann Jocelyn Claude!"

5

STUDY FOR FAMILY GROUP

"There can't be three of you!" cried Basil.

"Three?" The girl stared. "Three what?"

"Three girls who look so much alike."

"Who said anything about a third girl?"

The dog looked at the door as though he expected someone else. But no one came. He began to whimper. "Be quiet, Kai Lung!" But the dog continued to whimper. "There are only two girls who look alike. I, and my cousin, Kitty Jocelyn."

"Where is Kitty Jocelyn now?" asked Basil. "That's what I've come to ask you."

Sobel switched on the inter-office telephone and instructed a stenographer in the next room to take notes of the conversation. "Now, Miss — er — Claude, please go over your whole story from the very beginning. And omit no details. However irrelevant they seem they may have bearing on the case."

"I think this chair is the most comfortable." Basil pushed a leather armchair close to the district attorney's desk, so she had to cross the room to reach it. She thanked him with a smile, not realising he had done so in order to study her gait and gestures.

39

"Is one allowed to smoke here?" Without waiting for an answer, she took out a case filled with fat, oval cigarettes. As she bent her head to Basil's match, he watched the reaction of her pupils to the flame.

"Thanks." As she leaned back, her glance fell on the dog. "I hope you don't mind my bringing Kai Lung. I just couldn't leave him with Aunt Rhoda. He was Kitty's dog, and now she has disappeared."

"Disappeared!" interrupted Basil. "Why wasn't the Missing Persons Bureau notified?"

Ann lowered long lashes and lifted them. "The circumstances were — peculiar."

"If you'd only begin at the beginning!" pleaded Sobel.

"But that's so hard, isn't it? Because nothing ever really has a beginning. There's always something before that and something before that and so on. That's why modern authors always begin in the middle, though I do think it's awfully confusing, and I never get the characters straightened out afterward. This business of Kitty's disappearance began as a joke."

"A *joke*?" Basil was thinking of that body in the mortuary. "When did you last see your cousin?"

"The night of her coming-out party. Tuesday."

Sobel looked meaningfully at Basil. The body had been found in the snow early Wednesday morning.

"You spoke of an Aunt Rhoda," said Basil. "Do you live with your cousin and her stepmother?"

"I've only been with them the last four months. I never even saw them before then. You see, my mother married a poor man — Andrew Claude, the biological chemist, and—"

"Of course!" cried Basil.

"Oh, then you've heard of him!" She was pleased. "It makes me so cross the way people have always heard of the

Jocelyns (who never did anything but collar a lot of money), while nobody seems to have heard of Daddy who was worth all the Jocelyns put together! Of course he was much too high-brow to make any money, and Grandfather Jocelyn disapproved the marriage and left all his money to his two sons — Uncle Gerald, Kitty's father, and Uncle Edgar. Daddy died when I was thirteen and mother and I settled on the Riviera because living was cheap there."

Ann paused and looked about for an ash tray. "Thanks." She flicked the ash into the bronze tray Basil took from Sobel's desk. "My mother died last July. About the same time stocks went down and the little bit of money Daddy had left melted away. I didn't know what to do until I happened to see that Mrs Gerald Jocelyn and her daughter were at a hotel in Cannes. I hadn't even known they were in Europe — my mother was so completely cut off from her own family. But I took my courage in both hands and went straight to Aunt Rhoda and asked her if Uncle Gerald could get me a job in America. She told me he had died years ago and that she and Kitty had been living in Europe ever since. I'd heard some funny things about Aunt Rhoda. My mother used to say she was an adventuress who had 'captured poor Gerald' and all that sort of thing. But she really wasn't a bit like that. She was awfully attractive and young looking and beautifully dressed. And kind, too, because she took me on as her secretary. I don't know typing or short-hand, but she said she wanted someone to write social notes by hand when Kitty came out in New York that next winter. I was only too glad to do it for board and passage to America. If she hadn't helped me, I don't know what I could have done. The understanding was that I'd be free to look for a real job in New York as soon as the coming-out business was over.

"We spent the summer in Cannes and sailed in November.

The last few weeks we've been living in a house on Fifth Avenue that Grandfather Jocelyn left to Uncle Gerald. It has a ballroom, so Aunt Rhoda decided to have Kitty's party there, instead of going to a hotel. It was like getting ready for a big home wedding only a million times worse. There were people in and out of the house all the time."

At this point, Inspector Foyle interrupted. "I hope, Miss Claude, you'll be able to give us a list of all the people who came to the house the day your cousin disappeared. If possible, I'd like to know exactly what time each one came and left."

The wide, grey eyes gazed at him helplessly. "You've never had a coming-out party have you, Inspector?"

"I — er—" Foyle reddened. "Naturally not!"

"Oh, I'm not trying to be funny! I just meant that you don't know what it's like the day of the party — especially if you're having it at home. There's the caterer and his men, and the florist and his men, and two orchestra leaders and their men. Then there's a social secretary and her secretary, and messenger boys bringing flowers from friends and relatives, and one or two old friends who drop in to see if they can help, and one or two reporters hovering around in hope of copy and all the household servants in a dither. There were heaps of complete strangers dashing in and out all day! I couldn't begin to tell you when they came or when they left!"

"You'd better tell us whatever you can remember," said the district attorney. "Right through the day from the beginning."

"Well, I had breakfast in bed, but I don't know exactly what time it was. Then I took Aunt Rhoda's letters into her bedroom while she ate her own breakfast. After that, she and I drove to the bank to get Grandmother Jocelyn's pearls, for Kitty to wear that evening. She was out walking then with Victorine, Aunt Rhoda's maid. Afterward, we three lunched together — Aunt Rhoda, Kitty and me. And after luncheon, Victorine gave Kitty a massage, finger wave, manicure and so forth. Victorine's an artist at make-up. Victorine was the first person who told me I looked like Kitty. Of course I knew all along that we were about the same height and weight and shape — Kitty sometimes gave me her dresses when she got tired of them. And I could see we'd both inherited the Jocelyn colouring — grey eyes, black hair, and sallow skin. But I never realised that our faces were alike until Victorine said so. I had long, straight hair and rather thick eyebrows, while Kitty's hair was short and thinned and waved, and her eyebrows plucked to a fine line. That makes a lot of difference. I don't believe anyone but an expert like Victorine would have noticed that Kitty and I had the same features underneath all that."

"Surely your hair is short now?" Basil peered at the confused planes of the little black hat.

"Oh, yes — *now*." She snatched off the hat. Short, dark hair clung in smooth waves to a small head. "But I never bothered to have my hair cut or my eyebrows shaped in France. The upkeep is too expensive, and we never went to parties there or anything like that."

"When did you have your hair cut?"

"Tuesday — the night of the party. I didn't really want to, but Kitty said—"

"Suppose you take the events of the day in order."

"That's just what I was trying to do when you interrupted! Let me see now..." She pressed her fingertips to her forehead. "The next thing I remember is Mrs Jowett coming in with snowflakes all over her furs."

"Mrs Jowett?"

"Oh, dear, I'm afraid I'm telling this very badly! Mrs Jowett is the social secretary. She's terribly expensive, but you've just got to have her. She's *the* social secretary. I spent some time helping her sort out belated acceptances and regrets, and answering telephone calls for her — mostly photographers who wanted to take Kitty's picture, and reporters who wanted information about the party. You see a social secretary is a sort of campaign manager and press agent rolled into one.

"Where was I? Oh, yes. A little after six o'clock cocktails were served in the Murillo Room. It's really just a living room, but it's called the Murillo Room because they have the most ghastly marshmallow Madonna there by Murillo. Grandfather Jocelyn furnished the house so you can imagine what it's like. Not even one Cezanne, and of course no moderns.

"I went downstairs with Mrs Jowett. There were several people in the Murillo Room. Luis Pasquale, the South American artist, was shuddering every time he looked at that Madonna. Luis never paints anything but nudes, bottles, and guitars. He was always hanging around Aunt Rhoda in Cannes and he followed her over here.

"Then there was another of the old Cannes lot — Nicholas Danine. He's fantastically rich, but it's something horrible — poison gas or liquid fire. He lives in Europe, has a *château* near Beaulieu. Some people say he's Russian and some say he's Prussian, and yet he looks and talks like an Englishman.

"After a while Kitty came in, and then Aunt Rhoda with a grey-haired man she called Edgar. I knew it must be Uncle Edgar Jocelyn, though I had never seen him. Aunt Rhoda went to his office downtown when we first reached America, but he hadn't come to the house before. I thought of asking him for a job. But I simply didn't dare go near him. He looked so cross. He didn't recognise me, and no one introduced us.

"I must explain that none of these people ever noticed me particularly. I was both shabby and poor. I'm sure Aunt Rhoda and Kitty and Mrs Jowett were the only ones in the room who were really conscious of my existence.

"We were all tired and the cocktails were very welcome when Gregg — the butler — brought them in. Only Mrs Jowett and Danine chose sherry. Kitty was restless. I remember her wandering about the room, glass in hand, looking at cards on the flowers people had sent. There were so many they were all over the first and second floors and the air was heavy with their scent. Mrs Jowett complained of the stuffiness and made Gregg open a window.

"We were in the middle of our cocktails when Gregg announced Philip Leach. He was on the boat coming over and I suppose he really came to pick up some extra stuff about the dance for his column. He writes a gossip column for one of the New York newspapers under the name Lowell Cabot. Aunt Rhoda makes up to him because she's scared to death for fear he'll print something nasty about her and Pasquale.

"Some time after that Victorine, who's rather a privileged character, slipped into the room to tell Kitty that the dress she was going to wear that evening had come back from the dress-maker who had been altering it. And then the party broke up. Nobody seemed to need me, and I went upstairs to my own room and lay down and read. Oh, dear, it does take a long time to tell all this, doesn't it?"

"Have another cigarette," suggested Basil, soothingly.

"Thanks. Well, Gregg had told me they were sending up my dinner on a tray about eight o'clock, and I planned to go to sleep right afterward."

"Weren't you going to the dance?"

"Oh, no. Kitty did suggest it, but how could I? I didn't have a decent dress or a permanent wave or anything. You see, Kitty had been preparing for all this ever since she was born.

Looking out for her complexion and her figure and learning just enough French and dancing and music to make her civilised without the taint of intellect.

"About ten minutes after I got upstairs, Victorine tapped on my bedroom door and said Kitty wanted to see me. She was in her bedroom trying on her dress and she'd just discovered the skirt didn't hang properly. She'd got it in a hurry in Paris and tried to have it altered over here and still it wasn't right. It's all very well for a dress that's meant to be irregular to have an uneven hem line. But this one was white velvet with a marvellous circular skirt four-hundred inches around and it was supposed to fall in long, moulded folds, absolutely even.

"Kitty had sent out her own maid, Carter, to try and find the dressmaker who had been altering it. Meanwhile, Victorine. and I got busy with scissors and pins. Kitty didn't look worried at all. Indeed I never saw her look brighter or gayer. Usually she was pale, but that evening there was a pink flush in her cheeks and her eyes sparkled.

"We pinned the hem and then took off the dress. Victorine basted one side while I did the other. You can do that with a circular skirt, it's so wide. Kitty put a bed gown over her slip and lit a cigarette. Then she said, 'Heavens, how hot it is!' She took off the bedgown and opened all the windows. Victorine protested, but Kitty wouldn't close them. She began teasing Victorine about the French not liking fresh air. Suddenly I noticed that perspiration was rolling off her forehead in drops. That was odd, because it was still snowing outside, and the room was chilly with the windows open. She leaned her head on her hand and said, 'Gin always gives me a headache.'

"We'd finished the skirt by then and we tried the dress on Kitty. It hung perfectly. But just then Kitty tottered as if she were giddy and clung to the dressing table for support. She said her head hurt and she felt as if there were an iron band about her breast. She said, 'I can't breathe fast enough. It's so hot. Please turn off the radiator.'

"That frightened me for the room was quite cold by then. Victorine cried, 'You have fever!' and rushed out to get a thermometer. I made Kitty lie down just as she was, wearing the white velvet dress and I put a quilt over her. But she threw it back and begged me to help her take off the dress. The lining was damp and stained with perspiration. Her skin was hot under my fingers and she moaned, 'I'm so thirsty.' I got her a glass of water. Victorine came back with the thermometer and we took her temperature. It was one hundred and one.

"I went downstairs to get Aunt Rhoda. Snow was still falling outside, but the warm air inside the house was richer than ever with the sweetness of roses and lilac. Altogether too much like a funeral. Musicians were in the ballroom running over that tango called 'The Cup of Sorrow'. The dining room and breakfast room and a small reception room were all full of gilt chairs and little tables from the caterer, and in the Murillo Room they were putting up a portable bar.

"I found Aunt Rhoda in the hall talking to Mrs Jowett and a man from the caterer with a supper menu in her hand. She seemed to know something was wrong the minute she saw me. I suppose it was in my face. She left them and came forward and I said, 'Kitty is ill.'

"She was utterly astonished. She kept saying, 'But that's impossible! Kitty can't be ill at a time like this. Everything depends on her.'

"We hurried upstairs. Kitty lay panting with her eyes closed. Her hair was damp, her lips, bluish, and her tongue was very coated. Victorine was fanning her with a newspaper. 'It's malaria,' said Aunt Rhoda. 'She had it in Rome when she was eleven and she's never got the germ out of her system.'

"I said, 'Are you sure? She has a high fever.' Aunt Rhoda answered, 'Malaria always causes fever and perspiration. I wonder what brought it on tonight — of all nights!' I said, 'We must get a doctor.'

"But Aunt Rhoda shook her head and answered, 'Kitty never has a doctor for these attacks. She just goes to bed with quinine and the fever burns itself out in three or four days.'

"She sat down on Kitty's bed and spoke in her most persuasive voice: 'Kitty, dear, can't you make an effort to get up for the dance? You needn't go to Uncle Edgar's dinner — if you'll just stay up an hour or so to receive the guests you can go back to bed as soon as they're all here.'

"While she was talking, we could hear the notes of the tango, faint and far away. But Kitty seemed to have lost interest in the party. 'I can't get up,' she said rather irritably. 'I know you've been to a lot of trouble, but I can't help it. I feel rotten.' Then she began to laugh. 'I believe you care more about my party than you do about me! Why don't you have it without me? A debutante is really the least important person at a debut — like a bridegroom at a wedding. It's the family and the tradespeople who run the show that get the most out of it.'

"Aunt Rhoda was silent for a long moment. Then she rose with an air of decision and said to me, 'Ann, get the bottle of quinine in my bathroom cupboard. Victorine, put mademoiselle into a dry nightgown.'

"I was some minutes finding the quinine. When I came back, Kitty was laughing again. There was a reading lamp beside her bed, and she turned it until it shone full in my face. I closed my eyes in the glare of the sixty watt bulb, and I heard her say to Victorine, 'Well? Can you do it?'"

6

MASK

Ann Claude paused and looked at her audience. Basil's eyes were inscrutable. Morris Sobel compressed his lips and played with a fountain pen on his desk. General Archer looked uncomfortable. Inspector Foyle's face was a study in bewilderment.

Ann's hands trembled as she took out another cigarette. Again Basil held a match for her. She leaned back and exhaled. "Now I've come to the part that's so hard to tell." Her voice wavered slightly. "The part you wouldn't believe at first." She looked at Sobel. "But it is just what really happened.

"Victorine answered Kitty, 'But yes, *ma petite demoiselle*! Even if there were not such a strong family resemblance, I could do it. The upper part of the face is the only part that matters — eyes and eyebrows, nose, and upper lip. Change that and you change everything. That's why a half mask hides identity at a masked ball without covering the greater part of the face. In order to disguise anyone you need only alter the part of the face that is covered by a half mask, for that is the part on which recognition depends. And today, *maquillage* —

what you call *make-up* — is so ingenious it can change the expression of the eyes or the apparent shape of the nose and upper lip almost beyond belief! A little affair of *camouflage* — an optical illusion.'

"I opened my eyes then and Kitty cried out, 'Ann, do you understand? I've got the most absolutely priceless idea! There's never been anything like it before! It beats scavenger hunts hollow! You are going to take my place at the dance, and everyone will think you are I! Victorine says you'd be the image of me with your hair cut and your eyebrows plucked.'

"We all laughed — Kitty, Aunt Rhoda, Victorine and me. We were tired and Kitty's falling ill just before the party had been a shock. I suppose none of us was quite normal. Kitty was the first to stop laughing. She was flushed and exuberant.

"'You can do it, Ann!' she cried. 'You know you can! And it will be the most glorious lark! Just think of Philip Leach writing reams in his rotten rag about how *Kitty* looked at the dance — and it'll be you all the time!' Finally, I stopped laughing and gasped out, 'I couldn't do it — really I couldn't!"

"'But why not?' Kitty was getting more and more excited. 'I knew two girls at school who were twins and they used to have such fun confusing the teachers.'

"Aunt Rhoda joined in and said, 'I really think you could do it, Ann. It's only for one night and you've both lived abroad so long that no one coming this evening has seen either of you since you were children.'

"'Except Uncle Edgar!' I exclaimed.

"'He only saw Kitty for a moment this afternoon,' retorted Aunt Rhoda. 'He didn't even recognise you, Ann. He won't remember either of you clearly. Your Jocelyn cousins are the nucleus of the party. Most of the other guests are debutantes of the season and men on Mrs Jowett's "bachelor list". They only know Kitty from her published photographs. In her dress and make-up, you could deceive all of them.'"

At this point, the district attorney interrupted. "I can understand girls of eighteen playing a joke of that sort. But do you ask us to believe that a woman of your aunt's age and position would join in such a hoax?"

"I'm just telling you what happened," said Ann, desperately. "I was surprised myself, for though Aunt Rhoda is rather young-looking, and she always enjoys parties and gaieties, I never knew her to play a practical joke before. I was quite bewildered, but I managed to ask, 'What about Nicholas Danine and Philip Leach? Surely, they know Kitty well enough to see through an impersonation. And Luis Pasquale? Artists have keen eyes.'

"Kitty herself answered, 'We'll have to take Luis into the secret because he's known me for several years and you for some months. But Danine has only seen me half a dozen times. As for Philip Leach — that's part of the joke, putting it over on a reporter who's supposed to notice everything.' I let that pass because I had no more respect for Leach's ability as a newspaper man than Kitty. He looks more like a poet than a reporter. How he ever happened to become a gossip writer, I don't know.

"I did think of the servants, but Kitty wouldn't listen to any objections. 'Victorine's the only one who was with us before we reached New York,' she said. 'The others have only known us the last few weeks. If I move into your room, they'll be sure to think you're the one who's ill. And to make sure, I'll hide my face in the quilt if any maid but Victorine comes near me.'

"Victorine herself added, 'There is Madame Jowett. Mademoiselle Ann has been working with her the last few days and she has seen Mademoiselle Kitty several times. But Madame

Jowett wears glasses. If her glasses were mislaid this evening, there would be no danger of her suspecting anything.'

"'We both have a foreign intonation,' went on Kitty. 'To American ears, our voices sound more alike than they really are. I answered Mrs Jowett on the telephone the other day and she mistook me for you. Oh, Ann, don't you see it's just because the whole plan is so daring that no one will ever suspect the truth? Boldness is the essence of bluff. And even if somebody does catch you, nothing very dreadful can happen! Some of the old people may get a little stuffy, but I'm sure the young ones will think the whole thing a perfect scream! Oh, if only I could be there to watch you!' And she began to laugh again. I couldn't refuse. I'm human and I thought it would be rather a lark. And then, I felt I owed Aunt Rhoda and Kitty a good bit because they made it possible for me to come back to America.

"The rest of that night was like a dream. Even the memory of it is as unreal as the memory of a dream. Under Victorine's fingers, my face was as plastic as clay. She told me there were just five important differences between my face and Kitty's. Her eyes were set further apart, and had a slight greenish cast, while mine were a colder, bluer grey, and closer together. Her nose was a little longer, and her lips a deeper red. Her skin, that looked about the same colour as mine, was actually one shade darker.

"Victorine cut and thinned my hair and waved it with old-fashioned tongs, because there was no time for a permanent wave. She plucked my eyebrows to the acute angle of Kitty's. By removing entirely the part of the brows near the nose and extending them to the temple with a pencil, she made my eyes look as wide apart as Kitty's. She used two shades of face powder and this modelling with light and dark tones made my nose seem as long as Kitty's. She made my eyes greenish grey by putting a greenish yellow eye-shadow on the lids beside them. Finally she used two shades of lipstick, one over the other to make my lips seem the same shade as Kitty's.

"When she put me into the velvet dress and I looked in the glass, it was Kitty who looked back at me! All the outward signs of my identity had been blotted out in about two hours. For a moment I had a curious feeling that Ann Claude had ceased to exist. The dream was becoming a nightmare. I stared at myself and wondered, 'Am I Kitty Jocelyn? Is the girl who fell ill really Ann Claude?' I had a new mask — had I perhaps a new soul as well? I suppose I was tired and excited and scared to death or I wouldn't have thought of such things."

At this point, the district attorney looked at Basil Willing with sceptical eyes. The psychiatrist kept his own gaze tranquilly on the girl, and she continued:

"I wanted Kitty to see me in her dress, but Aunt Rhoda said, 'There isn't time now,' and put Grandmother Jocelyn's pearls around my neck. She told me she had telephoned Uncle Edgar that Kitty was too tired to come to the little family dinner he had arranged. Victorine brought me a light supper on a tray which I ate in Kitty's sitting room, and then Aunt Rhoda and I went downstairs and — I never saw Kitty again." Ann folded her hands in her lap with an air of finality.

"What happened?" asked Basil.

"At the dance? Nothing. Nothing extraordinary, I mean. But afterward—"

"Suppose you tell us some of the ordinary things that happened at the dance."

"Well — no one suspected that I was not Kitty — so far as I know. I heard some middle-aged women saying I looked 'so like dear Rhoda' — forgetting apparently that Kitty was only

Rhoda's stepdaughter. There were a lot of second and third Jocelyn cousins, and there were some distant cousins of Kitty's own mother — the only relatives she had on that side.

"I only saw Uncle Edgar for a moment, but I'm sure he didn't suspect. Mrs Jowett nodded and smiled when I came downstairs, but I noticed she wasn't wearing her glasses. Victorine had evidently contrived to have them 'mislaid'. I danced with Nicholas Danine and Philip Leach, but I'm sure neither of them suspected anything. Because of cutting-in, I only danced a few moments with each. I danced with Luis Pasquale several times, but of course he was in the secret. He didn't say anything about it, but I felt sure from the way he smiled that Aunt Rhoda had told him just as she had planned.

"I'm afraid I don't remember anything in orderly sequence. I just remember bits of things. It was my first American dance and I couldn't get over the way the stags huddled together at one end of the room with appraising eyes on the parade of girls. The lights glared, the rooms were hot, the air was close, and the two dance bands played alternately, so there wasn't a moment's peace. I made valiant efforts to eat indigestible food and drink imported champagne, until I began to feel sickish as well as tired. I wasn't enjoying Kitty's practical joke because I had no one to share it with.

"I remember the white dawn bleaching the colour out of everything, the flowers wilting in the warm air, the dirty dishes being carried out of the supper rooms, the musicians yawning as they packed their instruments, and sleepy boys and girls eating sausages and scrambled eggs.

"I dragged myself upstairs and found Victorine waiting for me in the hall. She took me to Kitty's suite and brought me a cup of hot chicken broth. Aunt Rhoda came in just as I was dropping off to sleep. I yawned and said, 'Is Kitty all right?'

And she answered, 'Everything is all right,' and then I fell asleep.

"I didn't wake up till about four o'clock the next afternoon. The low rays of the late sun were streaming in the windows. I got up and took a bath in Kitty's bathroom. Then I put on her dressing gown and rang for breakfast. The bell was answered by Victorine.

"'Where's Carter?' I asked. Carter was Kitty's own maid, the one sent out to find the dressmaker the night before. I had forgotten all about her until then. Victorine answered, 'Madame let Carter go with two months' wages.' And I couldn't get anything more out of her. She's awfully stubborn.

"When she brought breakfast, Aunt Rhoda came, too. I thought she looked older than I had ever seen her. There were new lines at the corners of her mouth and there were shadows around her eyes. 'How's Kitty?' I asked as I began to eat. Aunt Rhoda stared at me a full moment. Then she laughed. 'Really, Kitty, I don't know what you mean. Why do you speak of yourself in the third person?'

"I laughed, too. I thought she was joking, of course. There was no point in keeping up the impersonation before Victorine who was in the secret. I said, 'Well, I'm going to see her as soon as I'm dressed.'

"'Her?' repeated Aunt Rhoda.

"'Kitty, of course,' I answered impatiently. The joke was wearing thin. Aunt Rhoda said gently, 'I'm afraid you're not feeling well, dear. After all, it was a dreadful strain getting up for the party last night when you had such a fever.' Her fingertips touched my forehead lightly. 'I think it's gone now — no more than ninety-nine at most. But it must have left you weak. You'd better spend the day in bed.'

"I gasped and cried out, 'Aunt Rhoda, are you mad? Or am

I?' Again she stared at me a full moment. Then she said, 'I hope your mind is not affected, Kitty. But you have certainly been under a great strain, or you would not call me Aunt Rhoda. You must stay in bed and have a nice, long rest.'

"With that, she left the room. I looked wildly at Victorine and she said: 'Be calm, *ma petite demoiselle*.' That was what she always called Kitty. 'Repose yourself. You will feel better tomorrow.' And then she left me, too. I thought, *This is another of Kitty's practical jokes, but I don't like this one.*

"I got up and ran into the sitting room in bedgown and slip-pers. The door into the hall wasn't even shut, and there was no one in the hall that I could see. But I had an odd feeling that I was being watched. I raced upstairs to my own room where I had left Kitty the night before. I burst open the door shouting, 'I suppose you think this is funny.'

"The late sun was streaming through the windows. The room was neat and bare and empty as an unoccupied room in a hotel. There was no sign of Kitty, no sign she had ever been there. The bed was stripped of sheets and blankets — nothing but a mattress, a bolster, and a dust sheet. My trunk was gone. So were my two suitcases and my hatbox. My clothes, my toilet articles, my books and papers — all had vanished. One of the suitcases had contained my only means of identification — my passport; my two French *cartes d'identité*, one expired, one current; my birth certificate and my parents' marriage certificate; my mother's wedding ring with my parents' initials and the date of their wedding engraved inside; various letters addressed to me. The empty silence of that room was more eloquent than any words I ever heard.

"My knees weakened. I groped my way to a chair. After about ten minutes I pulled myself together and rang the bell for a maid. It was Hagen, one of the housemaids, who answered

— a rather stupid-looking girl. I decided to say nothing to her about Kitty. I only said, 'Where are the things that were here? The trunks and suitcases?'

"She looked at me curiously, and stammered, 'D-Don't you remember, Miss Kitty? Miss Ann has gone to California.' She wasn't just saying it. I could see she believed it. Suddenly, I remembered that Kitty's maid, Carter, had helped Kitty dress and undress ever since she reached America. Carter was the only one of the American servants who might know Kitty well enough to see through my impersonation of Kitty. Was that why Carter had been sent away?

"I was badly shaken, but I tried to keep my head. 'Did you see Miss Ann leave the house?' I asked Hagen.

"'Oh, yes, Miss Kitty. She left last night about ten o'clock when you were getting ready for the dance, dressed in that shabby black coat she always wears. Comes from Paris, she says, miss, but all I can say is, if that's Paris, give me New York!'

"'And her luggage?'

"'It went by express this morning — while you were asleep, Miss Kitty.' For an awful, moment, I wondered if they could be right. Suppose I really was Kitty Jocelyn? After all, my memories of being Ann Claude were the only evidence I had of my identity, and I knew that memory can be pure delusion. I've heard of cases of double personality with two separate memory trains, both apparently quite real.

"I had to get dressed, so I went back to Kitty's suite. Sitting on a cushion there was her little dog, Kai Lung. He came forward slowly, without wagging his tail, as he always did when Kitty appeared. He sniffed at my bare feet as if I were strange to him. Then he lifted up his muzzle and began to whimper. At last, I had a witness to my identity. They had got rid of Carter, but they had forgotten the dog! I think he saved my reason.

"I sat down and tried to think what I could do. I had no money for a lawyer, and I didn't know any lawyers. It would be hard to make a stranger believe my story. The only person I really knew in New York was a girl who had been at school with me in France — Polly Fraser. I knew she ran a bookshop and I had thought of getting a job with her when I left Aunt Rhoda. But I hadn't had time to see her in the few weeks since we reached America. I found her name in the telephone book and looked about for Kitty's telephone. It is one of those portable extensions and I soon found that it had been detached and removed. All that remained was the socket in the base-board. I ran into the sitting room and tried the door into the hall. This time it was locked. Like a fool I had walked back into a trap.

"Victorine brought me supper on a tray. I asked for the morning newspapers and she sent for them. They all had photographs of Kitty Jocelyn with the captions and list of guests I had helped Mrs Jowett prepare. The hoax had been only too successful. It would be almost impossible to prove that Kitty had not been present at her own coming-out party.

"That night, Victorine slept on a couch in the sitting room. I lay awake until nearly four in the morning. Then I slept the sleep of exhaustion until noon.

"Victorine insisted I stay in bed. She said I needed a rest and I saw no one else all day long. I had never realised before how enigmatic her face was. And felt sure she was stronger than I. She's pure peasant stock.

"On Friday morning, when she brought me breakfast, Aunt Rhoda came with her. 'You look much better, Kitty, dear.' Her sweetness was deadly. I couldn't understand how I had ever thought her attractive. 'Do you feel well enough to get up for dinner?' she went on. 'You're missing so much — moping like this. Nicholas Danine called yesterday afternoon and I had to tell him you were resting and couldn't be disturbed. It was most unfortunate. This evening we're going to the opera and I'm sure it would do you good if you feel equal to it.' Of course I said yes — it was my only chance to escape, I thought. But I was more puzzled than ever.

"Victorine dressed me with even more care than on the night of the dance. There was time for a permanent wave now and she spared no effort in getting my hair exactly like Kitty's in every swirl and dip. Kitty had an evening dress that was a very startling shade of clear vermilion. Victorine made me put it on. When I was dressed Aunt Rhoda came in and looked me over. Then she nodded to Victorine and we went downstairs together.

"Gregg greeted me with decorous cordiality and said, 'Good evening, Miss Kitty. If I may make so bold, I'm very glad to see you well again.' What could I say except 'Thank you, Gregg, I am much better'? I soon realised all the servants believed that I was Kitty Jocelyn and that Ann Claude had left the house.

"We dine at home with Luis Pasquale. He often comes to meals because he lives next door in the building that used to be the Jocelyn stables and coach house. The lower floor is a garage now and Aunt Rhoda lets Luis use the upper floor as a studio. During dinner I caught him watching me speculatively and I decided I liked him even less than I did Aunt Rhoda. And then I remembered Luis had been in the secret of the original hoax two nights ago. After dinner Aunt Rhoda began to play the piano in the music room. Luis was near me and I whispered to him, 'Won't you help me get out of this?' But he looked at me coldly and answered, 'My dear Kitty, I don't know what you're talking about!'

"Have you ever felt that your real self is entirely different from the artificial idea of you that other people hold and force you to live up to? It was like that, only a thousand times worse. We drove to the opera and went directly to the Jocelyn box. It belongs to Uncle Edgar, but he has been sharing it with Aunt Rhoda since she came to New York. He was there already and when I saw him a little hope stirred in my heart. For he had seen both Kitty and myself at cocktail time the afternoon Kitty fell ill. Even though he had been deceived by my impersonation of Kitty in the excitement of the dance, I thought he would surely recognise me when he saw me quietly at close quarters.

"But he greeted me as Kitty in the most matter-of-fact way imaginable. During the first intermission some of the men who had been at the dance came into the box. The Jocelyn cousins said, 'Hello, Kitty,' and the others said, 'Good evening, Miss Jocelyn.' Not one of them showed any doubt or hesitation.

"I couldn't stand it any longer. Just before the second act, I whispered to Uncle Edgar, 'Something dreadful is happening. I'm not Kitty at all. I'm Ann Claude and Kitty has disappeared. They say she's gone to California — I mean, they say Ann has gone to California — but that can't be, because I'm Ann and the whole point is: Where is Kitty?'

"Uncle Edgar simply stared at me. Aunt Rhoda leaned forward and I caught the words *delusion* and *over-wrought*. That was too much. I sprang to my feet and cried aloud, 'My name is Ann Claude! I'm not Kitty Jocelyn — I'm not!'

"Just then the lights were turned low and the orchestra drowned my voice. The people in the other boxes couldn't hear what I said, though they may have seen me stand up. Uncle Edgar whispered, 'We'd better take her home.'

"I felt limp and shaky. We left the box and went down to the car, Luis and Uncle Edgar walking on either side of me like jailers. When Uncle Edgar left us, Aunt Rhoda said, 'Of course, you won't mention this to anyone.' And he answered, indignantly, 'Of course not!' I realised then that I could count on no one to help me. I must find some way of getting out of the Jocelyn house by myself.

"On Kitty's bathroom door was an old-fashioned lock that must have been there in Grandfather Jocelyn's day. The key was in the lock. When Victorine wasn't looking, I slipped it into the pocket of my dressing gown — that is, Kitty's dressing gown. That night when Victorine went into the bathroom, I slammed the door and locked her in. Her shouting and pounding could not be heard in the rest of the house for the walls were old and thick, and the bedroom and sitting room cut off the bathroom from the hall.

"Then I had to deal with the locked door into the hall. Victorine had the key to that door with her in the bathroom. There was only one thing I could do — pick the lock. I had never picked a lock before, but I had all night to do it and it was the only way out. When there's only one way out you take it no matter how hard it is. I used up two eyebrow tweezers, a pair of sewing scissors and the wire from three kid hair curlers. Then I remembered a newspaper story about a man who was locked in an airtight strong room by gangsters and picked the lock with a thin dime just in time to save himself from death by suffocation. I hadn't a dime, but there was a nail file on Kitty's dressing table about the size and thickness of a dime at one end. I used that and by five o'clock in the morning I got the door open.

"I had to put on a suit of Kitty's because I had no clothes of my own. When I took a pair of gloves from her bureau drawer, I noticed a purse she had carried the morning she disappeared. I opened it and found she had left some change in it. The few dollars belonging to me had disappeared at the same time as the other things in my room, so I had no hesitation about helping myself. Then I picked up Kai Lung and walked downstairs. The front door is locked at night, and all the ground floor windows are barred as protection against burglars. I had no time to lose — it was nearly six now. I decided to gamble on the probability that the servants really did believe I was Kitty. I walked boldly into the kitchen. It was so early that only one of the maids was on duty. That was where Kai Lung came in. 'I'm taking him out for exercise,' I said in the most matter-of-fact voice I could muster. She wanted to get the key to the front door, but I said, 'Don't bother,' and went out the service door.

"I went to a restaurant first and got a cup of coffee and a morning paper. In the paper I saw an interview with the district attorney, Mr Sobel, in which he mentioned the Police Commissioner, General Archer, and then I remembered a niece of General Archer had been at the dance and I had talked to her several minutes. On the strength of that I went directly to Police Headquarters. One of Kitty's visiting cards was in her purse, so I sent it in to the Commissioner and — that's all."

Basil was the first to break the silence. "There's just one question I want to ask," he said, quietly. "What was your cousin's usual dose of Sveltis?"

"Sveltis?" The girl stared. "That reducing stuff? Why, Kitty never took anything like that. She was the last person in the world to reduce! She was always too thin." Then comprehension dawned in the wide, grey eyes. "Oh, I suppose you're thinking of that Sveltis advertisement she endorsed."

"It did cross my mind," admitted Basil, with a hint of irony.

She laughed. "That doesn't mean anything, you know," she explained. "The Sveltis people saw Kitty's picture in some magazine or newspaper, and they thought she'd look well in their advertisements because she was so thin. It's all done through an agency. Kitty got anything from $500 to a $1000 a throw, and I believe she got $2000 once. But she never used half the things she endorsed, and she certainly never took Sveltis. She was so anxious to put on weight that she used to have milk with all her meals."

7

DETAIL

It was late afternoon when Basil returned to the district attorney's office. Beyond the windows, the winter sky was a low, grey ceiling. Inside, desk lamps were lighted. The room could not have seemed more gloomy had it been underground.

Sobel poised his pencil over a scratch pad. "Now, Willing, do your stuff. Is it double personality? Or amnesia? Or just plain nuts?"

Basil smiled. "Officially, I am keeping Miss Claude under observation and preparing a detailed report on her mental condition for you."

"And unofficially?"

"She's as sane as you or I."

"Damn!" Sobel threw down his pencil.

"Sorry, DA," murmured Basil. "I can quite understand that neurasthenia or hysteria would be more convenient."

Sobel had the grace to grin. "It isn't that I want the poor wench to be nuts — but if she isn't, this is going to be one helluva case. Couldn't she be absolutely sane on every other subject and have just this one delusion?"

"What delusion?"

"That she's Ann Claude, when, of course, she's really Kitty Jocelyn. Society women are always having nervous breakdowns. See here—" Sobel began flipping through a typewritten manuscript. "This is in her statement: *'All the servants believed that I was Kitty Jocelyn and that Ann Claude had left the house.'* Isn't that just the sort of statement we always get from insane people? You know: *'All the servants believe that I'm John Smith when I'm really Napoleon Bonaparte.'*"

Basil lit a cigarette and leaned back in his chair, regarding Sobel through smoke. "Then who is the girl whose body was found in the snow? And how did she meet her death?" Sobel frowned, but Basil went on: "Ann Claude couldn't have known the body was warm when it was found in the snow, because the police kept that out of the papers. Yet when she described Kitty's illness she dwelt on the high temperature and profuse perspiration. Is that coincidence?"

"I suppose she identified the body as Kitty Jocelyn?"

"Not only that. She identified the clothes found on the body as her own. There were no laundry marks because she washed them herself, and after she went to stay with the Jocelyns, Rhoda's own laundress washed them. They were never sent to a public laundry. Then there's the evidence of the dog."

"You know I can't put a dog under oath—"

"Oh, it doesn't clinch anything," agreed Basil. "You'd have to prove first that the dog was Kitty's dog and that might be difficult. But I don't believe he belonged to the girl who brought him here: he didn't obey a single order she gave him. And it was suggestive the way he whimpered and watched the door."

"Okay. You win!" Sobel reached for the telephone. "We'll have the Commissioner and Inspector Foyle over here again."

As he replaced the receiver, Basil remarked, "I hate to think what might have happened to Ann Claude if that body had never been found."

"Where is she now?"

"At the clinic. But I advise you to let her go and stay with the friend who keeps a bookshop. A psychiatric clinic is a rather unpleasant place for a sane person."

"Always providing she's sane!"

"There are four simple, outward signs of serious mental illness," retorted Basil. "Excitement, depression, enfeeblement, and confusion. When you talked to her did she seem excited, depressed, enfeebled, or confused?"

"N-No but—"

"Neurologically she's in unusually good health — every reflex and reaction normal, perfect coordination and orientation, no nervous mannerisms. Her average free association time was 1.457 seconds — better than Jung's average for educated women. I discussed her story with her at length and she answered every question intelligently. I gave her a number of specialised mental tests, and she came through rather better than I imagine you would."

Fortunately, the callbox buzzed just then to announce the Police Commissioner and Inspector Foyle.

"Willing says she's sane," proclaimed Sobel. "And in that case her story is probably true."

Archer sat down heavily. "It can't be. The whole thing is unbelievable."

"No, Archer, I'm afraid it's only too believable." Basil perched on the arm of a leather chair. "The scheming stepmother, the dying debutante, and the modern Cinderella who took her place —dancing to the *Danse Macabre* — it all hangs together."

"But my niece Isobel was there, and it never occurred to her that girl was not Kitty Jocelyn!"

Foyle intervened. "I'm afraid that doesn't prove anything, Mr Commissioner. There are cases of mistaken identity in police records here and abroad where one fellow pinch-hit for another as witness where eyewitnesses under oath identified innocent men as crooks without meaning to — where dames identified dead bodies of guys they never saw before as their husbands. I don't know why it happens, but it does."

"The ability to recognise people is a pretty unstable thing," suggested Basil. "It's one of the first things to go in mental disease, and even in sane people it varies with light, distance, and the degree of familiarity. Most of the guests at the dance knew Kitty Jocelyn only through published photographs and they saw Ann in artificial light. They saw her in the Jocelyn house introduced as Kitty by Kitty's own stepmother. They saw Ann as Kitty because they believed she was Kitty and believing is seeing. But the dog who identified people by scent instead of sight was less easily deceived."

"Thanks for the lecture!" growled Sobel. "Suppose we get back to Kitty Jocelyn's murder — if it is murder. For all we know, it may be suicide or accident."

"I doubt if it was accident."

"Why?"

Basil put on his most pedantic manner because he knew it irritated Sobel. "The high spirits before death, and the extraordinary heat of the body after death, suggest one of the new pyretic drugs."

"Py-what?"

"Temperature-raising. They're often used as a basis of reducing medicines."

Sobel was startled. "That's funny!"

"Very, for if Ann Claude is telling the truth, Kitty never took Sveltis, or any other reducing medicine."

"Why didn't you tell me this before?"

"I wanted Lambert to make sure first. And then—" Basil smiled. "You haven't exactly encouraged my attempts at detecting."

"Let's hope it was suicide," muttered Sobel.

"Then why should she leave the house dressed in Ann's clothes?"

"It can't be murder!" cried General Archer. "Because — well, really! Edgar Jocelyn belongs to my club!"

"I'm afraid that's not evidence," said Sobel.

"But it's all so — so absurd! Who would want to murder a debutante on the eve of her coming-out party?"

"Whom are you putting on the case?"

"Will you take charge yourself, Foyle?" said Archer. "I'd like you to report directly to me."

"I'll do that, sir!" responded Foyle. "Are you putting a deputy on it? "

Sobel rearranged the pencils on his desk and Basil knew he was weighing "unpopularity in high places" against the promise of personal publicity.

After a moment his familiar grin came again. "No. I'm not sharing the limelight with anybody, Foyle. If I crack a case like this, I'll be famous no matter how many toes I tread on. The first thing to do is to see Kitty's stepmother — Rhoda Jocelyn. We could ask her to come down here in the usual way, but the circumstances are so extraordinary I'd rather take her off guard. Why not descend on the Jocelyn house as soon as possible — this evening?"

"Not me!" cried General Archer.

Sobel's grin was unashamed. "I have a perfectly good

excuse. Officially, I'm simply going there to notify Mrs Jocelyn that a dead body has been identified as her stepdaughter's. Willing, I want you to come with us, if you can spare the time. Mrs Jocelyn may try to pull a fast one and say that Ann Claude is screwy. You must hand her the line you've been handing us."

"I'd like nothing better," confessed Basil.

8

STUDY IN FALSE LIGHT

The Jocelyn house stood in the East Sixties on a corner of Fifth Avenue opposite the Park. It was grey stone, built on the same scale as the old ducal mansions of Europe. A steep flight of stairs under an archway led to the inner door. The outer door was glass with a wrought iron grille, delicate as black lace against the lamplight of the enclosed stairway.

Foyle rang the bell. After some moments, a footman came down the steps and opened the glass door.

"We have serious news of Mrs Jocelyn's stepdaughter," said Sobel, briskly. "We must see Mrs Jocelyn herself as soon as possible."

"What name, sir?"

"Morris Sobel, district attorney. This is Inspector Foyle of Police Headquarters. And Dr Willing."

"Very good, sir. Please step this way."

They mounted the steps under the arch and passed through the second door into a dimly lighted hall.

"Wait here, Casey," cried Foyle to one of the detectives

who followed. "Duff, you stick with us," he added to the police stenographer.

There were more steps and apparently endless corridors. Not a sound of traffic could be heard in the heart of the house. Another servant appeared. He had not the girth of most English butlers, but his manner was unmistakable. "If you will come this way, gentleman."

An elevator took them to the next floor, and they were shown into a drawing room. The soft green of old vegetable dyes glowed in the antique brocade that hung at the windows and lined the fragile Louis XVI chairs. In a fireplace of tawny marble a wood fire danced and whispered to itself.

Foyle wandered about the room, came to a double door-way, and opened it. There was a long vista of polished parquet. Crystal chandeliers shimmered faintly in the light of street-lamps filtering through curtained windows.

"Ballroom! That must be where the dance was held."

Foyle swung round. "Could this be the room where the cocktails were served?"

Basil smiled. "Unless I'm much mistaken, that's a Murillo over the mantlepiece."

Foyle and Sobel lifted their heads and stared. Before they could speak, a man and woman entered the room. "Mr Sobel? Inspector Foyle? How do you do? I am Rhoda Jocelyn. This is an old friend of the family, Mr Pasquale."

Her voice was low and dulcet. Basil understood at once what Ann Claude meant by "deadly sweetness".

"Do sit down," she went on, serenely, "and tell me what news you have of my little girl. I've been so terribly worried."

She was stately in a brocade gown of a rich and peculiar peacock blue. Her crisp, brown hair was flecked with grey, but her profile was still a thing of beauty. And then the whole effect was spoiled when she turned her face and you saw the morbid mouth — shapeless lips meeting in an obstinate line.

Pasquale looked like a middle-aged faun who had forsaken Arcady for air-conditioned drawing rooms. He had acquired gloss and a paunch in the process. His attitude toward Rhoda was a nice blend of romantic devotion and spurious domesticity. But Basil's clinical eye did not miss the unnatural pallor, the tremor of the plump, white hands, and the shrunken pupils of the eyes. He made a mental note: morphine addict.

"Well?" fluted Rhoda, clasping her hands on the arm of her chair and leaning forward.

Sobel drew a long breath. "Mrs Jocelyn, you must prepare for a shock," he said, bluntly. "We have reason to believe your stepdaughter is dead."

Under a film of powder, the olive cheeks took on a mottled look. Long, thin fingers plucked at a fold of the peacock blue dress. "Surely, there is some mistake, Mr Sobel."

"I don't believe so, Mrs Jocelyn. The girl died four days ago, and her body is in the mortuary."

Rhoda shook her head. "You have made a mistake, but a very natural one. Kitty Jocelyn, my stepdaughter, has a cousin, Ann Jocelyn Claude, who resembles her closely. I took this cousin as my secretary a few months ago. She left me last Tuesday evening — rather suddenly. There was some foolish girl's quarrel and Ann flounced out of the house saying she was going to California, and we were to send her trunks after her. We have heard nothing from her since. Of course we thought it was because she was still angry. It never occurred to us that anything had happened to her. None of us knew much about her private life. Poor child! It must be her body you have found." Rhoda's eyes defied them though her voice was calm.

"On whose testimony did you identify this dead body as my stepdaughter?"

But Sobel was prepared. "A young woman visited my office this morning and made a statement," he explained, patiently. "She said her name was Ann Jocelyn Claude. She said her cousin, Kitty Jocelyn, had fallen ill five days ago and that you had persuaded her to impersonate Kitty at a coming-out dance — as a sort of practical joke."

Rhoda's brows lifted. "That is preposterous! I never did anything of the kind!"

"This young woman stated that she never saw Kitty again after the dance, and that she, herself, was kept here a prisoner—"

"Mr Sobel, I'm sure you don't realise what you're suggesting! I can put the whole story in one sentence. The girl who talked to you this morning, claiming to be Ann Claude, is really Kitty Jocelyn. Luis—" she lifted a languid hand "— explain this dreadful situation to Mr Sobel and the others."

Pasquale turned toward them. "It is unfortunate that a family scandal should become known to strangers!" His voice rang indignantly. "But I suppose there's no help for it now. Mrs Jocelyn's unhappy stepdaughter has always been irresponsible — flighty. In plain language, a mental case."

Rhoda took up the tale. "You know what modern young people are, Mr Sobel. They burn the candle at both ends — cigarettes, cocktails, late hours — you can't stop them. It's really no wonder they break down so easily. Even when Kitty was a child, she was too imaginative — too introspective. She used to have imaginary playmates and hold long conversations with them. She became fond of her cousin, Ann, these last few months, and Ann's sudden departure the night of the coming-out party was a shock to her. That must be why she developed this fantastic delusion that she herself was Ann, and that the girl who had disappeared was Kitty! I'm sure you understand why I hesitated about going to a psychiatrist. I hoped Kitty would get over it in a day or so. I didn't want anyone — even a doctor — to know that she was…well, mentally unstable. The last few days have been a nightmare to us all. We didn't dare leave her alone for a moment. My friend, Victorine, slept in the sitting room adjoining her bedroom every night. But she locked Victorine in the bathroom and managed to leave the house this morning early, when the rest of us were asleep. We've been frantic all day. I didn't want to call in the police if I could help it, because of the scandal and unpleasant publicity. Now, from what you say, I gather that the poor, deluded child actually went to you with her absurd story that she was Ann and that Kitty had disappeared." Rhoda sighed. "It's my fault. I see that now. I should have called in a mental specialist at once."

The pleasant, plausible voice died away. Rhoda made a charming picture as she lay back in her chair. The luxury of the room lent her the authority of wealth. Both Sobel and Foyle were impressed. Sobel looked at Basil with a question in his eyes.

And then Rhoda overplayed it. "Perhaps it isn't too late," she murmured, her eyes focused on Basil. "Are you the Dr Willing who wrote *Time and Mentality*? Could I persuade you to take Kitty's case yourself?" The brown eyes were wide and luminous. "I will make it worth your while. Indeed I am prepared to pay almost any fee to get Kitty well again. You understand?"

"Mrs Jocelyn," said Basil, evenly, "the most disillusioning thing about being a psychiatrist is discovering how many kind relatives wish that other members of their family could be declared insane."

Her eyes flashed. He went on before she could answer: "I put the girl who calls herself Ann Claude through a series of mental and neurological tests this afternoon and I found no symptom of an unbalanced mind or diseased nerves. That means we cannot dismiss her testimony lightly as a delusion. You will have to give us some definite proof that this girl is Kitty Jocelyn and not Ann Claude — if you can."

Rhoda's painted lips parted, but no words came. Then she slid gracefully to the floor, apparently unconscious.

"See what you've done!" cried Pasquale, his face chalk white.

Basil scanned Rhoda with a cold, professional eye. He had dealt with the situation before and he knew the modern woman's vulnerable point.

"Ring for some water," he said to Pasquale, "and throw it over her head. Never mind the finger wave."

Rhoda opened her eyes and moaned. "I am very high strung, Dr Willing," she explained, with gentle resignation. "The least little thing upsets me and a shock like this is almost more than I can bear. My heart—" she pressed her hand to her left breast "—is not strong."

Pasquale helped her to an armchair with an ostentatious chivalry that was an indirect rebuke to the others. He set a small cushion at her back and a footstool beneath her blue sandals.

All Sobel's suspicions had returned. He faced Rhoda, one hand clenched behind his back, the other extended before him — his courtroom attitude. His voice had the edge it took on when he questioned an adverse witness. "Before you say anything more, Mrs Jocelyn, I want to make one thing clear.

The girl whose body has been identified as Kitty Jocelyn did not die a natural death."

"Oh, my God!" It was Pasquale.

Sobel turned in amazement. Unlike Basil, he had not noticed the symptoms of the morphine addict.

Pasquale buried his face in his hands and began to sob.

"You all seem to be kinda high strung round here," drawled Inspector Foyle.

"Luis! Pull yourself together!" Rhoda was so completely changed it seemed as if another person had entered the room. The languor, the stateliness, and the ghost of her youthful "charm" were gone. In their place was a hard, practical woman. Even her voice was different. The dulcet inflections gave way to a brittle, crackling tone. *"Luis!"*

Pasquale quivered like a big mould of white jelly. He ceased to sob, but kept his face buried in his hands.

Rhoda turned to Sobel. "Was it an accident?"

"The circumstances suggest murder."

Pasquale lifted his tear-stained face. It was a greenish white now. "Murder!" he echoed.

Rhoda looked at him with scorn. "Don't let them bully you," she said, quietly. "It's impossible that anyone should want to murder Kitty. She was only eighteen. She hadn't an enemy in the world. If this body has been poisoned, it is more likely to be Ann Claude."

But Pasquale was not listening. "I know nothing about it!" he protested. "I had nothing to do with it! I am innocent!"

Sobel concentrated on Pasquale, with a lawyer's instinct for the weaker witness. "The best way to prove your innocence is to make a clean breast of the whole truth. If you and Mrs Jocelyn conceal anything you know about the circumstances of this death, you may find yourselves charges as accessories after the fact. You might even be suspected of murder."

"Oh, no!" Pasquale spoke eagerly. "How could we be? Don't you see Kitty's death means ruin for both of us? That's why—"

"Luis!" Rhoda's eyes were terrible, but her voice was still under control. "I brought you here to advise me, not to betray me!"

"I am advising you, Rhoda." He spoke now as though they were alone. "Don't you see the police will find out everything sooner or later? They always do. For God's sake, tell them the truth now! Don't you realise it's a murder case and this is our only chance? We can't fight. Were licked!" His voice rose and cracked. "You should never have—"

"*Luis!*"

He sank back in his chair, mumbling. "If you don't tell them, I will. I — I'm not going to risk the electric chair for your sake." He shuddered. "To think it was all your fault!" He turned on Rhoda, but her eyes stilled him for a moment. Then he muttered, "You needn't look at me like that. You — you're inhuman, Rhoda. Like a cat that eats her kittens!"

Suddenly his lips parted, and he stared at her in sheer terror. "Mother of God!" he whispered hoarsely. "I — I wonder if you did poisoned Kitty? You always hated her!"

9

GENRE PICTURE

"Will you be quiet, Luis?" said Rhoda, in a level voice. Then she turned to Sobel. "If there is a possibility that Kitty has been murdered, it puts a new complexion on the matter."

"Then you admit that Kitty is dead?" demanded Sobel.

"I have no way of knowing. Both girls left the house. Obviously, one is dead. Which I don't know. But I will admit now that Kitty was the first to leave and it's true, I persuaded Ann to impersonate her at the dance. I had my own reasons for doing so. If you think they have any bearing on the case, I'll make a statement."

"That would be the wisest course," responded Sobel. "If you wish to send for your lawyer…?"

"No." Rhoda looked at Pasquale and he shrank from her glance. "I have nothing to hide. If Kitty is really dead, I have little to live for."

Inspector Foyle took charge. "Ready, Duff?"

"Okay, Chief." The police stenographer sat down at a frail

marquetry desk, took out his notebook, and unscrewed his fountain pen, stolid as the Recording Angel.

"We're waiting, Mrs Jocelyn," said Sobel. "First, I would like to know your reasons for letting Ann Claude impersonate Kitty at the dance."

Rhoda hesitated. There was no sound but Pasquale's choking sobs. Then she shrugged and began to speak in a flat, toneless voice, as if she were telling a tale about someone else, rather than confiding her own secrets.

Basil thought she took a masochistic pleasure in violating her own reserve. For years she had been acting a part. At last, she could indulge in the luxury of confession.

"When I persuaded Ann to impersonate Kitty at the dance, I let her think it would be a good joke — a lark — because that was the only argument likely to appeal to a girl like Ann. But to me it was a deadly serious matter. My own future depended on Kitty's success."

"I don't understand," said Sobel.

"It's quite simple. I am penniless."

Sobel gasped aloud. Basil smiled as he recalled she had offered him "almost any fee" a moment ago.

"Do you think I'd ever have allowed Kitty to endorse advertisements if we hadn't needed ready cash?" cried Rhoda, bitterly. "It was the only way I could supply her with pocket money and meet current expenses that couldn't be met with credit — servants' wages, passage to America, restaurant bills. The more familiar her name was to the general public the more credit we had with tradespeople. If you can't be rich, the next best thing is to be well known.

"This house and furniture are mortgaged — even the pictures. When they're sold there'll be almost nothing left after the mortgages are paid. I disposed of the Jocelyn pearls in

Paris — secretly. The necklace Ann wore at the dance is a replica of cultured pearls.

"I don't see why you all look so surprised. Surely, it's not the first time you've heard of a mother or stepmother gambling her last cent on a pretty daughter's first season? Many a family fortune has been rebuilt on a brilliant marriage. If they were honest, most mothers would admit that a coming-out party is always an investment and sometimes a speculation. I did it on a grander scale than most people — but then I've always done everything in a big way." She paused and opened a jade box on the table. It was empty. "Oh, dear! I've lost my cigarette case." Basil produced his.

"Thank you. Gerald Jocelyn, my husband, was anything but a businessman," she went on. "When he died, he left the bulk of his fortune to me, but the money had been so injudiciously invested that I had to choose between living on a narrow income or living on capital. I decided to live on capital, or rather, I decided to invest it in Kitty. She was certain to marry, and I determined she should marry well. From the time she was eleven I gave her an expensive education with that end in view. I knew she would provide adequately for me when she was married. Then I planned to marry Luis and settle down in Paris to a comfortable old age."

"Mr Pasquale's stake in the affair," muttered Sobel. Rhoda ignored the interruption. "I lived in Europe to avoid my late husband's family, but I decided to bring Kitty out in New York, because there is no *dot* system here. I got her clothes in Paris last spring at cut rates, on condition that photographs of Kitty wearing the clothes were used to illustrate fashion articles in American magazines. The De Luxe Advertising Agency saw these photographs and wrote offering her $1,000 to endorse a new nail polish. On the boat coming over we met Philip Leach, and he published a good deal about Kitty in his column. There were more endorsements, so she became something of a celebrity before she actually came out.

"Everyone assumed she was an heiress — even Kitty herself. She was less precocious about money matters than girls brought up in America and she left everything to me. The trust fund her father had created for her crumbled in 1929. She was really no better off than her cousin, Ann Claude. But neither of them knew it.

"As soon as we reached New York, I went to see my brother-in-law, Edgar Jocelyn. I didn't tell him our financial situation. I merely told him that I couldn't afford to give Kitty the sort of coming-out party she ought to have. As he was Kitty's nearest relative with no daughters of his own, he agreed to finance the party, and offered me $50,000. I induced him to make it $60,000, but he wouldn't go higher. I had hoped for $75,000.

"Now, perhaps, you are beginning to understand how I felt when Kitty fell ill a few hours before her coming-out party. Edgar Jocelyn had not given me a cheque for $60,000. He had merely promised to pay bills up to that amount when they were sent to him. Food, flowers, everything perishable had been delivered when Kitty fell ill. Mrs Jowett had already done her part in organising the party and she had made me promise her double the usual fee because it was all done at rather short notice. Both the orchestra leaders had refused other engagements in order to keep the date free for me and they had to be paid extra for that. Edgar would have to pay the bills whether the dance took place or not. I had no money for a second dance. Edgar had stated very positively that he would not give me anymore. I could not give a second party on credit alone. The tradespeople were beginning to suspect the truth.

"That party could not be postponed, and it was absolutely necessary to my plan of campaign for Kitty and myself. Had I told Edgar the truth he might have provided something for Kitty. But he would not have provided for me adequately. He has a divorced wife to support and when he dies his fortune will go to their children. For my sake, as well as Kitty's, her career could not be interrupted or side-tracked. Every detail had to go according to schedule, whether she was ill or not. And that is why I allowed Ann to impersonate her at the dance."

"Pretty desperate plan," remarked Sobel.

Rhoda looked at him. "I was desperate. Of course if I had dreamed Kitty was going to die during the impersonation I wouldn't have risked it. But it never occurred to me she was seriously ill. She used to have attacks of malaria in Europe with just those symptoms. I thought Ann would save the situation by taking Kitty's place at the party. Then Kitty would be up and about in a few days and everything would go on as I had planned. She had already attracted Nicholas Danine."

Rhoda extinguished her cigarette, asked Basil for another. "Ann played Kitty's part at the dance more brilliantly than I expected," she continued. "It's curious how a woman's personality responds to any change in dress or appearance. Everything went well until about three in the morning when Gregg said that Victorine wished to see me. I knew it was something urgent and exceptional or she wouldn't have interrupted me at the dance. I told Gregg I would see her in my own sitting room, but she met me in the hall. Her face was haggard.

"'Madame!' she cried. 'I went into Mademoiselle Ann's room just now to see how Mademoiselle Kitty was resting and she is gone!'

"We went to Ann's bedroom on the fourth floor. The

bedcovers were thrown back. Her nightgown, flung down on a chair, was not at all damp with perspiration, so she must have left some time earlier, for her illness made her perspire excessively. I said, 'She's not in the bathroom? Or in her own rooms?' Victorine answered, 'But no, madame, I have searched this entire floor and the floor below.'

"I said, 'See if any of Ann's clothes are missing.' Victorine looked into the closet and cried out, 'A black coat is gone. I remember it well. It was from the *Bazar de l'Hotel de Ville.* Mademoiselle Kitty must have dressed in Mademoiselle Ann's clothes and gone out!' Kitty's illness had been bad enough. Her disappearance was appalling. If anything happened to her now, all the money I had invested in her would be thrown away. I sat down and tried to think things out. My first thought was kidnaping. Then I saw that a kidnaper would have taken Kitty instead of Ann, because Kitty was the girl who was supposed to have money. And a kidnaper would have no way of knowing that the girl who passed as Kitty at the party was not Kitty, and that the girl who lay ill in Ann's room was not Ann. I concluded that Kitty must have left the house of her own free will: But why?

"I locked Ann's bedroom door and went down to my own sitting room. Then I told Victorine to find Luis and bring him to me. He was the only person to whom I could turn for help. As I waited, I could hear the dance music very faintly. It was nerve-racking.

"When Victorine came back with Luis, she said that Hagen, one of the housemaids, had mentioned seeing 'Miss Claude' leave the house by the front door sometime after ten o'clock wearing her black coat and hat. Neither Luis nor Victorine could suggest any reason why Kitty should leave the house wearing Ann's clothes. Her high fever, the lateness of the hour, and the snowstorm made it all the more bewildering. Luis cried out, 'It's madness!' We stared at each other as he repeated more slowly, 'Madness — can that be it?'

"We both recalled people who suffered from nervous breakdown, people who left their homes suddenly and wandered about for days with complete loss of memory. To us it seemed the only explanation of Kitty's disappearance. She must have put on Ann's clothes and left the house in a sleep-walking state.

"All that I told you about Kitty being imaginative and introspective was quite true. She was underweight and not strong. We had had an unsettled time the last few weeks, opening the house and getting ready for the party. Before that Kitty had had a long series of dress fittings in Paris. She was always tired after a fitting. It seemed possible that her nerves had broken down under the strain. Perhaps her collapse that afternoon had been more nervous than physical.

"At this point I realised for the first time what a boomerang publicity can become. Thanks to me, Kitty was a celebrity. If I asked the police to find her now, the newspapers would get hold of the story and I shuddered as I imagined the situation enlarged by the headlines. Such a scandal would ruin Kitty and me with her if the papers got hold of the imperson-ation story or unearthed anything about the true state of our finances.

"I decided then and there that the whole thing must be suppressed as ruthlessly as people suppress the appearance of a bastard or a kleptomaniac in the family. I said, 'We will not call in the police. We will get a discreet lawyer or a private detective to find Kitty.' But Victorine pointed out that Kitty's photograph had been published so widely that if she were wandering about the city in a dazed condition someone might recognise her before we had time to trace her. For a moment I was at a loss. It was Luis who—"

"No!" cried Pasquale, springing to his feet. "It was she who did it — not I! That woman hypnotised me, nagged me, bullied me! It's all her fault — I am innocent!" He collapsed in his chair, sobbing again.

Rhoda looked at him. A slight smile flickered at the corners of her mouth. "Really, Luis…"

The sobs died away.

"Well, then," murmured Rhoda, sardonically, "I pointed out that no one could identify a wandering girl as Kitty Jocelyn, so long as Kitty was still living at home and appearing in public places. The impersonation had succeeded. Why shouldn't Ann go on with it until we found Kitty?

"If Kitty were to disappear from public view and cancel all the engagements she had made for the next few days, there would be gossip, no matter what excuse we gave. But if Ann were to disappear it wouldn't cause a ripple. She was a stranger in America, and she had almost no money. She had no close relatives on her father's side, and she had lost touch with her mother's family so completely that her uncle, Edgar Jocelyn, had not recognised her that afternoon when he dropped in for a cocktail. She had only one friend in New York — some school friend who kept a bookshop. But this friend did not know Ann was in New York. No one would notice her absence. All we had to do was to tell the servants that Ann had gone to some far-off place — Canada or California. They would believe that, since one of the housemaids had mistaken Kitty for Ann when she left the house in Ann's clothes. We could send Ann's luggage by express to some station to wait until called for.

"The first day after the party it would be only natural for

Kitty to rest, so Ann could do the same thing in Kitty's room. The day after that she could appear dressed as Kitty in some public place, not too well lighted — the opera would be perfect. And by the third day Kitty might be found. We were gambling on the hope that we would be able to trace her before she fell into the hands of the police. She couldn't have gone far because she had so little money. Kelley and Reinold, the private detectives we consulted, were sure they could find Kitty without scandal in a few days."

"But they didn't," said Inspector Foyle, abruptly.

"Why didn't they look in the mortuary — where she was? That's routine in disappearance cases. And you knew she was ill when she left the house."

"I'm afraid we all assumed Kitty was alive," Rhoda answered a little too smoothly. "You see, we didn't take her physical illness very seriously. I had hopes that she would be able to take up her old life after a little rest without anyone knowing what had happened."

Basil thought: *She's lying. I wonder what is the real reason they "assumed" Kitty was alive?*

"We were faced with one difficulty," continued Rhoda. "What if Ann should refuse to go on taking Kitty's place? She's not a shrewd girl. When I took her on as my secretary she hadn't sense enough to insist on a salary in addition to her board and passage to America. But she is one of those deceptively docile people who turn mulish at the most inconvenient moments — usually when some fine-drawn and quite impractical question of right and wrong arises. With so much at stake, we couldn't risk a refusal, which might lead to the very thing we wished to avoid — scandal." Rhoda turned to Pasquale with a subtle smile. "Will you have hysterics again, Luis, if I say that it was you who overcame this difficulty?"

Pasquale lifted his head and moaned.

"It was really very astute of him," went on Rhoda, imperturbably. "He pointed out that it must be a rather peculiar experience to impersonate someone else in public. Ann had been through a great mental strain. We might be able to take advantage of suggestible condition. When Ann woke the next morning after the dance, wearing Kitty's nightgown, in Kitty's bed and bedroom, we would all speak and act as if we sincerely believed that she was Kitty. When she insisted she was Ann, we would pretend she was suffering from a delusion.

"No one in the house, but Luis, Victorine, and myself, had seen Ann and Kitty together since Ann's transformation. With her hair cut, she looked exactly like her cousin. The servants were sure to be deceived and treat her as if she were Kitty. Of course Kelley and Reinold had to know that a cousin was taking Kitty's place to conceal her disappearance. But they need not know the cousin was doing so involuntarily. When it was all over, we could get Ann to take the whole thing as a hoax — with a little persuasion — and—"

There was a sharp crack. Detective Officer Duff swore under his breath. He had broken the nib of his fountain pen.

"There's another pen there!" Impatiently, Rhoda swept across the room to the little marquetry desk. She snatched open a draw that contained an array of old-fashioned pens. In doing so, her elbow struck the ink well. It toppled and rolled. A shower of drops fell on the blotter, and a great spurt of black ink splashed down the peacock blue silk of her dress from waist to hem.

10

STILL LIFE WITH BOTTLE

R hoda dabbed at the stain on her skirt with a wisp of handkerchief, disgusted as a pampered and fastidious cat splashed with mud. "Will you wait while I go upstairs and change my dress?"

Foyle looked at Sobel, and Sobel shook his head. "I'm sorry, ma'am," said Foyle. "But I'm afraid we haven't time for that now. I want statements from Mr Pasquale and the servants. And I'll have to see Miss Jocelyn's rooms and go over the house. She was taken ill in this house. Some clue to her poisoning may be here."

Rhoda shrugged. "As you please. I'll do anything I can to help."

Pasquale's confidence was ebbing again. "I — I'm not under arrest?" he cried hoarsely.

"Not yet," returned Foyle.

Basil was amused at the change in the Inspector's manner. At the beginning of the interviews he had been a little over-awed. But now he had heard Rhoda's story, she was just another case. Perhaps the fact that the house was heavily mortgaged was not without its effect.

Foyle opened the door and strode to the head of the great staircase as self-possessed as if he were at Headquarters, "Hi! Casey!"

Gregg materialised out of the shadows in the lower hall. "I will inform Mr Casey that you desire his presence, sir."

"I want you, too," responded Foyle. "I've got to phone Headquarters for some more men — this place is as big as Madison Square Garden! I want you to round up all the servants in one room and hold them until I send for them. Casey, I want you take Mrs Jocelyn and Mr Pasquale into this next room and don't let 'em out of your sight or hearing."

Gregg was staring at Foyle.

"Well, what's the matter with you? Get going!"

"Begging your pardon, sir, but has Miss Kitty been kidnapped?"

Foyle eyed the man for a moment and then decided to trust him. "Not kidnapped. Murdered."

"Murdered!"

"Yeah. And don't spill it to the other servants until I've talked to them."

Basil and Sobel were left alone in the Murillo Room. Sobel yawned and looked at his watch. "Gosh! It's nearly midnight! We've been here for hours." He helped himself to one of Basil's cigarettes. "Funny to think of a woman like that talking so frankly. Or was she putting on an act?"

Basil stared into the fire. "People will say anything when they're suspected of murder. Even the truth, or part of it."

"Then it's possible Kitty Jocelyn left the house in a sort of sleepwalking state?"

"There've been such cases. The technical name is *fugue*. All mental diseases are a form of flight from reality — usually a mental form. In *fugue* there's physical flight as well. But it's equally possible that Kitty left the house in a perfectly sane condition for some reason of her own."

Sobel was silent. Then he said abruptly, "What would Rhoda and Pasquale have done if Ann had never escaped from this house and Kitty's body had never been identified? They couldn't have forced Ann to impersonate Kitty the rest of her life! It looks to me as if they had reason to believe Kitty was alive and could be found. Something they haven't told us."

"Either that or the exact opposite," returned Basil. "Suppose they did poison Kitty — knew she was dead and didn't want her body found and identified. Before she died, they invented a pretext to induce her to leave the house wearing Ann's clothes. Then they forced Ann to impersonate Kitty in order to conceal her death and prevent identification of her body. And they might have forced Ann to impersonate Kitty forever by pretending she was mentally unbalanced. Once they planted a doubt of Ann's identity in her own mind, she might have become insane eventually."

"Nice people. But why employ private detectives to trace Kitty? And why poison Kitty in the first place?"

"That's just it. According to their story, it was to their interest to keep Kitty alive so she could marry money."

"No wonder Rhoda was so frank about her poverty. It's a sort of psychological alibi."

"It and the private detectives," agreed Basil.

Sobel tossed his cigarette stub into the fire. "How long does it take this reducing drug to act?"

"A colleague of mine at the hospital says that a large dose

begins to act in ten to fifteen minutes and causes death in three to four hours — or a little longer."

"Then it was the cocktail?"

Basil nodded. "Can you imagine a better vehicle? No two taste alike. Most are cloudy from shaking. And they all contain two solvents — water and ethyl alcohol."

Sobel took a pencil and an old envelope from his breast pocket and began to write on his knee. "According to Ann Claude, Kitty had her cocktail between 6 and 7 pm and fell ill about ten minutes after taking it. That would make the probably hour of death between 10 and 11 pm — say midnight at the latest. According to Rhoda, a housemaid saw Kitty leave the house sometime after 10 pm wearing Ann's clothes. Her body was found about ten blocks from this house at dawn next morning. It all fits."

Basil lit a cigarette and handed his case to Sobel again. "I suppose you realise that limits the suspects to people who were in this room at cocktail time?"

There was a moment's silence.

"Sure of that?" queried Sobel.

"Everyone else who had cocktails here that day was alive and well at the dance afterward. That means only one cocktail was poisoned. Who could have known which one was to be Kitty's until it was handed to her in this room?"

The door opened and Foyle came in, mopping his brow with a big blue and white handkerchief. "Well, I've got things organised!" he announced. "As soon as the rest of the boys get here, we'll see the servants and check on Mrs Jocelyn's statement. If only they'd called us in when Kitty first disappeared!"

"Or when she first fell ill," added Sobel. "I shall want a list of everyone who was here for cocktails that day."

"You can have it right now." Foyle took out a notebook and flipped over the pages. "I made a list of them when I heard Ann Claude's story." He began to read in expressionless singsong. "First, I put the family: *Rhoda Jocelyn, Kitty's stepmother; Edgar Jocelyn, Kitty's uncle; Ann Jocelyn Claude, Kitty's cousin and Rhoda's secretary.*"

"Really, Inspector," broke in Basil, "you don't think Ann Claude—"

"We always suspect the party who first reports the crime," answered the Inspector, grimly.

"Do you? If I happen to come across a crime, I'll be careful not to report it then!"

"I think you can rule out Ann Claude," said Sobel, "As a rule, murderers only report their own crimes to the police when they can forestall others by doing so. But we might never have proved murder at all if it hadn't been for Ann Claude's story."

"Maybe she didn't know that." The Inspector resumed his singsong: "Second, I put friends: *Luis Pasquale, artist; Nicholas Danine, director of a German explosives company.*"

"A chemical industry," murmured Basil.

"What's that got to do with it?"

"Nothing, perhaps. Go on."

"Third, I put the people who were interested in the coming-out party in a professional way. They are: *Mrs Jowett, social secretary; Philip Leach, gossip writer. And, last of all, I put the servants: Gregg, the butler and Victorine, Rhoda Jocelyn's maid.*"

Gregg appeared in the doorway. "The other detectives have arrived, sir. And some journalists at the front door. They seem to have followed the police car and they're asking for you."

"Blast!" cried Foyle bitterly.

But Morris Sobel revived like a parched flower at the first

drop of rain. "I'll handle them, Inspector," he said swiftly. "You needn't bother. I'll take them right off your hands. It's getting pretty late, anyway, and I don't believe you need me now. Coming, doctor?"

Basil felt as though he'd been asked to leave a play at the beginning of the second act. "If the Inspector doesn't mind, I'd like to see this through."

"Sure. You stick around, doc. Maybe you'll see some o' those psychic fingerprints you talk about."

Foyle grinned broadly. Sobel turned away, smiling. "Gregg," went on Foyle, "I'd like you to show us Miss Jocelyn's rooms next."

They went to the next floor in an elevator, and Gregg led the way to a sitting room, bedroom and bathroom *en suite*. Old French pieces, in grey and faded olive green, furnished the rooms. The chairs were upholstered with oyster-white brocade. In the sitting room, an open hearth was paved with porcelain tiles.

As soon as the photographers had finished taking pictures, the Inspector and his men went through the rooms, dictating to Duff anything they thought worthy of record. Closets full of dresses and coats, each with its own hanger and silken cover. Shoes on silver mounted trees. Dresser-drawerfuls of fine under things scented with orris. But no clues.

"What about the desk?" asked Basil.

Foyle sat down before it and went through its papers swiftly. First came a few letters addressed to *Miss Katherine Jocelyn* with European stamps.

"Can you translate these, doc?"

Basil looked over his shoulder. "French and Italian. Old school friends. Nothing useful there, Inspector."

Next came some letters in English with American stamps

— invitations, bills, advertisements. Hairdressers begged Kitty to patronise them. Photographers implored her to pose for them. And the De Luxe Advertising Agency offered her $1,000 for an endorsement of cigarettes. No address book. No love letters.

"But moderns don't write love letters," observed Basil. "They telegraph or telephone."

"Well, here's a sort of account book." Foyle smiled involuntarily as he noticed two errors in elementary arithmetic. "And a cheque book." There was a cheque for $50 made out to *self* and signed *Katherine Jocelyn*, which had never been torn out of the book, and which could never be cashed now.

"Not a very business-like young lady," remarked Foyle. "No wonder her stepmother was able to run things and get away with most of the money."

He looked up to find Basil had left him and strolled toward the bathroom.

"What's that?" Basil asked Duff, standing beside something that looked like a small, enamelled safe.

"It's an electric refrigerator, doctor. Lots of cold cream and such stuff inside."

Basil opened the door and glanced at the collection of perfumed and tinted unguents. "A few cents' worth of mutton fat would do the trick just as well." He shut the door and his glance swept the bathroom settling upon a cupboard with a mirror door.

"Looking for anything particular, doc? Or just looking?" Foyle's voice came from the next room.

"Just looking." Basil opened the mirror door and eyed toothpaste tubes, mouth washes and antiseptic lotions. "Now, we'll go through Mrs Jocelyn's rooms," said Foyle. "See if you can get Casey on the phone, Duff, and ask him to bring her upstairs."

As Rhoda met them in the upper hall, she seemed less at ease. Perhaps the ugly splash of ink on her handsome dress had shaken her self-possession. That one stain was enough to make her look defiled. It was almost symbolic. The word sent Basil's mind off on a new train of thought that opened up curious possibilities.

"What's in there?" demanded Foyle, as they passed several closed doors.

"Nothing, sir."

Gregg opened a door and they saw an empty room, the furniture swathed in dust sheets.

"Economy," said Rhoda, briefly. "Only a few of the rooms are in active use."

Her own suite was at the farther end of the hall. The sitting room, on a corner, had twice as many windows as Kitty's. It was furnished, preciously, in rosewood.

"I really can't imagine what you expect to find here," murmured Rhoda, with a flavour of irony.

"Just routine, ma'am," answered Foyle. "After all, this is a house where murder has taken place."

"The rooms are dusted thoroughly every day." This time the irony was obvious as she watched one of the detectives who carried a fingerprint kit.

Basil went into the bedroom but did not linger there. They could hear his footfalls scrape on the tiles of the bathroom floor. He came back to the sitting room carrying something wrapped in his handkerchief.

"Mrs Jocelyn," he said, with unusual gravity. "Your step-daughter endorsed a reducing medicine known by the trade name of Sveltis. The endorsement implied that she took it regularly. Is that true?"

"Of course not." Rhoda seemed irritated by the naiveté of such a question. "Kitty didn't need reducing medicine. She always had a lovely figure. That was why Sveltis asked her for her endorsement."

"Would you be prepared to swear that Miss Jocelyn never took Sveltis?"

"Naturally! She's been thin ever since her first attack of malaria in Rome when she was eleven. You can see it in that photograph on the table just behind you."

It was an enlarged snapshot framed in silver — a ten or eleven-year-old girl with hollow cheeks and long, thin legs standing among the pigeons in front of St Mark's, Venice. For a moment Basil wondered why Rhoda should keep such a photograph in her sitting room. Then he realised it was one of the properties in the little drama of maternal devotion she had been playing.

He turned back to her, eying her own tall, slight figure. "Did you ever take Sveltis yourself?"

She stared in astonishment. "Really, Dr Willing!" As he seemed unimpressed, she added, "Certainly not!"

"Did anyone else in the household take Sveltis?"

"I don't suppose the servants could afford it, but I really don't know. Why do you ask?"

Basil ignored the question. "Did you or your stepdaughter ever own a bottle of Sveltis?"

"The Sveltis people sent Kitty a sample bottle with her cheque. We laughed about it. I remember her putting it in the scrap basket, in this very room."

"When was that?"

"A few weeks ago — in November, I think."

"But the endorsement first appeared last spring?"

"Yes. They were very slow about sending Kitty her cheque. We had to write several times."

"You're sure neither of you took Sveltis?"

"How many times must I tell you Kitty was actually under-weight? Her Paris physician will testify to that. He tried to build her up by getting her to drink milk with all her meals, but it didn't do much good."

Basil was unwrapping the object in his handkerchief.

He was careful not to touch it with his fingertips. "Mrs Jocelyn, how do you explain that this bottle of Sveltis was in your bathroom cupboard — half empty?"

Foyle peered over Basil's shoulder.

The Sveltis bottle was "modernistic" as the advertisement promised — crystal and black enamel, in chic contrast to the pale yellow of the tablets inside. The label was less lyrical in its claims than the advertisement, for labels are subject to stricter regulations. Blown in the glass was the silhouette of a nymph with inhumanly attenuated thighs, and legs repre-senting at least three fourths of her body to keep the ideal of willowy perfection constantly in the mind of anyone taking Sveltis. The round, black cap was embossed in gold with the familiar slogan: *Science Says Sveltis is the Sane Way to Reduce*. Even the letters were tall and narrowly spaced as if they had been reducing, too. As a final touch of luxury, a thick tassel of yellow silk dangled from the cap.

Covering his fingertips with his handkerchief, Basil unscrewed the cap and spilled one or two of the tablets into his palm. The edges had crumbled a little and there was a fine yellow dust in the bottle.

"I — I don't understand," gasped Rhoda. For the first time, she looked really disconcerted. "I remember distinctly throwing out the sample bottle the day it came. And Kitty never took the stuff."

"You mean she never took it intentionally," said Basil.

"Oh! You think it was Sveltis that—?"

"I don't know yet." He was wrapping his handkerchief around the bottle.

Rhoda leaned forward eagerly. "If she'd been taking Sveltis, then it might not be murder after all? It might be an accidental overdose?"

"Exactly."

"Well—" She smiled, twisting her fingers together. "Maybe I was a little too positive. Maybe she was taking Sveltis without telling me."

"But she was taking milk to put on weight," said Basil, softly. "Her Paris physician will testify to that, you say. Ann Claude has done so already. And the photograph of her as a child shows she has been thin for years. She never needed reducing medicine."

Rhoda was silent. Her mind seemed to be darting hither and thither, like an animal in a trap, looking for some loophole — some way of going back on her former testimony that would be convincing.

"After all," her breath came quickly. "If I had known anything about the murder, I would hardly keep the poison openly in my own bathroom would I?"

"Maybe you weren't expecting us tonight," said Foyle, without emotion. "Or maybe you were so smart you thought we wouldn't suspect you if we found the poison there — openly, as you've just pointed out."

When she had left the room under Casey's watchful escort, Foyle looked at the Sveltis bottle again. "Damn!"

"What's the matter?"

"Well, doc, you and I know these fool endorsements don't mean a thing. But once the defence lawyers get busy, how can the DA convince a jury that a girl who was advertised all over the country as taking Sveltis, really never touched the stuff and so couldn't have taken an accidental overdose?"

Basil's eyes held the Inspector's as he answered, slowly, "The murderer thought of that."

11

TRIPTYCH

B asil lit his last cigarette with characteristic deliberation. "Don't you see it can hardly be coincidence if Kitty Jocelyn was poisoned by an overdose of the very product she endorsed?" He clasped his hands behind his head and blew a long plume of smoke. "When she signed that testimonial, she signed her death warrant. She gave the murderer a unique chance to make the murder look like an accident. *'Just slip a Sveltis tablet in your evening cocktail...'* Somebody slipped in more than one and the cocktail wasn't his."

Foyle whistled. "Premeditation — if we could prove it!"

Basil nodded. "Yes, I think we can assume malice afore-thought. The most striking thing about this crime is its malicious ingenuity."

"We-ell," Foyle tugged at his lower lip. "I wouldn't put anything past Rhoda and Pasquale."

Basil frowned. "If Sveltis was the poison used, it doesn't look like Rhoda — so far."

"Why not?"

"No one could choose Sveltis to poison Kitty without

hoping her murder would be attributed to an accidental over-dose she had taken herself. That was too obvious for the murderer to overlook. His plan must have been based on the fact that Kitty was the girl who announced in advertisements that she was taking Sveltis. So the last thing he wanted was Kitty's body unidentified. But Rhoda delayed and almost prevented the identification by making Ann impersonate Kitty after she disappeared. And Rhoda has just testified that Kitty never took Sveltis. We could not have proved that with Ann's testimony alone. Then there's a little psychological point — not conclusive, but not wholly negligible. Poisoning, like klep-tomania, arson, and cruelty to animals, is often associated with sexual repression."

Foyle grinned broadly. "I get you, doc! With Rhoda and Pasquale, it isn't repression."

"Pasquale might have committed the murder alone — without Rhoda's knowledge," Basil went on. "She didn't plan the impersonation until after Kitty fell ill from the first effects of the poison. The murderer might have poisoned Kitty, and then found himself forced to help Rhoda's impersonation plot against his will."

"Or against her will," put in Foyle. "That maid — she had plenty of opportunity to poison Kitty."

"I don't believe either Victorine or Ann poisoned Kitty because they happen to be the only people who could have prevented the impersonation. It depended on Ann's resem-blance to Kitty and Victorine's skill at make-up. Either one could have stopped it at the beginning by refusing to partici-pate. Had either one been the murderer, she would have done so, since it was the impersonation that ruined the murderer's plan."

The Sveltis bottle, still wrapped in Basil's handkerchief,

went into Foyle's coat pocket, the yellow tassel dangling outside.

"How do you suppose this thing got into Rhoda's cupboard? Is it a plant to throw suspicion on her?"

"Possibly. Or it may be she is mistaken about the sample bottle being thrown out."

"But why is it half empty?"

"Perhaps the murderer came across it and took the missing tablets to poison Kitty, avoiding a purchase of Sveltis which might have been traced to him."

"Doc, you're making my headache!"

Foyle rose and stretched himself with a mighty yawn. "Let's tackle the servants and call it a day. Or rather a night." He glanced at the clock on the mantelpiece. "Believe it or not, it's 1:10 am!"

Downstairs in the Murillo Room once more, Foyle threw himself into a light chair that creaked ominously and placed thick-soled boots on a footstool covered with *petit point*. "We'll start with you, Gregg."

Duff again seated himself at the marquetry table and opened his notebook.

"I was butler to the late Lord Chisholme, sir. When he died, I came to America. This is my first post over here."

"How long have you been with Mrs Jocelyn?"

"Only six weeks, sir. We were all engaged through an agency when she reached New York in November. With the exception, of course, of Victorine, Mrs Jocelyn's own maid, who came with her from France."

"Ever see Miss Kitty take a medicine called Sveltis?"

"Why, no, sir. I suppose she must have taken it in her own room. Because she did endorse it, didn't she?"

Basil made another mental note: Apparently the servants

never realised Kitty did not take Sveltis.

"Gregg, did you mix and serve cocktails the afternoon of the coming-out party?" continued Foyle.

"Yes, sir."

"Did anyone else help you serve them?"

"No, sir. That's just the sort of thing I mean when I say we are under-staffed. I should have had the footman or at least a parlour maid to help me."

"Did you leave the cocktails standing anywhere after they were poured into the glasses?"

"No, sir. I brought them directly from the pantry to this room — as soon as I poured them out."

"Did everyone have the same cocktail that day?"

"Mrs Jowett and Mr Danine had some pale, dry sherry. Everyone else had Bronx cocktails."

"How were they made?"

"Gin, Italian vermouth, orange juice, and bitters."

"Horrible!" murmured Basil, who disliked cocktails made with fruit juice. "Do you recall the colour?"

"The colour, sir?" Gregg was puzzled. "They were the usual colour for Bronx cocktails — a pale yellow."

Basil thought of the pale yellow of the Sveltis tablets. "Was any food served?"

"There was a bowl of unpitted Spanish olives on ice," said Gregg, precisely. "And Mr Danine had a biscuit with his sherry. That was all."

The Inspector tugged at his lower lip. "Do you remember if Miss Jocelyn had more than one cocktail?"

"To the best of my recollection, no one had a second cocktail, sir, except Mr Leach. He always has several."

"Gregg, I'm going to be frank with you. The medical evidence looks as if Kitty Jocelyn was poisoned when she drank that cocktail."

Gregg paled. "I — I had no idea. Of course, when I left England, they warned me people were always being — er — bumped off in America. But, somehow, I never quite believed it until now."

"Did you use more than one shaker?"

"No, sir. They were all mixed in the same shaker."

"That means that Miss Jocelyn's cocktail was poisoned after it was poured out and passed to her," ruminated Foyle.

Gregg smiled wanly. "That's fortunate for me, sir."

"Of course you might have poisoned the cocktail yourself just before passing it to her." Foyle's tone took the sting out of his words. "But I don't believe you did."

"Certainly not, sir!" cried Gregg, earnestly.

"Did you notice anyone touching her glass after she had taken it?" asked Basil.

Gregg frowned in a concentrated effort at recollection. "Miss Kitty was a very impulsive young lady, if I may say so, sir, and she was restless that afternoon — excited because of the party. She fidgeted and roamed about the room with her cocktail in one hand and a cigarette in the other. Every now and then she'd put the glass down and pick up one of the cards attached to the flowers that had come and read the name on it. All the people were scattered about the room. Miss Kitty was near each one at one time or another."

"That's helpful!"

"I suppose it could have been done then, sir — when she set down her cocktail glass. Oh, no!"

For the first time there was emotion in Gregg's voice. He turned startled eyes on the Inspector. "There couldn't have been poison in that cocktail, sir!" he said, confidently.

"Why not?"

"Because Mr Pasquale drank half of it."

For a moment there was no sound but the whispering of the fire. Then Foyle was hurling questions at Gregg. Miss Kitty had set down her glass half full and turned away from it for a moment. Mr Pasquale had set down his own glass near it. When he went to pick up his glass, he took Miss Kitty's — by mistake, he said afterward. Miss Kitty claimed the cocktail as hers just as he finished it. He apologised and offered her his own which was untouched. Gregg himself had offered her a fresh one. But she said she didn't want any more. And soon afterward she went upstairs. Gregg was absolutely sure Mr Pasquale had taken a full half of the cocktail — he was standing directly behind Mr Pasquale at the time. And he was sure that Mr Pasquale had not been ill. On the contrary, he had been in the best of health the last few days, though he was always a rather moody and excitable sort of gentleman, if Gregg might say so.

"What a case!" Foyle took out his blue and white handkerchief and mopped his forehead once more. Impossible ideas were flitting through his mind. Could the poison have been in something she had at luncheon? But Willing said this poison began to act in "10 or 15 minutes". Had some other poison been used? Or could the poison have been in Kitty's cigarettes? Or in the olives served with the cocktails? Or in the quinine they gave her after she fell ill? She might have had a genuine attack of malaria at first. One thing seemed certain. It couldn't have been in the cocktail if Pasquale drank half of it. And that meant the suspects were not confined to the people present at cocktail time.

"Are you sure this was a blunder on Pasquale's part?" Basil was asking Gregg. "Isn't it possible he drank from Miss Jocelyn's cocktail glass deliberately?"

"Oh, no, sir. He was quite astonished when she said it was her glass."

Basil seemed satisfied with the answer. Foyle wondered just what he was driving at. "That's all, Gregg. We'll see Mrs Jocelyn's maid next."

"Mademoiselle Victorine? Very good, sir."

With her long upper lip and high-necked black woollen gown, this mistress of the art of make-up was herself completely innocent of face cream, powder, or lipstick. Her face was dry, brown, and crinkled as a walnut shell. A large mole on her chin sprouted three black bristles. Her nails were clean, but unvarnished and short as a surgeon's. She folded large, flexible hands across a flat abdomen, and waited for them to speak.

"Siddown," said Foyle.

"*Monsieur?*"

"Golly, she don't speak English! You tackle her, doc." Victorine received the news that Kitty had been murdered with more stolidity than Gregg. Basil had an impression of peasant stoicism and peasant avarice. This was a nature that would show amoral, feudal loyalty to anyone who paid high wages — as long as there was a reasonable prospect of those wages being paid.

"I suppose you will be returning to France soon?" said Basil, conversationally.

"To France?" Victorine was puzzled. "Madame has said nothing…"

"Oh, not with Madame Jocelyn. You doubtless know that she has suffered very grave financial reverses. It is probable that she will live in a small hotel in future, and unlikely to afford any servants — even a maid."

Some emotion stirred in the depths of Victorine's eyes.

"It is not possible!" Her glance flitted about the room.

"This belongs to Madame — the furniture alone—"

"All that means nothing," answered Basil. "It has been devoured by debts and mortgages. You know what it is — a mortgage?"

"*Bien sûr*. But I never divined that madame—"

"But of course you didn't. If you had, you would scarcely have taken the risk of being charged with criminal conspiracy for Madame Jocelyn's sake — as you did when you played jailer to Mademoiselle Claude. But now I'm sure you realise that your best chance of escaping serious charges is to tell the exact truth. *Monsieur l'Inspecteur* Foyle wishes to hear everything that happened to you the evening of the dance."

"Very well." In a sour voice, Victorine confirmed everything that Ann had told them.

"You promenaded with mademoiselle the morning of the day she fell ill," said Basil. "Where did you go?"

"We went to an art gallery and a linen shop. Then we walked home."

"You went nowhere else?"

"Ah, no! Mademoiselle was walking in order to exercise. It is good for the skin."

"Did she have anything to eat or drink with you?"

"Nothing."

"When was the last time you saw her?"

"About nine o'clock the evening of the dance. I went to the room of Mademoiselle Claude, where Mademoiselle Kitty reposed. All the windows were open, and it made cold in the room. I scolded her and closed the windows. She was still in a state of excitement, but she was no longer gay. She seemed restless and depressed. She said, 'Victorine, it is annoying to fall ill so suddenly. I really thought that doctor in

Paris was telling the truth when he said I was rid of malaria.'"

"Then she said nothing to suggest suicide?"

"Mademoiselle believed it was all simply an attack of the malaria. I thought so too, and I did not linger in her room. I had much to do that night, for I was charged with the rooms where the ladies who came to the dance made their toilets and left their cloaks. I didn't go back to see mademoiselle again until about three in the morning. Then I discovered she was gone."

"Didn't she notice anything out of the ordinary the day of the dance?" urged Foyle in a stage whisper.

Basil repeated the question in French.

"*Si!*" Victorine's black eyes gleamed suddenly. "One thing seems to me a little strange, now I recall it. A little moment before the cocktails were served, I was passing the library door. It was closed but I heard voices — quarrelling voices loud, and, oh, furious!"

"You heard what was said?"

"Ah, that, no! The door is thick."

"But the voices were loud. You didn't listen?"

"*M'sieu!*" Victorine folded her hands.

"Possibly you recognised the voices?"

"I recognised the woman's voice." Her thin lips curled in a malicious smile. "It was Madame Jocelyn," she said slowly, savouring the name. "I am certain of it."

"And the other was a man?"

"A man, yes. It was not a voice I knew well, but I think it was the voice of the gentleman Edgar Jocelyn."

. . .

"WAS THAT JUST SPITE?" demanded Foyle after Victorine had left the room. "Maybe you shouldn't have told her Rhoda was broke."

"We would never have got a word out of her if I hadn't," retorted Basil.

A timid tap on the door announced Hagen, the second housemaid. She looked no more than eighteen or twenty, a strapping Brünhilde with full bosom and buxom thighs straining the seams of her black uniform. There was a high colour in her cheeks, but her lips were pale, parted and dry, because she breathed through her mouth. Foyle wondered if that made her look more stupid than she really was.

"Speak English?" he began, not to be caught again.

"Y-Yes, sir." Her voice was unexpectedly harsh. "Full name?"

"M-M-My name, sir?" She swallowed. "M-M-My name Hagen."

"Now, my dear," said Foyle, not unkindly, "I've sent for you because you saw someone you took for Miss Claude leave the house during the dance. That right?"

"Y-Yes, sir. B-B-But—" She paused and mastered her tendency to stutter. "It was Miss Claude."

"You saw her in a good light?"

"Well, n-no," she admitted. "It was after dark an' I didn't see her face. I only saw her back as she went out the side door. But I'd know that shabby black coat of hers anywhere. She used to wear it every day."

Basil looked at his watch, and then looked at the girl, his eyes on her throat. "I'm afraid that identification wouldn't stand up in court," replied Foyle. "As a matter of fact, it was not Miss Claude, but Miss Jocelyn wearing Miss Claude's coat."

"But when I saw Miss Kitty the nex' day—"

"It wasn't Miss Kitty you saw the next day," explained Foyle, patiently. "It was Miss Ann with her hair cut and waved and her eyebrows plucked, so that she looked like Miss Kitty.'

"But then…" Hagen fixed her glassy, blue eyes on Foyle. "What's become of Miss Kitty?"

"She's been murdered," answered Foyle. "Poisoned."

"P-Poisoned?" The colour bled from the girl's cheeks. "Oh," she moaned, "I'll be next, I know I will!"

"Snap out of it!" cried Foyle wearily.

Basil interrupted. "What makes you think you'll be poisoned?"

"The food, sir!" she wailed. "Ever since I've been here, it's tasted bad."

"Have you mentioned this to anyone?"

"Oh, yes. I k-keep tellin' the housekeeper an' Mr Gregg. But they won't take no n-notice of me. An' then the chef gets mad an' he won't speak to me now. He's F-French an' he says because I'm G-German I don't know what good cookin' is. But I'm not German — I'm American. I was brought to America when I was three years old an' I don't know a word of German an' I do know what good cookin' is an' the food they give me here tastes bad. Somebody's trying to p-poison me!" The fat tears rolled down her round cheeks. "One of those f-fiends you read about in the p-p-papers !" She choked and buried her face in her apron.

Foyle shook his head slowly. "Now we'll have to have all the food analysed."

"Lambert will love that," murmured Basil. "If I were you, I'd take my meals outside the house for a while."

"I c-certainly will, sir!" Her voice was muffled by the apron.

110

"Have you quarrelled with anyone in the house?"

"N-Not exactly. But when I was dustin' one day, I b-broke a flask of hand lotion M'm'selle Victorine brought from Paris."

"What did she say?"

"She didn't say anythin'. She just looked at me. It was awful. I'd rather have had her say things—"

"Did Victorine ever show antagonism toward Miss Kitty?"

Hagen stared. "Oh, no. She was fond of Miss Kitty."

When Hagen had gone, Foyle said, "Well, there's no doubt about her innocence. She's too dumb to commit murder."

"If she'd had her adenoids removed and her teeth straightened when she was a child her whole personality might have been different," remarked Basil. "I wonder why she was so frightened?"

"Frightened? She was just dumb!"

"Her pupils were dilated and there was a little pulse visible in her throat. I tried to time the beating and I made it around 22 to a quarter of a minute — that is about 88 to the full minute."

"Anything over 80 is excessive in most people. She was probably scared because I told her Kitty had been poisoned."

"No. Her pulse was going fast before you told her about Kitty. And yet it looked normal to me when she first came in. Something else that she heard or saw in this room must have startled her."

Foyle stared all around the room. But he could see nothing out of the ordinary — nothing that had not been there all along.

12

CARICATURE

The other servants denied knowledge of the Sveltis bottle.
All seemed to believe that Kitty had been taking Sveltis
herself. The chef explained at some length that "*cette 'Agen*"
was a hysterical woman and a miserable Boche insufficiently
civilised to appreciate the delicate shades of taste that were the
glory of the true French kitchen.

"This sure is a queer set-up," said Foyle, when the inquisi-
tion was over. "Wages not paid on time, half the rooms in the
house shut up in dust sheets, house and furniture mortgaged,
money for a coming-out party supplied by a relative, pocket
money from testimonials and indirect advertising, everything
else bought on credit — and then the build-up of Kitty in the
newspapers as 'the loveliest debutante of the season' … Well, I
guess we've done all we can tonight."

"Aren't you going to take a look at Pasquale's quarters next
door?" suggested Basil.

"Oh, Lord, I suppose we must! There are several things I
want to ask that fat slob."

The former coach house stood between the Jocelyn house

and an apartment house. On the ground floor was a double doorway wide enough to admit a carriage and pair. Above was a studio window, once the opening to a hayloft.

Pasquale took out a latch key. A spiral stairway brought them to the "love nest", as Foyle insisted on calling it behind Pasquale's back. It was furnished in the modern French manner — pale wood, with a figure like watered silk, in suave lines unbroken by corners, mouldings or ornaments. Basil marvelled at Rhoda's folly in squandering money here. But there was something catlike about Pasquale which would always demand the cream of life — doubtless why he had chosen the role of an old woman's darling. His morphine habit, his slack, unexercised muscles, and his full, feminine contours all seemed part of the same trait — self-indulgence. How could such a man achieve the selflessness of the artist? The answer was quite simple: he couldn't.

Foyle stood before an easel; arms akimbo, eying an unfinished canvas in which a nude, who seemed to have been recently flayed, sat on top of a taxicab, playing a guitar under an ominously stormy sky, while three watermelons and a toothbrush occupied the foreground. "That how you earn your living?" demanded Foyle.

"Oh, no." Pasquale smiled with gentle superiority. "Rhoda — Mrs Jocelyn — has saved me from the humiliation of prostituting my genius in the marketplace so I can devote myself to pure self-expression."

Basil had seen painting equally subjective produced by mental patients in a hypnotic state, and it had often helped him in diagnosing their secret thoughts. For that reason, he studied every detail of Pasquale's psychoanalysis in paint. Was it imagination — or did the face of the nude really bear a faint resemblance to Kitty Jocelyn, hardly more than a pictorial echo?

Pasquale eased his fat body into one of the low chairs and lit a cigarette. "You're quite at liberty to poke around." He waved a plump, white hand.

"Thanks," said Foyle, not without sarcasm.

Basil dropped into a chair opposite Pasquale. "Just what did you mean by your remark that Mrs Jocelyn had always hated her stepdaughter?"

Pasquale had recovered all his assurance when he found he was not under arrest. "Rhoda was always jealous of Gerald Jocelyn's affection for his first wife's child. That's why Kitty was sent off to school when she was hardly more than a baby. It was only after Gerald died, and Kitty began to mature, that Rhoda realised Kitty's beauty was a marketable asset — about the only one Gerald left her. Then she kept Kitty with her and spoiled the girl. But the old hatred was there underneath. Rhoda's had several husbands but she's never had any children. No maternal instinct. Something to do with glands, I think. And," he chuckled, "even a motherly woman Rhoda's age could scarcely be expected to love a stepdaughter so much younger and prettier than herself."

Something caught the light and winked at Basil from the edge of the rug. A bit of broken glass? He stooped and picked it up. A platinum ring set with a rose diamond. He lifted his eyes and saw Pasquale watching — his face a sickly, greenish grey. It was not particularly warm in the studio, but a bead of sweat gathered on his forehead.

Foyle had seen the whole thing. "That your ring, Mr Pasquale?" he demanded, sharply.

"Er — yes — of course." Pasquale ran his tongue over his lips. "I — er — mislaid it."

"It looks like a woman's ring. Suppose you try it on." Even his little finger was too fat. He couldn't get the ring past the first joint. He gulped and muttered, "I haven't worn it lately. It's an heirloom. Belonged to my mother. I keep it for sentimental reasons."

"The platinum setting looks modern."

"I had the diamond reset."

"For sentimental reasons?"

Pasquale's eyes shifted and he wriggled in his chair. "Well, Inspector, to tell the truth..."

"That'll be a novelty!"

"...this ring belonged to a little friend of mine and I couldn't let her down by telling you about her — could I? She was here the other night and took it off when she washed her hands. I found it after she'd gone and then I — er — mislaid it myself."

"What's the name of this little friend? She must be worried about her ring. Let's phone her right now and tell her it's okay — if she can identify it."

Again Pasquale's eyes shifted. "I — well — the truth is — I — er — don't know her name or address."

"Not even her phone number?"

"No. She was — well, what you would call a pick-up."

"How convenient! Of course it didn't occur to you to advertise—"

"No. She said she was married. Her husband—"

"You think of everything — don't you? Does Mrs Jocelyn know about your picking up little friends?"

"Of course not!"

Basil glanced inside the ring. Someone must have worn it for some time. The jeweller's name and mark were obliterated.

Foyle slipped the ring into his pocket. "I'm keeping this for the present."

Foyle went through the rest of the flat briskly. The tiny kitchenette looked as if it had never been used. Pasquale explained that he got most of his meals at the houses of friends. One of Rhoda's maids kept the place clean. No, he didn't pay her anything. Why should he? There was an enormous, built-in bathtub worthy of Imperial Rome, furnished with a shower curtain of coral, oil-silk, a rubber air-cushion to sit on, and a shelf with an electric lamp and an ash tray, for reading and smoking in the bath. Tinted and scented soaps and bath salts glittered on a glass shelf, flanked with toothpaste and bicarbonate of soda.

"What's that thing?" Foyle pointed to a machine not unlike a bathroom scales in appearance. A loop of webbing dangled from it.

Pasquale lounged forward and pressed a button. The webbing began to vibrate violently with a humming sound. "It's for reducing my hips," he explained candidly.

"Have you ever tried Sveltis?" Basil's tone was casual.

"That Persian stuff?" Pasquale's voice betrayed no emotion. Evidently Rhoda had not seen fit to tell him about the Sveltis bottle found in her bathroom closet while they were both under the vigilant guard of Detective Officer Casey.

"No," he went on, "some say it's none too safe."

"Kitty Jocelyn tried it," said Basil. "Unintentionally."

"Oh, no! Kitty never took it. She only endorsed it. She was actually trying to put on weight."

"I said *unintentionally*."

Pasquale's jaw slackened. "You mean…?" He gasped. "It was — that?"

"We believe so. And the medical evidence suggests that it

was slipped into the cocktail she drank the afternoon of the dance. The one you finished by mistake."

Pasquale sat down on the edge of the tub grasping the shower curtain with both hands for support. "Good God!" He looked as if he were going to retch. "Then it might have killed *me*!"

"Yeah." Foyle regarded him a little unsympathetically. "Wouldn't that have been just too bad?"

"Why you should be alive and Kitty dead, is something of a puzzle," said Basil. "It may be the cocktail wasn't poisoned after all."

"But — suppose it was? Oh, God!" Pasquale buried his face in his hands.

Basil and Foyle looked at each other. Could this be acting?

"You may be able to help us," pursued Basil. "Do you remember if Kitty's cocktail tasted different from your own?"

Pasquale gulped. Then words tumbled out of his mouth. "Hers was too dry — drier than my own. I remember wondering if Gregg had used two shakers with French vermouth in one and Italian in the other."

"Are you sure that the dry cocktail you drank by mistake was Kitty's cocktail?"

"She said so. I don't know anything about it! I wish you'd let me alone! I don't see why I have to be bullied and harassed just because Kitty is dead! I won't be able to do any work for a month after this!"

"Work!" Foyle stared at the nude on the taxicab.

Outside, the police car was waiting.

"I want something to eat," said Foyle. "There's an all-night cafeteria near here."

As the car started, Foyle took out a small tin box with the familiar words *sodium bicarbonate*.

"Feeling bilious?"

Foyle opened the box. It was full of a fine, white powder. "Happy dust," he announced.

"Happy dust? That's poetry, Inspector!"

"No, doc, it's morphine — crook slang," explained Foyle, earnestly. "I pinched it in the bathroom when you were asking him about the cocktail. On the shelf with the toothpaste and other things. So obvious I nearly missed it. This'll be a jolt for the Narcotic Squad. They thought they had things pretty well sewed up."

"Couldn't you have arrested Pasquale for being in possession of a narcotic?"

Foyle grinned. "I want him to get some more — soon. That's why I pinched this."

"So you can trail him and nab the distributor?"

"Yeah. Poor devil! He'll have to have it — even if he guesses he's being trailed." Foyle replaced the box in his overcoat pocket. "He had nearly an ounce there, and I've known it to go as high as three grand an ounce during a shortage. He can't make much dough out of those pictures. Do you suppose Rhoda buys it for him?"

"It's possible."

"That would explain her hold on him. But how in heck can you explain his hold on her?"

"At her age, he's as necessary to her as morphine is to him," answered Basil.

The cafeteria was decorated in geometric patterns of red and gold. There was not another customer in the place. Basil took a ticket from the machine and sauntered over to the steam table, selecting a sandwich and a salad. Foyle joined him at the table carrying a tray laden with corned beef and cabbage.

Foyle leaned back with a sigh of repletion. "The thing that

interests me most is that Sveltis bottle we found in Rhoda Jocelyn's bathroom. Maybe you psychologists never heard of it before, but a crook nearly always makes on fatal blunder—"

"—that gives him away to the police in spite of all his efforts to hide his crime!" chanted Basil.

"You can laugh all you like, doc, but it's true. When the fingerprint boys get busy on that bottle, I bet we'll have something!"

Basil's eyes twinkled. "The clue that interested me the most was Rhoda Jocelyn's upsetting that ink bottle!"

13

ABSTRACTION

"What?" The Inspector stated at Basil in amazement. "That was just an accident! I don't get you, doc. Did Rhoda Jocelyn spill the ink on purpose? Do you think she wanted an excuse for going upstairs before us? She did say she wanted to change her dress, but Sobel wouldn't take a chance on it."

"Nothing like that. It was really an accident."

"Then what do you mean when you call it a clue?"

"That's the sort of think I mean by psychic fingerprints. You see, Freud and his followers have a theory that the human body cannot set itself in motion by mechanical chance, and therefore no individual human act is ever accidental. In unhealthy people, the cause may be disease or abnormal growth, palsy can cause a slip of the hand, brain tumour can cause slurred speech. But in healthy people, thoughts and feelings are the only spark plugs of the human engine and it cannot move unless they are ignited, directly or indirectly. Even a reflex is regarded as a fossilised feeling."

"So what?"

"So unintentional acts, or blunders as we call them, cannot be purposeless accidents. If all individual human acts are caused by thought or feeling, then any act not caused by *conscious* thought or feeling must be caused by *unconscious* thought or feeling."

"But I though awkward blunders were due to not paying attention?" protested Foyle.

"No acts are more graceful than those purely inattentive," returned Basil. "Sleepwalkers perform amazing feats of skill. Athletes, musicians, and conjurors practice in order to acquire the smooth action of habit — which is unconscious. Wild animals, like snakes and panthers, are models of grace because they are unconscious.

"According to this theory, awkwardness or abstraction is not due to lack of conscious attention, but to conflict between conscious and unconscious. This conflict is liable to occur when the consciousness represses the unconscious. Then the unconscious can only express itself by speaking through dreams and works of art, or by acting through blunders. Once you recognise an unconscious purpose in blunders, you'll find that the unconscious seems to use great skill and precision in attaining its purpose in defiance of the conscious will."

"Then the kids are right when they say accidentally-on-purpose?"

"Perfectly right if Freud is right. Even accidental deaths that involve individual human action — a doctor making a mistake in a prescription, or a chauffeur running a car into a tree — may be unconscious suicides, or unconscious murders."

"I can just see how that would go down with a jury!"

"Apparently, the only true accidents are coincidences: that is, accidents known to involve more than one active factor, such as an accidental meeting of two people on the street, or the accidental meeting of two chemical substances, without human intervention."

Foyle considered this. "Then Rhoda Jocelyn had some unconscious purpose for upsetting that ink bottle and spoiling her own dress?"

"Exactly. And if we knew what that purpose was, we'd know a lot more about Rhoda than she would ever tell us of her own free will. Blunders, like dreams, are messages in code. By decoding them we are able to eavesdrop on the unconscious and get at the truth. For no one can control his blunders any more than he can control his reflexes or his dreams. The unconscious cannot lie. The blunders a suspect makes, the things he drops and breaks and forgets, his stumbling and stuttering, might tell the psychologist as much about his mind as the marks on a bullet tell the ballistics expert about the gun from which it was fired."

"There's been only one blunder in this case so far," began Foyle.

"No." Basil cut him short. "There've been at least four. Pasquale drank half of Kitty's cocktail — by mistake. And he claims himself that he *mislaid* a diamond ring. Rhoda not only splashed her dress with ink — she lost her cigarette case. It's too soon even to guess why. Psychic clues have to be studied and sifted like physical clues."

"Does losing a thing count as a blunder?"

"Of course. To 'lose' a thing is merely to *forget where you put it*. You see, all blunders are mental diseases in miniature — the insanities of the sane. Forgetting or losing something is amnesia on a small scale. A slip of the pen, changing only a word or letter, is produced by the same mental process as the pages of automatic writing recorded by self-styled mediums."

"It all sounds pretty psycho — well, screwy to me, doc. How do you decode a blunder anyway?"

"If you were to get a bill and a cheque by the same mail, and you lost the bill, and didn't lose the cheque — I should conclude you were unusually greedy or unusually hard up. If an engaged girl were to lose a valuable engagement ring, I should conclude she wasn't very deeply in love. You might be quite unconscious of your greed. The girl might believe herself sincerely in love. In decoding a blunder, you ask yourself what unconscious wish could be back of it. Why should such-and-such a person want to do such-and-such a thing? The idea is that no one ever does anything he doesn't want to do — either consciously or unconsciously."

Foyle brought his fist down on the table with a crash. "I might have known there was a catch in it! Suppose these suspects don't make any blunders?"

"Most people make several blunders every week of their lives."

"Maybe, but suppose the guilty one just doesn't make any at all?"

Basil smiled a little sadly. "He's the one person who's absolutely sure to do so. The criminal who pretends he is innocent has to repress all his natural impulses of flight, fear, and triumph. He has to lie and lying is a form of repression. It invariably sets up conflicts, which in turn cause blunders. That's why awkwardness and guilt have been associated from time immemorial. Not only that, but he has to repress his conscience, and that causes as much mental trouble in civilised people as the repression of animal instincts."

"What about that one fatal blunder of every crook you were just talking about? Like the pieces of rope the murderer forgot in the Titterton case. When a criminal makes an obvious mistake that can lead only to his capture what unconscious purpose can cause it except remorse and the wish to give himself up to the police?"

After they paid their cheques, Basil said, "One thing about this case puzzles me."

"*One* thing?" Foyle laughed.

"Yes. Why did Pasquale himself suspect Rhoda of murder when, apparently, she had every reason for keeping Kitty alive?"

Foyle sighed. "This sure is one murderer who doesn't seem to have made that one fatal blunder."

"Give him time, Inspector. He will!"

Outside, the morning papers had been on the street for several hours, and the newsboys were shouting: "Debewtante Moidered ! Read Allaboutamoideruvadebewtante!"

Basil bought a paper:

BODY IN SNOW HOT
HOW DID KITTY JOCELYN REACH 78TH STREET? WAS COCKTAIL FATAL?
EXCLUSIVE INTERVIEW WITH DISTRICT ATTORNEY SOBEL

"I wish he wouldn't talk so much," grumbled Foyle.

"He didn't talk as much as you think," answered Basil, his eyes on the paper. "Not a word about the impersonation, and no mention of Sveltis by name — merely 'a reducing medicine'."

The newspaper in question had padded out its scant array of facts with, on the gossip page an article on "Kitty Jocelyn as I Knew Her" by Lowell Cabot. On the woman's page, the sob sister who ran the sweetness-and-light department suggested that *"there is a lesson for all modern girls in the terrible fate of Kitty Jocelyn"*, without specifying how Kitty's modernity had caused her murder. And, of course, there were photographs. *Kitty Jocelyn at Cannes* — in a bathing suit. *Kitty Jocelyn with a Friend on Fifth Avenue* — the friend was Victorine.

14

DEVELOPMENT OF A BOTTLE IN
SPACE

As Foyle appeared outside the district attorney's office Monday morning, he was dazzled by two flashlight bulbs and a flood of questions.

"What's the 'Mystery Man' doing here?"

"Is he mixed up in the Jocelyn case?"

Foyle had no idea what the newspaper men were talking about. But he kept his own counsel and went into the private office.

"Sorry I'm a bit late…" His voice trailed off as he saw Sobel was not alone. Of the two other men who faced him, one was obviously a clerk or secretary. The other was just as obviously a personage. His eyes were sombre under arched brows and heavy lids, his mouth set in lines of tragedy. One gloved hand was holding a gold topped Malacca stick as if it were a rapier or a whip.

"This is Inspector Foyle, Mr Danine," explained Sobel.

"Oh…" The brows lifted slightly, and the hooded eyes settled on Foyle. They were a pale, cold blue. "I am glad you are here, Inspector Doyle…"

"Foyle." The Inspector corrected him involuntarily.

"I beg your pardon — Foyle, of course," said Danine, affably, without a trace of foreign accent, except for the slight hissing of his *s*. "I have just been telling the district attorney what a shock the news of Miss Jocelyn's terrible death was to me. I am — I was very fond of Miss Jocelyn." He paused. With a visible effort, he went on. "I might as well be frank, Inspector. I had hoped to make Miss Jocelyn my wife."

Foyle muttered something scarcely articulate.

"Thank you, Inspector. I am indeed grateful for your sympathy. As I was just telling Mr Sobel, I have decided to offer a reward of $10,000 for information leading to the capture of Miss Jocelyn's murderer. If there's anything else I can do, please call on me."

"It's very generous of you, Mr Danine."

Sobel was beaming. Foyle listened stolidly to the exchange of courtesies. The more the guy talked the less he said. What was that crack about words having been invented to conceal thoughts?

"Now if there are any questions you wish to ask me…?"

"None, Mr Danine." Sobel's voice was unctuous.

"Just a minute, sir," Foyle intervened. "There's one question I'd like to ask."

"Indeed! And what is the question?"

"Were you actually engaged to Miss Jocelyn?"

Danine seemed on the point of resenting this bluntness. Then he capitulated with a slight shrug. "No, Inspector. I had not spoken to her, but…" he smiled, wistfully "…she must have known my feeling for her. Women always know these things — even very young women."

"I'm afraid I must ask an even more direct question," went

on Foyle. "Have you any reason to believe that Miss Jocelyn returned your — er — feelings for her?"

"Look here, Foyle!" cried Sobel. "That's unnecessary!"

"It's all right, Mr Sobel." Danine spoke with gentle resignation. "I cannot answer your question positively, Inspector Coyle, but I believe Miss Jocelyn was not wholly indifferent to me. Of course I am not a young man, but — well, I was offering her the utmost devotion and a position in life — er — shall we say commensurate with her own? Few young men can give either of these things. Youth is selfish, Inspector. It is only in middle age that a man learns what love should mean — pure un-selfishness." He rose with an indolent suppleness that was almost feline.

But Foyle detained him.

"One more thing, Mr Danine. Can you think of anyone who might have wanted Kitty Jocelyn out of the way?"

Danine shook his head. "It's incredible! A lovely girl of eighteen — on the threshold of life! How could she have an enemy?" He sighed. "If that's all, I'll ask you to excuse me now."

"I'll take you out my private door," said Sobel. "That way you'll escape the reporters."

"Oh, yes, the reporters! But I have no wish to escape them: I thought if I told them about the reward I am offering it might help things along."

Sobel was taken aback. He had been planning to announce Danine's reward in an interview of his own. With ill grace, he told his secretary to bring in the newspaper men. But if Nicholas Danine felt tension in the atmosphere, he didn't show it as he greeted the reporters.

I guess he's as much of a limelight hound as the DA, thought Foyle. *And that's saying something!*

With amazing docility, the great man allowed the photographers to have their way with him.

"I was very fond of Miss Jocelyn," he repeated. "And I am offering a reward of $10,000 for any information leading to the capture of her murderer. I had hoped to marry Miss Jocelyn, and I followed her to this country with that intention. And now... really, I am tired. I have suffered a great shock. You have your story. Please let me go. If you wish to see me again, Inspector Boyle, you'll find me at the Waldorf ." Danine made his way to the door.

"Well, what do you make of that, Duff?" demanded Foyle in the privacy of his own office.

Before Duff could comment, the telephone rang. He answered it and then looked over at Foyle. "Edgar Jocelyn. The Commissioner is passing the buck to you."

Foyle took the telephone.

"Are you in charge of the Jocelyn case?" The voice was pitched low, but it was resonant with repressed rage.

"Yes I—"

"Well, I'm Kitty Jocelyn's uncle — Edgar Jocelyn. I talked to General Archer on Sunday and he told me to call you this morning. Look here, Inspector, there must be some mistake! That girl whose body was found in the snow Wednesday morning can't be my niece, Kitty, because I saw her at the opera on Friday night. Her stepmother refuses to see me now and General Archer actually asked me to believe some nonsense about Kitty's cousin being at the opera in her place. I will not have the Jocelyn name butchered to make a Roman holiday for the yellow press."

"If I could see you and talk with you, Mr Jocelyn—"

"All right, I'll be at your office in fifteen minutes."

Foyle looked at the pile of letters and reports and interdepartmental memoranda on his desk, which he had not had time to touch since yesterday. "I could come to your office any time this afternoon, Mr Jocelyn, but I can't see you this morning."

"Make it two-thirty!"

"Two-thirty will suit me perfectly."

"Well, it doesn't suit me at all, but I must see you. You know the address? It is in the telephone book under Industrial Finishing Company." Edgar Jocelyn hung up without saying goodbye.

"That story in the papers this morning sure got results," ventured Duff. "First Danine and now Jocelyn."

"I'm a lot more interested in the guys who don't want to see me than I am in the guys who do," retorted Foyle. "See if you can get hold of a mug called Philip Leach. He writes for some newspaper under the name Lowell Cabot. Gossip stuff."

The Inspector began going through the papers on his desk. The first was a report on the Sveltis bottle from the fingerprint department.

"Couldn't get that guy Leach, Chief," announced Duff. "Got his office and they say he ain't there and they dunno where he is."

"No?" Nothing ever surprised the Inspector. "Well, get Minna Hagen down here sometime this morning. Her finger-prints were found on the Sveltis bottle."

"Okay. And there's the dope on Danine, Chief."

The Inspector took two slips of paper, and began reading a transcript from *Who's Who*:

DANINE, Nicholas, Order of Merit. Commander of the Legion of Honour. Stockbroker. *b.* 1884, *Educ.* Paris. Numerous gifts to the Victoria and Albert Museum and the Oriental Section of the Louvre Museum, including Hispano-

Moresque faïence and Chinese scroll paintings of the Yuan dynasty. *Address*: Château Alys, Beaulieu, Alpes-Maritimes. *Clubs*: Marlborough; Cercle de l'Union.

The second slip was a cable from Scotland Yard:

Your inquiry X L 6392 Nicholas Danine little authentic information available. Rumours assign birth variously Odessa Stockholm Budapest parents alleged Russian. Stockholder various munition companies including Poudrerie de Sainte Gudule Paris since 1913. Nationalised by Blum government 1937. Balka Prague since 1919. Kochleinekessel Munitionsfabrik Bremen since 1932. Corporacion de Munición de Argentina Buenos Aires since 1936. First became public figure as economic adviser Wallachian Delegation Palermo Conference 192 r. Testified Royal Commission Armaments 1936 claiming retired active business though admitting still shareholder companies aforesaid.

Unmarried. Associated various women latest Suzy Comminges Theatre Dharlequin Paris this autumn. Fanatically averse personal publicity, never interviewed.

Signed Chief Inspector Linden Records Scotland Yard.

Foyle pursed his lips in a soundless whistle.

BASIL REALISED that now there was no longer any question of Ann Claude's sanity he had no official standing in the case.

"But that won't prevent my calling on Lambert in my private capacity," he told himself. "And if he should happen to mention the Jocelyn case I certainly won't change the subject!"

131

After luncheon, he found Lambert in his laboratory, solemnly shaking a stoppered flask to and fro under the weary gaze of Inspector Foyle.

"He's been doing that for the last half hour," explained Foyle.

On the table stood two black and crystal Sveltis bottles with long yellow silk tassels.

"Find any fingerprints on the bottle?" asked Basil.

"A few of Kitty Jocelyn's and a few of Minna Hagen's. I had her down at my office for further questioning this morning. She wept and said she'd only touched the bottle when she was dusting the bathroom cupboard. She didn't recall when she first saw it there or how long it had been half empty. Mebbe that's true and mebbe it isn't. We'll give her a day or so to think it over, and then we'll grill her again."

"She hasn't the brains to commit a murder like this."

"No, doc, but she's the very stuff accomplices are made of. Weak as water — easily scared — and dumb."

"Have you any report on the food and liquor from the Jocelyn house?"

"Bill, my assistant, analysed it this morning," put in Lambert. "There was no trace of poison."

He paused in shaking his flask and held it up to the anaemic light of the winter day. The upper layer of the contents was turning a ripe, reddish purple.

"So that's that." He set down the flask.

"So that's what?" demanded Foyle.

"A positive Derrien reaction. This flask contains twenty Sveltis tablets and that purple colour shows that Sveltis contains di-nitro-phenol."

"What about the body?" asked Basil.

Lambert was washing his hands at the sink. "This morning

I tested a steam-distilled extract of kidney tissue concentrated by evaporation," he said over his shoulder. "And I found ample evidence of 2, 4 di-nitro-phenol, or, to use the more explicit term, hydroxy di-nitro-benzene 1, 2, 4."

"Hy-di-what?" cried Foyle.

"And to think we have compulsory education in this country!" said Lambert, sweetly. "I'll call the drug by its French name *thermol* — even you should be able to remember that. I made a quantitative analysis of the kidney tissue this morning, and there's no doubt Kitty Jocelyn had an unusually large dose. It's difficult to estimate the exact amount because some of the poison is usually eliminated by vomiting and urination before death. But I would put it as high as 6 grams — that is, about 90 grains troy, or over 1000 milligrams per kilo body weight. She weighed 105 pounds — roughly 52 kilos — 10 milligrams per kilo is the recognised fatal dose, though the drug is so capricious lesser doses have proved fatal. As one doctor puts it: 'The so-called medicinal dose and the fatal dose are sometimes the same.' But the ads say the blasted stuff is harmless!"

Lambert smiled. "They also say it's based on an old Persian beauty secret."

"And it isn't?"

"Well, it's the first I've ever heard that the ancient Persians knew anything about nitro derivatives of the benzene ring."

"If the stuff is as dangerous as all that, I shouldn't think you could buy it without a prescription," pursued Foyle.

"You can't buy it in New York city," responded Lambert. "But any New Yorker can buy it freely outside the city limits — in New York state or Connecticut, or any state in the Union except New Jersey, California, and Louisiana. There's no federal law to control the sale of such things, as in Canada, and local legislation lags behind medical opinion. Naturally, business racketeers take advantage of this and exploit products like Sveltis. According to the American Medical Association there are twenty-three forms of thermol reducing medicines on the market now under various trade names. They all advertise in the more sensational newspapers and magazines, and several have been advertised on the radio. But I believe Sveltis is the only one that goes in for what advertising men call 'class appeal'."

"Could Kitty Jocelyn have taken this poison in an unpitted olive?" asked Basil.

"Not unless she ate a great many. Each Sveltis tablet contains 300 milligrams of thermol. She must have had twenty tablets."

"Was it thermol that caused that queer heat of the body after death?" queried Foyle.

"That's characteristic of thermol poisoning," answered Lambert. "In one case, where the dose was 9 grams, the post-mortem temperature was 115° Fahrenheit. As a dead body loses heat at the average rate of 2° an hour, you can see for yourself how long it might remain warm if it were protected from wind by snow."

"And the yellow stain on her face?"

"Sometimes it's on the face. Sometimes it's on the hands, or neck, or abdomen. The internal organs and secretions are usually yellow as well."

"If all the symptoms are so well known, why didn't that mutt Dalton put me wise when he first did the autopsy?"

"But they're not well known. I've just been making a special study of them — that's why I have them so pat. It was Basil who tipped me off that the poison might be thermol."

"And I only thought of thermol when I found Kitty's name connected with reducing medicine in advertisements," added

Basil. "I didn't know enough about the drug to recognise Kitty's symptoms when I read the autopsy report."

"Oh, yeah? Well, all I got to say is — you're a fine bunch of experts!"

"Thermol is a comparatively recent discovery," returned Lambert with dignity. "Dalton isn't the first medical examiner to be stumped by it. In one of the cases I found in the *Journal of the American Medical Association*, the doctors who conducted the autopsy wrote quite frankly: *'We were unable to propose an intelligent guess regarding the cause of death.'* It was only after they found thermol tablets among the dead person's belongings that they got at the truth."

"If Kitty Jocelyn had been larger, we might have got onto thermol sooner," suggested Basil. "Her body was naturally thin with long, narrow bones, and I think that inhibited any thought of reducing medicine at first."

But when Inspector Foyle got hold of an idea, he held it in such a firm grip that Basil could almost hear him telling it to "come quietly".

"I *still* don't see why Dalton thought it was heat stroke!"

Lambert smiled again. "Because it was heat stroke."

"Huh?"

"Internal heat stroke. As you doubtless know, life is a form of combustion or fire which we call metabolism. If the rate of metabolism is speeded up, more heat is generated inside the body, and it affects bodily organs the same way the external heat of a tropic sun affects them. Thermol is a bellows that blows upon the fire of life — a 'catalyst of the vital process', as van Uytvanck says. It is used as reducing medicine because it burns up body tissue, including fat. Small doses cause high colour and a glow of warmth and well-being — that's why the advertisements claim that Sveltis is a tonic and beautifier as well as a reducing medicine. But they do not mention the fact that even small doses may cause blindness, skin rash, or impaired sense of taste, while the victim of a large dose is *literally cooked to death* by a fire inside the cells of his own body."

Foyle could not repress a shiver.

"Do you realise that this is the first thermol murder in the history of crime?" Lambert spoke with a bright and bird-like interest. It occurred to Foyle that chemists were really more hard-boiled than policemen.

"There've been a number of accidental deaths from thermol reducing medicines, and one suicide. But the Jocelyn case is the first murder. Standard textbooks on medical jurisprudence have very little about the stuff. The 1935 Douglas Kerr cites a short article from the *British Medical Journal* and the 1922 Dixon Mann has a few paragraphs under di-nitro-benzene. But neither describe the startling symptoms that come from taking a large dose of thermol internally. The cases they mention are mostly those of munition workers who were poisoned externally."

"Munition workers?!" Foyle bounded from his chair. "Don't tell me thermol is used in making munitions?"

"Why not? Is there anyone in this case connected with munitions?"

"Is there?!" It was Foyle's turn to laugh at Lambert. "Just wait until you see the evening papers! Nicholas Danine — that's all."

"That's interesting," admitted Lambert. "For no one ever thought of using thermol as reducing medicine until the war came and people noticed that the workers who handled Shellite, containing thermol, were losing weight."

"To think of drinking an explosive in order to reduce!"

Foyle shook his head wonderingly. "Is there anything else this hell-broth is used for?"

"Most poisons have more than one commercial use. Thermol has been tried in England as a vulcaniser for crepe rubber. In this country, it's used as a fabric dye, and as an insecticide for plant lice. And in chemical research it's used as a colour-indicator for hydrogen ion concentrations in the Michaelis technique."

"What's that?" groaned Foyle.

"It's quite simple. The alkalinity—"

"Skip it!" said Basil, firmly. "Never let him get started on research, Foyle!"

"Isn't there some way of proving that the thermol you found in Kitty Jocelyn's body was given her in the form of Sveltis?"

The Inspector's voice was plaintive, but Lambert's reply was an unqualified negative.

"Sveltis tablets are triturate, and the only ingredients besides thermol are sugar, to disguise the bitterness, and soda bicarb to increase solubility. Both are so common their presence in a dead body would prove nothing. There's no distinction between the chemically pure thermol, used in reducing medicines, and the commercial thermol, used in explosives and dyes, that can be determined after they have passed through a living body. Outside the body, commercial thermol is a dingier yellow than pure thermol, and it has a faint bitter almond odour, while pure thermol is odourless. There's the usual variation in melting point. But once in the body, both stain tissue the same canary yellow, both speed up metabolism, and both are transformed by the body itself into other compounds. If an extremely impure commercial thermol had been used, I might have found traces of the mono-nitro-phenols. But their absence proves nothing, since their presence depends on the degree of impurity."

As Foyle rose to go, his glance fell on a mound of brilliant yellow powder in a glass vessel.

"What's that?"

"The Eastman Kodak Company's purest thermol. I check the tests on Sveltis and the kidney distillate, by making the same tests on that and comparing results."

"Huh! This case is sure costing the city a pretty penny!"

Lambert was puzzled. "Thermol is not expensive. Even when it's chemically pure, it costs only 75 cents a hundred grams. Commercial thermol is only 23 cents a pound if bought in barrels of 350 pounds each."

Basil balanced one of the Sveltis bottles in his hand. "About 50 tablets, containing 300 milligrams each, with a little sugar and soda. And this is the Boudoir Size — Price $10.00. Somebody's making a reasonable profit…" He eyed the lissom lady blown in the glass. "A skull and crossbones would be more appropriate. But the modern buccaneer doesn't sail under the Jolly Roger. He would regard that as the wrong kind of publicity."

Foyle was peering gingerly into Lambert's microscope. "There are your real murderers, Inspector."

Lambert showed him how to focus it. "Two nitro groups in the para position to the hydroxyl group in the benzene ring. Poison is just a pattern — a design for dying."

"I don't see anything like that!" objected Foyle. "I just see some little yellow rectangles."

"Nobody has ever seen the benzene ring. It's more complex than many machines, and yet so small it's invisible."

"Then how do you know it's there?"

"I don't." Lambert grinned. "Chemistry is like mathematics

— based on pure fiction. It requires more imagination than poetry and more faith than religion."

"Could the bouquet of gin and vermouth disguise the bitter almond odour of commercial thermol?" inquired Basil, abruptly.

"But it couldn't have been the cocktail, doc!" insisted Foyle. "Pasquale is still alive and kicking."

Basil turned to Lambert again. "Would it be possible for two people to have six grams of thermol each and one die and the other not?"

"I never heard of anyone having so large a dose without dying, but there are constitutional variations in reaction to any drug. Some we don't understand and some we do. For instance, drunkards and malaria patients are more susceptible to thermol than normal people."

Foyle brought his big fist down on the table so the glass vessels rang.

"For the love of Mike! You'll break something!" cried Lambert.

"It may interest you to know that Kitty Jocelyn was subject to chronic malaria," said Basil, slowly.

Lambert was interested. "That's rather horrible. It seems almost — planned — doesn't it?"

An idea came to Basil. "How does thermol affect drug addicts?"

"Depends on the drug — naturally!"

"Well, let's say morphine."

"I don't believe there's any special effect, but we'd better make sure."

Lambert went over to the bookcase and took down an index volume of *Chemical Abstracts*. Then he searched through another volume.

"Hello! Was that a guess or second sight? Here's a French-man, Cahen, who's discovered that rabbits, habituated to morphine, are less susceptible to thermol than normal rabbits. The experiment has never been tried on human beings, but it is possible that a human morphine addict would be immune to larger doses of thermol than ordinary people."

Basil's eyes met Foyle's. The same question occurred to each, but it was Foyle who voiced it: "D'ye suppose Pasquale knew that all along?"

15

PORTRAIT OF A LADY

The newspaper that employed Philip Leach was housed in its own building, with editorial offices on the eighth floor.

Foyle showed his gold badge to the boy on guard at the entrance.

"I want to see Philip Leach."

"Aw, gee!" The boy's eyes shone. The *Tales of Terror* he was reading fell to the floor. "He ain't here, Inspector. Has he bumped somebody?"

"What's his home address?"

"Honest, I dunno."

"Then take me to the managing editor."

The managing editor was sitting at a desk about a third of the way down the huge city room.

"Well, Inspector?" His eyes we weary.

"I'm looking for Philip Leach."

"Why?" The voice was deceptively soft. "Has he been shoving queer money? Or rubber cheques?"

"Is that what you'd expect him to do?"

141

"No. Only — you're looking for him…" The editor leaned back in his seat. "What do you expect him to do?"

Foyle ignored the question. "I tried to reach him by phone here this morning and I was told he couldn't be reached. How come?"

The editor smiled. "Mr Philip Leach has not honoured us with his presence since last Tuesday, and we can find no trace of him. Durkin's doing his stuff. When he does show up, he'll be fired."

Foyle collected his thoughts. Tuesday — the night of the Jocelyn dance. "Then that article in this morning's paper on 'Kitty Jocelyn as I Knew Her' was not written by Leach at all, in spite of the fact that it was signed 'Lowell Cabot'?"

"Of course not. It was faked from clippings in the morgue."

"But you must know the fellow's home address!"

The editor drew a horseshoe on his blotter. "The Harvard Club. We phoned. But Annie doesn't live there anymore. He calls now and then for letters — they don't know where he lives. They have only this address — his office. Lots of people have been asking for him here. Some of them seemed pretty anxious."

"He must have a lot of invitations and phone calls doing work like that," said Foyle. "Do they all go to his club?"

"Yes. He was usually at the club in the morning and at the office in the afternoon."

"When was he last at the club?"

"Tuesday afternoon. Early." The editor was watching Foyle's face. "Interested?"

Foyle answered with another question. "Why didn't you notify the police when Leach disappeared?"

"The police?" The editor drew another horseshoe. "My dear Inspector, I don't have hysterics and yell 'Police!' every time one of the men goes on a binge. Leach has done it often enough. But this time he'd done it once too often. If you find him, you can give him my compliments and tell him to go boil his head."

"Have you noticed any change in his manner lately?"

"He's changeless, Inspector. Perennial." The editor drew a third horseshoe.

"How would you describe him?"

The editor smiled. "Slippery."

"I mean what was his height and weight? And the colour of his hair and eyes?"

"About 5 feet 11, and about 150 pounds. Brown hair and eyes."

"Don't you know anything about him? Where he came from and who his father was?"

"I'm afraid not, Inspector. He walked in here one day in 1930 with a scandal story. It was hot news and I bought it. After he'd brought in several more stories, I gave him a column. He had a talent for journalism in chrome and ochre. His scandal stories always reminded me of Van Gogh's sunflowers and cornfields. No mistaking the colour — if you get what I mean. And that's all I know about the lad."

"Any photos of him?"

The editor consulted the photographic department by telephone.

"Just one. A group. Not very good of Leach, but it can be enlarged. Aren't you going to tell me why you want to see Leach?" The editor's drawl was silky.

"I'm afraid I can't at present. It's nothing much."

"Nothing much! And an assistant chief inspector is making inquiries in person!"

"When did you last see him yourself?" countered Foyle.

"Tuesday — about 7:45 pm."

"Sure of the time?"

"Positive. He had an appointment with me at seven to map out some stories on the season in Florida, and he was only three-quarters of an hour late. Said he'd forgotten to wind his watch."

FOYLE SEEMED thoughtful as he re-entered the police car.

"Too early for Edgar Jocelyn," he informed Duff. "I'm going to drop in on that social secretary dame, Mrs What's-Her-Name."

"Jowett," supplied Duff.

"She might give us a line on this bunch we couldn't get in any other way."

Mrs Jowett's office on 57th Street was spacious and sparely furnished in cool neutral colours. The only highlight was a copper bowl containing white chrysanthemums on her desk. Beside it was a photograph in a tortoise-shell frame showing a girl about fifteen or sixteen with a round, noticeably chubby face. Scrawled below it were the words:

To Mother from Janey.

Foyle liked Mrs Jowett the moment he saw her. But then he had a weakness for large, placid, smiling women who made him think of sunlit farm kitchens and freshly baked bread. His own mother used to give him a slice of such bread with butter and brown sugar, and he could imagine Mrs Jowett giving the same thing to the girl in the photograph when she was a few years younger. He wondered what quirk of fate had induced such a woman to become a social secretary.

She didn't look clever, but she did look immensely capable, and — Foyle groped for a word. Feminine wouldn't do. It implied weakness and there was nothing weak about Mrs Jowett. He wondered if there were such a word as "mulierity" to describe that strength of the elemental female instincts which corresponds to virility in the male.

"I guess you know why we're here, ma'am," he said a little awkwardly.

She nodded. "It was like a nightmare when I saw the papers this morning. Of course I scarcely knew Kitty Jocelyn. She was only one of many girls I'm bringing out this season. I never met her until she reached this country a few weeks ago, and I only saw her about half a dozen times altogether. But she was beautiful and young and it's monstrous to think of her being murdered."

"Well, I guess it does seem monstrous now. But when we find the murderer, we'll probably find it was all quite commonplace and natural. Now I just want to ask you a few questions."

Duff opened his notebook and began to take shorthand notes.

"I wish you could do something to keep my name out of all this," said Mrs Jowett, impulsively. "I've been arranging a coming-out party for the Police Commissioner's niece, Isobel Archer, to take place next Thursday, and General Archer himself telephoned me this morning telling me to go on with my plans as if nothing had happened. But most of my clients are not so considerate. I've had five cancellations today."

Foyle suppressed a smile. It was so like Archer to "stand by" Mrs Jowett with slightly patronising loyalty. It would never occur to him to suspect anyone so respectable of having anything to do with the crime, and just because he was Police Commissioner and supposed to know all about the case, he might be able to save her from the professional ruin that threatened.

"I'm afraid there's nothing I can do about the publicity, ma'am — much as I'd like to. Kitty Jocelyn's name has always been news, and—"

"I had nothing to do with that!" Mrs Jowett was emphatic. "Indeed I protested about it again and again. Each time, Kitty promised me she would stop publicising herself. But she didn't."

"Then you had nothing to do with the arrangements for Kitty's endorsement of Sveltis?"

"Sveltis?" Mrs Jowett's brow wrinkled.

"One of the products Kitty endorsed. The ad came out in the sensational fiction magazines."

"I never read any fiction magazine except *Harper's* and the *Atlantic* and I don't believe they print advertisements of reducing medicine."

Foyle looked up sharply.

"How did you know that Sveltis was a reducing medicine?"

Something in Mrs Jowett's face suggested that she was not quite so simple as Foyle had assumed at first.

"I don't know," she answered. "I suppose I must have seen one of their advertisements somewhere and forgotten about it. But I never knew that Kitty endorsed it. Though all the usual announcements of her normal social activities went through my office before they reached the newspapers, I assure you I had nothing to do with her testimonials. She dealt directly with the De Luxe Advertising Agency which specialises in that sort of thing. As a rule, I don't bring out girls who make themselves as conspicuous as Kitty Jocelyn."

"Why did you make an exception in her favour?"

"Because Mrs Jocelyn offered me double the regular fee," replied Mrs Jowett, almost too readily.

Had she been rehearsing the reply to such a question in her own mind?

"When Mrs Jocelyn wrote me from Europe last spring asking me to take charge of her stepdaughter's debut in New York this winter, I replied that it was impossible without giving my reasons. But they were clear in my own mind. Kitty had publicised herself too sensationally and, though I had never met Mrs Jocelyn, I had heard unsavoury gossip about her and this Luis Pasquale. It was purely a matter of business with me — not a question of taste or morality." Her eyes twinkled. "I'm afraid I grade debutantes as impersonally as a meat packer grades cattle. By insisting on certain conventional standards among the girls I bring out, I am able to charge much higher rates than I would be if I were indiscriminate. These standards do not necessarily exclude the new rich — not from our 'B' lists anyway. But they must exclude the *declassée*. Girls' schools are conducted on the same principle for the same reason."

Again the twinkle appeared. "I suppose you might call it 'commercialised virtue'."

"When did you change your mind about Kitty Jocelyn?"

"This autumn, when Miss Jocelyn and Kitty reached New York, they walked into my office unannounced and begged me to reconsider."

"Rather short notice, wasn't it, ma'am?"

"Very short notice, but money can do almost anything. It has been a bad season this year and, as I say, Mrs Jocelyn offered me double the fee I generally receive. So I decided to stretch a point in Kitty's favour, comforting myself with the reflection that people are much more tolerant of self-advertisement and other things today than they were even a few years ago."

"I didn't know social secretaries were so — so business-like," remarked Foyle.

Mrs Jowett smiled. "You must be thinking of my predecessor? Miss Severance. I was one of her assistants until she retired. She was a member of a New York family; she had a great many friends here, and it was all a labour of love to her. I am a very different sort of person, Inspector — the widow of a country doctor with few friends in New York, and no pretensions to any social importance of my own. I don't particularly enjoy the work. To me, it is simply one of the few ways a comparatively untrained woman can earn her bread and a little butter. I turned to it when my husband died, because I knew Miss Severance. Her brother has a place in the country near the village where I used to live."

Foyle fished something out of his pocket and laid it on the desk — a platinum ring, set with a rose diamond.

"Ever see that before?"

Mrs Jowett peered through her *pince-nez*.

"I don't know whether I have or not. That type of ring is so common."

"Yes — worse luck!" Foyle returned it to his pocket. "Now there's something else, ma'am. Do you know any way we can get hold of Philip Leach?"

"If you can't reach him through his office or the Harvard Club, I really can't suggest anything else."

"Do you know where he came from in the first place?"

She shook her head. "He's one of those amiable, well-dressed young men who appear suddenly at parties and night clubs without anyone knowing just who they are or where they come from. The scarcity of presentable young men is responsible for it, I suppose."

"What about the other folks who had cocktails at the Jocelyns' the afternoon of the dance? Can you give us a line on them?"

"The only one I knew at all was Edgar Jocelyn. I have had charge of several weddings and coming-out parties given for young cousins of his and I've always liked him."

"What about Ann Claude? She worked with you that day of the party, didn't she?"

"Yes. I felt rather sorry for Ann. It must have been hard for her to watch all those preparations for her cousin's party when she had never had a coming-out party of her own. But if she was envious, she didn't show it. She has character."

The Inspector felt curiously baffled. "Didn't you notice anything out of the ordinary in the Jocelyn household the day of the dance? Anything at all?"

Mrs Jowett hesitated. "There were two little things," she admitted finally. "But I'm sure that neither one has any bearing on this dreadful crime."

"Let's hear them."

"Well, the first one is simply the fact that there were some red roses sent to Kitty the day of the dance without any card attached. We couldn't even discover the name of the florist, for the boy who brought them had disappeared, and the servants had unwrapped them and put them in the Murillo Room with other flowers by the time we noticed them. Kitty thought the card must have been lost. I thought it more likely the roses had been sent anonymously. Debutantes as spectacular as Kitty are always getting anonymous letters — begging letters, threatening letters, and letters that are sheer nonsense."

"What became of all this fan mail?"

"It was destroyed each day. Mrs Jocelyn forbade Kitty to answer begging letters and the others were utterly silly."

"And I suppose, the roses were thrown out, too?"

"Oh, yes. They were thrown out before the dance began, because — curiously enough — they had begun to fade. As for the second thing, I'm afraid it's even more irrelevant. There was an uninvited guest at the dance — a gate-crasher."

"At the dance," repeated Foyle. "I suppose that means he didn't enter the house until 11 or 12 pm?"

"No. You see this man confessed that he had concealed himself in the house during the afternoon."

For a moment Foyle was speechless. Then he cried, "Could this fellow have been hiding in the Murillo Room when you were all having cocktails?"

"I don't know where he was hidden."

Mrs Jowett didn't seem to realise the significance of this possibility.

"What was his name and address?"

"I never thought of asking him."

The Inspector's face fell. "How did you happen to catch him?"

"There have been a great many gate-crashers this season. In order to circumvent them, I present each male guest with a *boutonniére* when he gives up his card of invitation at the entrance and ask him to wear it during the evening. I use a different flower at each party, and no one knows beforehand what flower it is to be. It's a nuisance, but you must do something to identify regularly invited guests."

"Why not fingerprint them?"

"We may have to come to that!" Mrs Jowett laughed. "Let me see… it was about two o'clock when Gregg told me he had noticed a young man wearing a gardenia, instead of the white rosebud that was given each man that night. Gregg had left this boy in Mrs Jocelyn's study with a footman and I went there at once. I rather expected to find someone I knew by sight, for most gate-crashers are friends of girls who are themselves invited. But this one proved to be a complete stranger.

"He was perfectly cool. I thought he must be a thief. Gregg searched him and found he had taken nothing except two supper menus. That was rather odd, wasn't it? He admitted frankly that he was a gate-crasher and told me he had sneaked into the house that afternoon and hidden himself until the party began. I asked him why and…" she smiled reminiscently, "he gravely informed me that he was writing a PhD thesis in anthropology entitled: *The American Coming-out Party Considered as a Survival of Primitive Puberty Celebrations*, and that he had come to the Jocelyn dance purely in the interests of science to gather data for his thesis.

"I wasn't in the mood for that sort of thing. I told him I was going to call the police and see if he wasn't liable to a charge of burglary. He was quite ludicrously frightened. And just then who should come into the room — without knocking — but Luis Pasquale."

Her lips puckered as if the name had left an unpleasant taste in her mouth.

"He was most officious. He insisted that this gate crasher should be allowed to go scot-free. I failed to see that the matter concerned him in any way. But he began to make so much noise about it I was afraid he would attract the attention of the people at the dance, and that would almost certainly have led to scandal, for Pasquale's position in the household is equivocal, to say the least. So I gave in and let the gate-crasher go. Instead of being grateful, he stared at us with the utmost impudence and said, 'I suppose I may keep the two supper menus?'

To my amazement Pasquale replied, 'By all means!' I made Gregg escort the gate-crasher to the door in order to make sure he really did leave the house, and that was the end of the incident."

"Can you describe him, ma'am?"

"No. I didn't get a very clear view of him for I had most unaccountably mislaid my glasses that evening, just before the dance, and I don't see well without them. I can only tell you that he was tall and young."

Mrs Jowett was beginning to look tired under the rain of questions. A muscle in her left eyelid twitched slightly. She stretched her hand toward an old-fashioned phial of smelling-salts on the desk, and then thought better of it.

Foyle couldn't help thinking that a smelling-salts phial would be a very convenient way to carry poison without arousing suspicion. He was ashamed of the thought as he lifted his glance to her broad, motherly face. That was the trouble with being a policeman. It made you suspect everybody.

"Well, ma'am, this testimony of yours may prove important. Can you spare the time to come to Police Headquarters tomorrow? Your statement will be typed by then and you can read it over before you sign it."

"I'm rather busy tomorrow. Couldn't you type it now? My secretaries have typewriters."

Foyle looked at Duff and nodded. Duff went into the outer office and soon the clatter of typewriter keys was faintly audible through the closed door.

Foyle's glance reverted to the photograph in the tortoise-shell frame.

"Your daughter, ma'am? She's real cute looking."

"Yes." Mrs Jowett's voice was suddenly vibrant with emotion. "She died last May."

"Oh — I — I'm sorry." The Inspector was abashed. "I have five…" he stumbled on. Anything to fill that aching silence. "Three girls and two boys. We live in Flatbush." He told her all about them.

When Duff returned, Mrs Jowett adjusted her pince-nez and read the statement through word for word.

"That's quite correct. Shall I sign it here?"

"Please, ma'am." Duff, who had been trained to handle the toughest gangsters, subdued himself to a heavy gentleness with Mrs Jowett.

She accepted Duff's fountain pen and wrote rapidly.

"Thank you, ma'am." Duff picked up the document and looked at it mechanically. Then he stared. "Say, ain't your name 'Jowett'?"

"Certainly."

"Well," Duff grinned, "that ain't the name you've written here. You've written the name of the dead girl. See?"

He pointed to the signature: *Catharine Jocelyn*.

"Oh, dear!" Mrs Jowett gasped, her cheeks a delicate pink. "How stupid! This terrible thing has upset me so, I really don't know what I'm doing!"

She crossed out her blunder and wrote *Caroline Jowett* in a clear, firm hand.

COMPOSITION IN YELLOW

The business offices of the Industrial Finishing Company
suggested a cathedral. Lighting was indirect as if
filtered through Gothic windows. Walls were panelled in linen-
fold oak; chairs and tables were Jacobean. The rest of New
York might be rocking with excitement over the crime
involving Edgar Jocelyn and his family, but here, in his own
offices, well-schooled voices were hushed reverently, and footfalls fell softly on plush carpets.

A high priestess with cultured pearls and equally synthetic
voice was languidly incredulous when she heard that Inspector
Foyle had an appointment with Mr Edgar Jocelyn. But she
condescended to pass the information on by telephone to Mr
Jocelyn's private secretary, and after twenty minutes or so he
appeared — portly and episcopal.

"Mr Jocelyn will give you a few moments now." He might
have been intoning: *"Let us pray!"*

He led Foyle and Duff down dim corridors where the only
sound as the eternal clicking of typewriters, until at last they

reached a cheerful room with windows overlooking lower Broadway and the harbour.

Edgar Jocelyn rose to greet them — tall, grizzled, with the pale Jocelyn eyes under black brows.

"This is a horrible business, gentlemen," he said, gravely. "As I told the Police Commissioner over the telephone, there must be some mistake. This dead body was found early Wednesday morning. My niece, Kitty, was dancing at her own coming-out party until dawn on Wednesday. I myself saw her and spoke to her two days later at the opera."

Foyle met Edgar Jocelyn's directness in kind.

"The girl you saw at the opera was not Kitty Jocelyn."

Edgar had "given" them rather more than "a few moments" before the story of the impersonation was made clear to him. Then he forgot all about his board meeting. The shadows lengthened and the sun became a fiery red ball beyond the Western windows before they reached the real purpose of the visit. Edgar's own testimony.

All his reserve was gone. The shock had loosened his tongue like wine, and apparently it never occurred to him that he himself might be under suspicion. He seemed rather to assume that he was conducting the investigation himself, as Kitty's next of kin. Was he consummate actor? Or was it merely the naïveté of a man who had always been protected from the more brutal realities of life by the power of money?

"Would it surprise you to hear that your niece was killed by an overdose of Sveltis, the reducing medicine that she endorsed?"

"Sveltis!" Edgar's astonishment certainly seemed genuine. "I didn't even know it was poisonous."

"It contains thermol."

"I never heard of the stuff. I'm a businessman, not a chemist."

"A large amount of the drug was found in your niece's body, proving that she had a fatal dose."

"Couldn't it have been an accidental overdose?"

"Rhoda Jocelyn and Ann Claude have testified that Kitty never took Sveltis and that she didn't want to reduce. According to them, she was actually trying to put on weight at the time of her death. The autopsy proved that she was underweight."

"They would know," admitted Edgar.

Foyle tried a new tack. "Do you suspect anyone who had cocktails at Mrs Jocelyn's Tuesday afternoon?"

"That's an embarrassing question, Inspector, but, in the circumstances, I'll try to answer it. Rhoda — my sister-in-law — is out of the question. Her whole heart was centred on Kitty's coming-out, and she would not have done anything to interfere with that. It can't be Ann Claude — her mother was a Jocelyn. Mrs Jowett is a very simple, pleasant woman; I can't imagine her killing anything larger than a mosquito. They say Nicholas Danine is unscrupulous in his business methods, but I think he's too successful to commit murder. Most murderers seem to be unsuccessful people who can't dominate their environment in any other way. That leaves Luis Pasquale and Philip Leach. Frankly, I know nothing about them. They're what I call 'gilded gypsies' — people without roots. The sort you meet at Monte Carlo. You see, I don't really suspect anyone, but I suppose it might be Pasquale or Leach or one of the servants, because it *couldn't* be anyone else."

The Inspector said nothing. He had often found silence a more effective way of making people talk than questioning.

Edgar Jocelyn seemed as anxious to escape from that accusing silence as lesser men.

"To tell the truth, I was rather upset when I saw the sort of people Rhoda was gathering around Kitty," he hastened to add. "I'd been occupied with business affairs, and though I'd seen Rhoda here in the office, I hadn't been to the house since they reached America, until I dropped in that afternoon of the dance. They were not a nice gang. Especially Pasquale. I told Rhoda he'd have to go, but she refused to send him away. And there wasn't much I could do because I naturally didn't want Kitty involved in a public scandal. Good Lord, if I'd been firmer, I might have saved her life and avoided the worse scandal of murder!"

"Did you have this talk with Mrs Jocelyn in the library?"

"Why, yes. How did you know?"

"One of the servants passed the door and heard voices quarrelling."

Edgar frowned. "We were not *quarrelling*," he said with patent distaste for the word. "I was merely protesting against the extremely bad taste of allowing Pasquale to live in the studio over the old coach house. I suppose I'm old-fashioned, but when I was young these affairs were managed with some regard for appearances!"

"There's one more thing I've got to ask you, Mr Jocelyn. Just how was your father's fortune cut up between you and Kitty's father?"

"Is that really necessary?"

"I'm afraid so."

"Well, my father left me the old house on Long Island, and my brother Gerald — Kitty's father — got the town house where Rhoda is living now. The rest of the fortune was divided equally between us. Ann Claude's mother — my sister — got nothing, and when Gerald and I offered her a settlement, she refused it. The breach that had occurred when she married Claude never healed."

"Did you and your brother both inherit stock in this Industrial Finishing Company?"

"Oh, no. Our money was all in Western mining stock originally. I sold mine and invested in the IFC at the end of the war, when it, like other American dye firms, acquired certain German patents that became available as part of our reparations. My brother Gerald sold his mining stock, too. But he invested in foreign bonds and railroad shares which have depreciated since."

"Mrs Jocelyn told us she was hard up."

"Did she?" Edgar was none too pleased. "It's largely her own fault. She's the most recklessly extravagant woman I've ever known. I always told Gerald he should tie everything up in a trust fund. But Rhoda got round him, and he left nearly everything to her outright. Poor Gerald was a perfect fool about Rhoda. For some years he was a widower with a little girl, and we all thought he'd never marry again. But he went West to inspect some of my father's mining properties and met her in Nevada. She was not — er — appreciated in New York, and that's one reason they went abroad to live."

"Then Kitty Jocelyn had no money to leave anyone at the time of her death?"

"None whatsoever."

"Was her life insured?"

"Not to my knowledge."

"And you gave Mrs Jocelyn the money for this coming-out party of Miss Jocelyn's?"

"Kitty had to have her chance in life. I am her nearest relative and I have no daughters of my own. I provided a fairly round sum — $60,000."

"To a guy like me who makes only six grand a year it sounds like plenty," remarked Foyle. "Was it a gift outright? Or was Miss Jocelyn going to pay it back if she married some rich fellow?"

"Of course not!" Edgar Jocelyn's pale face flushed angrily. "It was a gift, and I was only too glad to do it for Gerald's daughter. There was no question of her paying me black!"

A sudden silence was emphasised by the moaning of a foghorn in the bay.

"Are you getting this down verbatim, Duff?" asked Foyle, without turning his eyes from Edgar.

"Yes, chief. Every word."

"Mr Jocelyn, do you know if anybody was in love with your niece?"

"I do not.'

"What about Nicholas Danine?"

"His name was mentioned in connection with Kitty's. That's all I know about it. I should certainly have opposed such a marriage. I don't believe in marrying foreigners."

Again Foyle produced the diamond ring. "Do you recognise this?"

"I can't say I do. Every woman I know has at least one diamond cut like that. They all look alike to me."

Foyle rose.

"Is that all?" Edgar didn't try to hide his relief.

"For the time being. We'll get this statement typed so you can read it over and sign it. Tomorrow will do for that."

"I see… Well, don't hesitate to call on me again, if you need me. I'm naturally anxious to do anything I can to help."

There was no sound of typewriting in the corridors now.

159

The episcopal secretary, leading the way to the elevator, took a short cut through empty offices. They passed a display room where samples of coloured fabric were on view in glass cases, like precious objects of art and *vertu*.

Suddenly Foyle stopped in his tracks. "Are those IFC dyes?"

The secretary looked surprised.

"Why, yes. We pride ourselves on our fabric dyes," he intoned. "We maintain a big research laboratory that is constantly seeking improvements."

Foyle frowned and peered into the showcase before him. It contained four samples of silk taffeta — lemon, canary, butter colour, and burnt orange.

"That's a nice, bright yellow. What chemical composition do you use for that?"

The secretary was bewildered. He forgot to be episcopal.

"Why — I believe they're all in this book."

It was a huge tome on a centre table. On the left-hand pages were pasted samples of coloured cloth about two inches square. On the corresponding right-hand pages were trade names of each colour and the chemical names. Usually there were two chemical names — the dye compound itself and the intermediate compound from which the dye compound was made.

The secretary switched on a light.

"Here are the yellows," he said. "The four you noticed are Citron, Buttercup, Goldenrod, and Sunset."

As Foyle turned the pages, his frown deepened. He read every page devoted to the yellows and their intermediates.

"Very interesting. Thanks."

He closed the book with a snap. "Come on, Duff."

They left the secretary staring after them.

VIEW IN ORIENTAL PERSPECTIVE

W hen Basil rang the bell it was Ann Claude herself who opened the door. The living room of the little flat above the bookshop was furnished with taste, but it was undeniably small. Street noise came from the windows, and a smell of frying onions from the hall — a contrast to the space and stillness of the Jocelyn house. Reluctantly, Basil's mind played with the fantastic idea that Kitty's illness had been a genuine attack of malaria at first, and that Ann had found some way to poison Kitty after the impersonation began, hoping to slip into Kitty's shoes permanently.

Impossible! cried his heart. *But his head answered: Poisoners are often neglected people — poor relations, old maids, servants, who have few normal outlets for initiative and who enjoy the secret power poison gives them over the lives of others.*

"Polly, do come here!" Ann was saying. "This is the man who decided I was sane after all. He's half Russian and the only man I know who would look all right in 18th-century dress!"

"Hello, Dr Willing!"

Polly was as plain as Ann was pretty, but like most plain girls today, she was very carefully dressed.

"Is this an official visit?" Ann curled herself up on the window seat.

"Of course it's official!" put in Polly. "Kitty was poisoned, and your father was a biological chemist. You're their number one suspect!"

She would not have said such a thing had she realised that Ann was actually under suspicion. Ann herself knew better. Her face was suddenly white.

Basil tried to reassure her. "You're not legally obliged to answer any questions at present. But it would be a help if you could tell us a little more about Kitty Jocelyn. What sort of girl was she?"

"That's rather difficult." Ann's voice was low and even. "You see I only knew her about four months."

"I'll make allowances for that."

"Well, then — Kitty was good-natured and generous. And she was also self-indulgent. She was easy-going with herself as well as others. She was neither good nor bad — just human. There was a streak of cynicism in her nature — that was part of her environment. She might have done things that were venal or dishonest, but I can't imagine her doing anything cruel. That's why I can't understand how anyone could have wanted to — to kill her."

"Now this a rather important question," said Basil. "Did anyone show surprise when you first appeared at the dance impersonating Kitty?"

Ann was silent for a few moments. Her simple cotton house dress and artlessly brushed hair made her look younger. Basil had a glimpse of what she must have been like before

Victorine turned her into a replica of Kitty. "Dr Willing," she answered finally, "I can't remember anyone who looked surprised." Basil made one more effort.

"Did anything happen at the dance that you haven't told us? Anything out of the ordinary, however slight?"

Colour rushed into Ann's cheeks. "There's one thing I didn't tell you. But you'd hardly call it out of the ordinary."

"Yes?"

"It was Nicholas Danine. I think he'd had too much to drink. When we were alone, he was rather tiresome. Wanted to paw me."

"Don't boast!" sang out Polly.

"That's why I didn't mention it before. I knew everyone would think I was boasting or lying or something nasty."

"Tell us all about your other conquests, my child," said Polly, wickedly.

"Don't be an idiot!" retorted Ann. "You know what dances are. Even Philip Leach tried to kiss me, but Rhoda had warned me that he was a philanderer who made love to everybody."

As Basil left the building, he caught sight of Sergeant Samson looking in the window of the bookshop.

"Interested in *Elizabethan Minor Poets*?" asked Basil, reading the title over his shoulder.

"Like heck I am!" The Sergeant was bitter. "Everybody who was at that Jocelyn cocktail party is being watched and I would draw a girl who lived over a bookshop. Now if I'd got Danine, I'd be snug as a bug in a rug at the Waldorf bar."

"But if you'd drawn Pasquale you might have to spend your time in the Museum of Modern Art!"

A few blocks farther up Madison Avenue, Basil met General Archer's niece, Isobel.

"Oh, Dr Willing! *Do* tell me all about the Jocelyn case! I'm definitely thrilled, but I just can't get Uncle Theodore to tell me half the things I'm dying to know. I was actually at that dance when it was happening. Isn't that too devastating for words? I'm so glad Aunt Emily brought me to New York this winter! Things like that never happen in Boston!"

Basil regarded the foolish, delicately painted face with a certain distaste.

"Do you recall anyone looking surprised when Ann Claude first appeared at the dance dressed as Kitty?"

"Oh, no. You see I didn't get there until after she appeared. I suppose that was just when poor Kitty was dying. Really, I never dreamed that Sveltis was poisonous, and I—"

Basil said something about an appointment and got away. He was to regret this later…

That evening Basil wrote out a careful summary of Ann's latest testimony, and Tuesday morning he took it to Inspector Foyle.

"Danine again!" cried Foyle when he read it. "Honest, doc, that guy is driving me haywire. I thought he'd be hard to get hold of — a big shot like him. Instead o' that, he's bothering the life out of me! Called up again this morning and said he must see me this afternoon. He's got a new idea about the case."

"And do you distrust Greeks bearing gifts?"

"He isn't Greek, he's Russian." Foyle was always literal. "I wish you'd come along with me."

"Nothing I'd like better!"

"Honest? Gee, doc, I wanted to ask you to come with me yesterday when I saw Mrs Jowett and Edgar Jocelyn, only I didn't quite like to. Maybe you can get some sense out of Danine if you talk to him in his own lingo."

Basil was twisting a ring on the littler finger of his left hand. "I rather think we'll get more out of him if he doesn't know I understand Russian. It's an old trick, but a very useful one."

As the police car drove uptown, Basil drew the ring from his finger. It was an uncut emerald with a crest rather crudely engraved.

"This ring belonged to my mother's father," he explained to Foyle and Duff. "Danine might recognise the Russian workmanship. So…"

He slipped the ring into his breast pocket.

"Now I'm safe. *Willing* doesn't sound very Slav, and, of course, Basil is a perfectly good Anglo-Saxon name. Danine has no way of knowing that it happens to be a translation of *Vassily* in my case."

At the hotel, they learned that Danine was in one of the tower apartments. His secretary came down to show them the way. Foyle recognised the correct and colourless young man who had been with Danine in the district attorney's office. Basil recognised a product of Eton and Oxford. As they went up in the elevator, he mused on the ironies of the system that had made this elaborately educated youth secretary to the man whose education was defined by the elastic word "Paris" in books of reference.

Not that Paris isn't educational, Basil reminded himself.

The elevator came to a stop. They were shown through a hallway into a drawing room with many windows.

"Whew!" The Inspector whistled softly.

Manhattan Island and all its streets and rivers were spread out far below — a realistic relief map with glass and metal fixtures blinking in the last rays of the pale winter sun.

"Clever of the cartographer to make the little dolls down there actually moving, isn't it?" said Basil. "They almost look as if they were alive. But not quite. He should have set the mechanism at a faster rate. That slow crawl destroys the illusion of life."

"It gives me the willies!" Foyle backed away from the window.

But Basil lingered. "You know, Foyle, it's like those Chinese and Persian paintings where ordinary objects are distorted by a bird's-eye view. But I never realised before that height — like opium — can distort time as well as space."

"Better come away from that window, doc! Some guys go nuts looking down from a height and then the papers say: 'Fell or Jumped'."

"Sorry to keep you waiting, Inspector."

Nicholas Danine had entered the room without making a sound.

"This is Dr Willing, Mr Danine," explained Foyle. "He's in the district attorney's office. If you don't mind, I'd like him to hear your new theory."

The arched brows rose a little.

"Not the Dr Willing who wrote *Time and Mentality*? This is indeed a pleasure."

"And I brought along Officer Duff to take notes," added Foyle.

"Please sit down," responded Danine. Basil recognised the hissing of the Slav *s*, and the cold, pale, slightly blurred blue eyes of northern Russia. "Perhaps you will join me in some sherry?"

Danine was as familiar as if they were his oldest friends, dropped in for a little chat before dinner. Basil reflected that only a Russian could create an atmosphere of intimacy so spontaneously and so insincerely. It was not the first time his mixed blood had helped him to understand international situations.

"I have some rather rare Amontillado," Danine was saying. "No? Well, at least a cigarette!"

The hand that pushed the box across the table was the narrow, tapering hand of a man who had never done manual labour.

"Tell me, Inspector Foyle, what progress have you made?"

"Not much." The Inspector answered shortly.

"And my reward? No responses?"

"Dozens, hundreds. But all from cranks and crackpots."

"Cranks? And what?"

"What Dr Willing here calls neurotics."

"Oh." The voice was enigmatic, the face veiled in drifting smoke. "I wonder if someone like that could be responsible for poor Kitty's death. Surely no one but a neurotic would poison such a charming girl."

"Is that the new theory you wanted to tell me about, Mr Danine?"

"No." Danine leaned back in his chair, his head canted to one side, his eyes half shut. "Has it occurred to you that the poison might not have been meant for Kitty at all? That she might have taken a cocktail intended for some other person?"

"But who else?"

Danine's smile had a fine edge.

"Couldn't the poison have been meant for…me?"

"For you! Why?"

"We-ell." The slim hand made an eloquent gesture. "There is an absurd prejudice today against anyone connected with the munitions industry — even against a mere salesman like myself, who peddles munitions, as another man may peddle bonds or neckties, in order to earn a living with no technical knowledge of the thing he sells. It's absurd but natural, for the mob mind is incapable of realism. That's why all folk art from children's drawings and primitive religious art to fashion drawings, pornography and caricature is based on emotional distortion and symbolism. The munition maker has become a symbol and a scapegoat like the Scarlet Woman. The mob vilifies him virtuously — and then proceeds to glorify all the emotions and economic customs that really cause war."

Danine looked down from the window at the creeping, foreshortened men and women far below.

"I must confess I can feel neither pity nor sympathy for people who reason in such slovenly fashion!" Again came the slow, subtle smile. It was impossible to tell if he were in earnest or not. "Who can look down from a height and see them crawling like flies or lice on the crust of our planet and still believe in the sanctity of human life?"

Basil followed his gaze. "Do you never get dizzy up here?"

"Oh, no! I thrive on the heights, Dr Willing! There is only one thing I fear." Danine's eyes were dreamy.

"And that is?"

"Poverty. In my youth, I lived in that prison without walls — a partial death, like ignorance, disease, or celibacy. Today, when a beggar stops me on the street, I can always tell if he's actually starving or not, for I know — only too well — the peculiar smell of a starving body. Poverty is more cruel than war. It lasts longer."

With a jerk, Foyle hauled the conversation back to the murder.

"Were any of the folks at the cocktail party peace hounds

who might have tried to poison you because you were a munition maker?"

Danine's brows lifted.

"Well, the butler, Gregg, was an ex-soldier, I believe. And it was he who served the cocktails. Some ex-soldiers are fanatical pacifists."

"That's so." Foyle turned to Basil. "Didn't you say he was a shell-shock case?"

Basil frowned. "That is scarcely sufficient evidence for accusing Gregg."

"I wonder if any of the others could be pacifists?" ruminated Foyle. "Did you meet the Jocelyns for the first time in Cannes' last summer, Mr Danine?"

"Yes." Danine lit another cigarette. "Kitty and her stepmother, Miss Claude, Victorine; the maid, and Pasquale, the *cavalière servente* were all there. I was attracted to Kitty at once. A charming child! Artemis in a white bathing suit."

"None of that bunch are the stuff fanatics are made of," said Foyle. "Unless it's Victorine. She's French and the French had a pretty tough time in the last war. Did Victorine ever act queer toward you, Mr Danine?"

"I have no recollection of it."

"Well, I guess that's all for the present." Foyle rose. "We'll keep this idea of yours in mind, Mr Danine."

"There may be nothing in it." Danine was deprecating. "But it just occurred to me, and I thought I'd pass it along. After all, I have made more enemies in my 53 years than poor little Kitty in her 18."

He touched a bell. A manservant entered the room moving as silently as his master, an old man, tall, bent, and white-haired. He, too, had blurred, blue eyes, deep-set under heavy eyelids. His hands were also narrow and tapering, with almond-shaped nails.

An idea came to Basil.

"Was this man with you at Cannes last summer?"

"Oh, yes." Danine moistened his lips with his tongue.

"Sergei goes with me everywhere. I couldn't get along without him!"

"Then I wonder if I might question Sergei? He would certainly know more about Victorine than you."

"As you please!" Danine's voice had lost its blandness. "But I warn you, that you won't get anything out of Sergei. Like most Russians of his class, he is lazy, stupid, and super-stitious."

"Indeed?" murmured Basil. "I know so little about Russians of any class."

The room had been growing darker for some time. Now, like a theatrical trick, lights began to appear in the great build-ings outside until they looked like giant honeycombs, each window a cell loaded with shining, yellow honey.

Danine switched on a table lamp and spoke to Sergei in Russian. His tone was the ordinary, dispassionate tone of a man speaking to a servant. If Basil had not understood the language he would never have guessed that the words were interlarded with personal abuse:

"These men wish to question you — you filthy swine! Answer without lying — if you can!"

Sergei showed no sign of emotion. "You speak English?" asked Basil.

"Oh, yes." Danine answered for Sergei. "He is quite a linguist."

"What is your full name?" went on Basil.

"My name is Sergei Piotrovitch Radanine, sir," came the reply in excellent English.

"How do you spell that? Slav names are so difficult…"

Sergei produced a Nansen passport.

"I see. Thank you. Now I want to ask you about Mrs Jocelyn's maid, Victorine. I understand you knew her in Cannes last summer. Is she a pacifist?"

"Not to my knowledge, sir. But I talked to her only two or three times — no more."

"In French, I suppose?" inquired Basil.

Danine answered again. "Yes, Sergei has picked up quite a little French as well as English. But you see it's hopeless trying to question him. You'll get nothing intelligent out of such *canaille*."

"Hey! Wait a minute!" Inspector Foyle thought he had been quiet long enough. "Let me handle this bird."

"As you please, Inspector Coyle." Danine's voice was dry.

"Say, are you trying to be funny, Mr Danine? My name's *Foyle! F* — that's the first letter — *F!*"

"I'm so sorry, Inspector. Just a slip of the tongue. Quite unintentional, I assure you."

"Huh!" The Inspector turned to Sergei. "You a Communist?"

"No, sir"

"Oh, yeah? What's the Russian for 'come clean'?"

"There is no such expression in the Russian language," interpolated Danine.

"Well, Sergei, what were you before the revolution?"

"A soldier, sir."

"And after that?"

"I worked on a French railway on the Riviera. When the

franc rose and the Americans and English stopped coming, I lost my job."

"I ran into him at the *Bureau des Etrangers* in Nice." Danine took up the tale. "His *permis de travail* had expired and he was having some trouble getting it renewed. He seemed a fairly capable fellow, so I arranged things for him — I have a little influence in France — and took him on as my servant."

"Well, you certainly ought to be grateful to Mr Danine," remarked Foyle.·

A peculiar expression crossed Sergei's face. But he answered simply, "Yes, sir."

As the Inspector's party rose to go, Sergei moved forward to open the door for them. He had to pass Danine. At that moment, there flashed into Danine's eyes a look that startled Basil. In all his experience of abnormal emotions, he had never seen hatred more naked and unashamed.

"That guy Danine talks too much," said Foyle as they stood on the sidewalk, outside the hotel. "All that guff about folk art. I hope I never have a Russian witness again as long as I live! Do you think there's anything in this idea that the poisoned cocktail was intended for him and Kitty Jocelyn just got it by mistake?"

Basil smiled. "Have you forgotten Gregg's statement? And Ann Claude's? Danine took sherry the afternoon of the dance. It seems most unlikely that the poisoner would confuse a Bronx cocktail with a glass of sherry. Certainly no butler would be likely to do so, and therefore Kitty could hardly have been served with the glass of sherry intended for Danine."

"Then it was all moonshine! And you knew it and you were just stalling him along!"

"I'd like to know why he hates his servant," remarked Basil. "Hate is so intimate."

Before Foyle could answer, a voice shouted: "Hold it!"

A flashlight bulb went off in their faces. "Well, I'll be—"

Duff sprang forward and seized the photographer by the shoulder.

"Now, Inspector, be a sport! It's for the Occidental News Service and we represent one hundred and forty-nine newspapers in North and South America!"

"Let him be, Duff. We're not going to smash your plates, buddy. But I want to know how you knew I was going to be at the Waldorf this afternoon?"

"Somebody tipped me off. I don't know who it was — honest, Inspector. Somebody rang me up at the office this morning and said you were coming here at 4 pm to see this guy Danine, about the Jocelyn case."

Foyle let the photographer go and turned to Basil. "Who could have known that except Danine himself?"

Basil smiled. "Precisely."

"Where now?" asked Duff.

"What about dinner with me, doc?" suggested Foyle. "I'd like to talk this over with you."

"Why don't you two dine with me? Juniper is always able to rustle up something at short notice. And I want Duff to bring his notebook."

"Okay. Do you mind going to Lambert's first? There's something I want to ask him, and he'll be at home by now."

Lambert lived on Riverside Drive. A maid showed them into a chilly study.

"Too much wind," explained Lambert. "We burn twice as much coal as we would in any other street. What about a little experiment with an aqueous solution of ethyl alcohol?"

"Experiment is right," retorted Basil, eying the bottle of

corn whisky. "If I die, tell the reporters I was just another martyr to Science."

"Listen, I came here on serious business," protested Foyle. "I found out yesterday that Kitty Jocelyn's uncle, Edgar Jocelyn, is president of a dye company — the Industrial Finishing Company."

"Dye companies are often called finishing companies, or processing companies," put in Lambert.

"I was in his office and I happened to see some samples of fabric dyed yellow. Of course I remembered your saying that thermol is used as a commercial dye. So I looked up all the yellows in the chemical dictionary of IFC trade names. But not one of 'em was made from thermol."

Lambert's face broke into an insolent smile. "Someday all detectives will be chemists!"

"Oh, no. Psychiatrists," insisted Basil.

"I didn't just look under *thermol*," cried Foyle, hastily. "I looked under *di-nitro-phenol* and *di-nitro-benzene* and I looked at the intermediates as well as the dye compounds, and I didn't find a thing. The book may have been doctored before my visit, so I want you to tell me how I can find out if the IFC makes a thermol dye, without letting Edgar Jocelyn know what I'm after."

Lambert's smile became a chuckle.

"You poor babe in the woods! You *would* look up the *yellow* dyes!"

"Well, blast it, the stuff is yellow!" exploded Foyle. "I saw the crystals under your microscope!"

Lambert's chuckle became a roar. He swallowed some whisky the wrong way and Basil had to pound him on the back.

At last, he got his breath and wiped his eyes.

"Colour is scarcely a constant factor in chemicals! You remember my telling you that thermol is used as a standard colour-indicator for hydrogen ion concentrations in the Michaelis technique? Obviously, that would be impossible if its colour never changed. Warmed with sulphur and sodium sulphide, thermol yields a black dye for fabrics, not a *yellow* dye, Foyle, mavourneen. The IFC markets it under the trade name Sulphur Black."

"Black!"

Foyle was startled.

18

DRY POINTS

"And now," said Basil, when dinner was over, "if I'm to be any help, I must know everything about the case that you know — everything."

"You do know everything that happened up to Monday morning," replied Foyle. "I'll go one from there."

As he went on to describe the events of the last few days, Basil put in a question now and then, and Duff prompted his superior from the shorthand notes of the case. At the end, Foyle himself was surprised to find how clearly he had remembered every detail. He did not realise how skilfully he had been led from one association to another by a man whose profession was to stimulate the memory of his patients and make them recall forgotten incidents of their past.

"I'm up a tree, doc," he concluded. "Every lead peters out the minute you go after it. For three solid hours, I questions those private detectives that Rhoda employed to find Kitty when she first disappeared, and I couldn't get anything useful out of them. They admitted they knew that Anne was taking

Kitty's place but claimed they didn't know she was doing it against her will. And they had the nerve to say that it never occurred to them to search the hospitals and mortuaries because Rhoda was so sure Kitty was alive. Can you beat that for crust?

"My men have combed all the fashionable hotels, renting agencies, real estate firms, and residential clubs for Philip Leach, and not one of 'em has any idea where he lived. He musta slept on a bench in the park! I got a photo of him from his editor and the boys are showing it around to the taxi men outside the Harvard Club and the night spots where he used to hang out. But nothing has come of it so far.

"Then there's that gate-crasher. We haven't found hide nor hair of him. As if we hadn't enough suspects without his butting in!"

"I'm afraid that's a habit with gate-crashers," said Basil. "What about the men who've been trailing Pasquale? You were sure he'd try to get some more dope when you — er — confiscated his supply."

Foyle grinned ruefully. "Mebbe I was a bit too sure that time! The men tailing Pasquale say that the only day he left the house, he didn't go anywhere except Carnegie Hall and the Viviane Galleries."

"What day was that?"

"Monday."

"Monday. Then he went to the Strauss concert and the Reynold exhibition?"

"Yeah. Mullens said the exhibition wasn't so bad, but the concert was something fierce. And as if all this weren't enough to drive me cuckoo, the Sveltis company has started kicking because some of the papers have begun to mention Sveltis by name as the reducing medicine that poisoned Kitty. Of course they were bound to do that sooner or later in a case masking as big a splash as this one."

Foyle drew a folded sheet of paper from his breast pocket.

"I made a list of all the blunders in the case, doc," he said, a little sheepishly.

"How many are there altogether?"

"Nine." Foyle began to read in the singsong he reserved for the written word:

1. *Why did Rhoda Jocelyn upset that ink bottle?*
2. *Why did Rhoda Jocelyn lose her cigarette case?*
3. *Why did Luis Pasquale drink from Kitty Jocelyn's cocktail glass by mistake?*
4. *Why did Luis Pasquale mislay a woman's diamond ring in his own rooms?*
5. *Why did Philip Leach forget to wind his watch?*
6. *Why did Mrs Jowett mislay her glasses?*
7. *Why did Mrs Jowett sign* Kitty Jocelyn*'s name to her typewritten statement instead of her own?*
8. *Why did Edgar Jocelyn say black when he meant to say back?*
9. *Why does Nicholas Danine call me* Coyle *and* Royle *and everything except my right name,* Foyle*?*

"Not nine — eight," objected Basil. "According to Ann Claude's story, Mrs Jowett did not lose her glasses. Victorine hid them purposely. When Rhoda and Victorine were planning the impersonation, Victorine said to Ann, *'Mrs Jowett wears glasses. If her glasses were mislaid this evening there would be no danger of her suspecting anything.'* When blunders are used as evidence, it's important to make sure they are genuine blunders. Otherwise, they haven't the same psychological significance."

"Well, then, we've got eight of your psychic fingerprints." Foyle's grin broadened as he used the phrase. "But, honest, I can't think of any explanation for any of them."

"I doubt if there is any clue in the early stages of a case that cannot be interpreted in more than one way," responded Basil. "That's equally true of psychic clues and physical clues and it's one of the detective's greatest handicaps — if he has any pretensions to intellectual honesty. I can explain seven of these eight blunders tentatively. But so far I cannot guarantee that any of the explanations is the right one."

"Well, let's hear them anyway."

Basil took a carton of cigarettes from the table drawer. "Better light up. It'll take some time... Edgar Jocelyn's blunder follows such a classic pattern that to most modern psychologists it would be proof positive that he was lying when he told you he had never heard of thermol. The blunder occurred shortly after you told him that thermol, or di-nitro-phenol, was an ingredient of Sveltis, and that it had been used to poison Kitty. He promptly denied that he had ever heard of the drug. We know now that his company, the IFC, makes a fabric dye called Sulphur Black. He might not have known that businessmen don't always know every detail of the technical side of their business. But do you believe it's merely coincidence that he uttered the word *black* when his tongue slipped? I don't. As I see it, he naturally began to think about Sulphur Black the moment you mentioned di-nitro-phenol. His effort to repress normal expression of that thought set up a conflict, which, in turn, produced that minute split in personality we call a slip of the tongue — and Edgar blurted out unconsciously one of the very words he was trying to repress

179

consciously — *black*. The reason he said *black* instead of *sulphur* was because *black* happened to be similar in sound to a word he did want to say — *back*. Word blunders are often rhyming or alliterative. The poet's muse is simply a higher development of this tendency of the unconscious."

Foyle pondered this. "Of course Edgar Jocelyn did say he was not a chemist, but a businessman."

"He rather went out of his way to say it, didn't he? And Danine went out of his way to assure us that he was just a salesman with no technical knowledge of the thing he sells. Quite a touching epidemic of modesty in the chemical industries, isn't there?

"The key to Mrs Jowett's blunder may lie in her own exclamation: *'I wish you could do something to keep my name out of all this.'* Her conventional sense of duty induced her to tell you everything she knew about Kitty's circumstances. But in doing that she was repressing a conflicting wish to have as little to do with the Jocelyn case as possible, because of the scandal which might ruin her professionally. When she came to sign her statement, that suppressed wish to keep her name out of the case rose to the surface. Her unconscious 'counter-will' boldly wrote another name in place of her own — a stratagem that was futile and yet symbolic, like that of the unhappily married woman who signs her maiden name by mistake. The dead girl's name was probably chosen for the substitute signature because it had the same initials as Mrs Jowett's own name, and that appealed to the unconscious love of alliteration. You see the same tendency in criminals who unconsciously select aliases with the same initials as their own."

"Golly, that's so! They nearly always do." Foyle was impressed almost in spite of himself.

"The fact that Rhoda spilled ink on her dress has an even

simpler explanation. Blunder by which you soil or injure your-self are usually symptoms of hidden self-disgust. Suicide from remorse is only an extreme form of the impulse that can express in 'accidents' as trivial as stubbing your toe when that impulse is suppressed. Rhoda has plenty of reasons for feeling self-disgust, but without this evidence of the state of her unconscious mind, we might have believed her too insensitive to feel it.

"As for her losing her cigarette case — there is a famous psychiatrist who always loses his pipe when he's been smoking too much. Rhoda has been under a terrific strain the last few days, and she lit one cigarette after another during our inter-view with her. The loss of her case may be the symbol of an unconscious impulse to preserve her own health from too many cigarettes.

"Perhaps the most suggestive of all these blunders is Philip Leach's forgetting to wind his watch last Tuesday evening. Though we have never seen Leach or talked to him, we know from that blunder that he was most probably in a state of despair the day of the murder. Forgetting to wind a timepiece is obviously symbolic of dread or indifference to the future. Freud and his immediate followers go further and claim that it is a symptom of the desire to commit suicide, thrust far below the threshold of consciousness because it conflicts with moral ideas and self-preservation. In my own clinical work, I have always found it associated with varying degrees of discourage-ment and despair, even in cases where the patient was cheerful on the surface and quite literally unconscious of his inner sense of failure.

"In Pasquale's case, there are at least two perfectly good hypotheses to explain his drinking half of Kitty's cocktail by mistake. First: Pasquale is the murderer and he knows all about thermol. He slips a dose into Kitty's cocktail and then deliberately drinks half of it, pretending he does so by mistake, and gambling on the hope that his morphine habit has made him immune. By doing this, he hopes to divert suspicion from himself, and make it almost impossible to prove that the cocktail poisoned her, which in turn would make it impossible for us to limit suspects to people at the cocktail party.

"Second: Pasquale is not the murderer and he has no idea Kitty's cocktail is poisoned. His mistaking it for his own is a genuine blunder, and the key to its significance lies in fiction and folklore. There's a scene in Meredith's *Egoist* where a man first shows his passion for a girl by deliberately touching his lips to a glass her lips have just touched. And I believe that sharing the same cup of wine is part of both the Russian and Japanese marriage ritual. Pasquale himself told us that Rhoda was jealous of Kitty's youth. Naturally Pasquale hungered for youth, but he had to hide that hunger because he was dependent on Rhoda. There you have the old cycle again — wish, conflict, repression, and then the wish expressing itself vainly and harmlessly in the involuntary pantomime of a blunder. According to this second hypothesis, it was only the luck of the shiftless and good-for-nothing, that Pasquale's morphine habit should save him from a horrible death."

"Then you believe Pasquale had fallen for Kitty?" asked Foyle.

"Nothing so deep and lasting as that. Just 'such stuff as dreams' — one of those fleeting, animal impulses that betray themselves in blunders and reveries and works of art. You remember the nude in Pasquale's painting had a slight resemblance to Kitty?"

"And why did Pasquale lose that diamond ring?"

"That's the one blunder I won't attempt to explain even

tentatively at this stage of the case. We don't know enough about the ring itself as yet to construct a useful working hypothesis."

"What about Danine?"

"Well, what about him?"

"You know. His calling me Doyle and Boyle and so on."

"We-ell, I don't want to hurt your feelings, Inspector…"

"Aw, shoot! I can take it!"

"When Abraham Lincoln wished to rebuke a certain Lord Hartington for tactlessness, he kept addressing his victim as 'Lord Partington.' In that way, he classed Hartington with 'Mrs Partington' — a symbol of gaucherie in those days — and implied that he really couldn't be bothered to remember Hartington's correct name. Lincoln did that deliberately, but most modern psychologists are familiar with the unconscious snub. Poor Danine has to be friendly with us now in order to avoid trouble. But unconsciously he is annoyed at having to bother with us at all and he expresses that annoyance by not taking the trouble to remember your name. Since poverty is the only thing he fears, wealth must be the only thing he respects. Think how galling it must be for him to have to defer to men who pay as little income tax as you and me!"

Foyle's face reddened and he looked sternly at Duff.

"What are you grinning about?"

"Nothing, chief — nothing at all," cried Duff, hastily. "But there's one question I'd like to ask, Dr Willing."

"Fire away!"

"What about Minna Hagen's stuttering? Don't all speech defects count as blunders?"

"Golly, I *forgot* about that!" exclaimed Foyle. "What does that prove about my unconscious mind, doc?"

Basil smiled. "Perhaps your unconscious mind remembered what I told you the other day — that only the blunders of physically normal people can be trusted as psychological evidence. Minna Hagen is afflicted with adenoids and difficulty in breathing. Her stuttering has no more psychological significance than a slip of the hand in a person with palsy, or the nasality of speech in a syphilitic. There are cases of purely psychological stuttering, but she is not one of them and so we cannot count her speech defects as blunders."

"Well…" Foyle helped himself to another of Basil's cigarettes. "The way you explain them, doc, there are only four blunders out of the eight that sound as if they might prove useful to us — Edgar Jocelyn's *lie*, Rhoda Jocelyn's *remorse*, Pasquale's *interest in Kitty*, and Leach's *despair* the day of the murder."

"But I said these explanations were only tentative," protested Basil. "We may have to revise several of them before we solve the case. Rhoda's remorse may be due solely to her part in the plot against Ann Claude and have nothing to do with the murder at all. On the other hand there may be some other explanation of Danine's calling you Boyle and Coyle which would make that a psychological indication that he committed the murder. Psychic fingerprints have to be analysed and correlated with other factors in the case as laboriously as physical fingerprints before you can reach any definite conclusion. And that takes time. Do you know what's really the most amazing thing about this murder?"

"There are so many amazing things about it, doc." Foyle spoke wearily.

"But what's the most amazing thing of all? The thing that's conspicuous by its absence?"

"Give it up."

"Motive!" cried Basil, with sudden intensity. "Where's the

motive? In most crimes a detective starts with a number of suspects who have motives, and his job is to fasten means and opportunity on one of them. But here we have the reverse a lot of people with means and opportunity, and not one so far with a logical, compelling motive!

"All our witnesses insist that no one had reason to hate Kitty and so far as we know no one profited by her death. Rhoda and Pasquale were depending on her to make a brilliant marriage and she was killed before she was even engaged. Edgar Jocelyn had just pledged a large sum of money for her coming-out party and she was killed before the party. Mrs Jowett, like the tradespeople, was actually making money out of Kitty's debut, and nothing could be better calculated to harm Mrs Jowett professionally than the scandal of this murder. All the servants, including Gregg and Victorine, owed their jobs to Rhoda's exploitation of Kitty's debut. Now Kitty is dead, and Rhoda's bluff is called, she will have to close the house and dismiss the entire staff. If Danine did want to marry Kitty, why should he poison her? I can't believe that such a competent cynic would love any girl enough to murder her and risk his own neck for jealousy or disillusion. Even to Philip Leach, Kitty must have been at least a source of copy for his column. Ann Claude gained nothing by Kitty's death except a rather terrifying experience. I have played with the idea that Ann might have poisoned Kitty through envy, or a desire to slip into Kitty's shoes permanently through the impersonation. But I have never taken that idea seriously. I consider Ann too intelligent to envy Kitty's rococo life, and too normal to be a poisoner. When I tested her mental condition at the beginning of the case, I was unable to find any tendency toward abnormality, while I did find every evidence of intelligence.

"To sum up, among all the people known to have been at

the cocktail party when Kitty was poisoned, there is not one who had a motive apparently."

"Not only that," added Foyle, soberly. "But most of 'em scarcely knew Kitty at all! Her uncle Edgar hasn't seen her since she was a kid. Mrs Jowett and Gregg had never seen her until she came to this country about six weeks ago. It would have been physically impossible for these three to have known Kitty before then. The years when Kitty was in France and Italy, Edgar Jocelyn and Mrs Jowett were in America and Gregg was in England. My men checked up on that, and they've been unable to trace any previous personal connection between Kitty and these people or their families. So far as we know, Philip Leach only met her on the boat coming over. The only suspects who knew her at all well are those who were on the Continent the last few years — Rhoda, Pasquale, Victorine, Danine, and Ann Claude. I can't help thinking one of them must be the murderer."

Basil smiled again. "You think it bad form to murder someone you don't know really well? Doubtless it is! Yet none of the five you mention, who knew Kitty well, had reason to hate her, as far as I can see. There are only two motives for murder — hate and greed. Emotions like fear and jealousy and revenge are simply variations on the theme of hate — Chaucer's '*colde wrathe*'. No one profited by Kitty's death. Therefore someone hated her. But who? And why? If we had an inkling of the motive, all the rest would fall into place. For the ingredients of this crime were assembled as symmetrically as the atoms in a molecule or the elements in a work of art."

"Pasquale's an artist!" cried Foyle, hopefully.

"But he has no sense of design!" Basil's eyes twinkled. "Have you forgotten his painting of the nude on a taxi cab? We can almost acquit him on that evidence alone! This was not a *sur-réaliste* crime. The murder as first planned was severely classic-architectural. The thing that spoiled it was the intrusion of romantic elements not in the original design — Rhoda's impersonation plot, and Kitty's leaving the house in Ann's clothes — for whatever reason."

The sudden peal of the telephone made Foyle jump.

Duff answered it. "For you, chief."

"Hullo?" As Foyle listened, his eyes grew brighter. "Okay." He slammed the receiver back into its cradle. "One of the boys has got hold of a taxi driver who remembers driving Leach away from a night club a few days ago. And where do you think he went? Washington Heights — of all places! What was a gilt-edged gossip writer doing out there in the sticks?"

19

DRAWING FOR VALENTINE

Wednesday morning, a police car sped north until it came to the hill between the Hudson and the Harlem Rivers, where Madame Jumel's white house still stands on its own lawn, overlooking the Polo Grounds and the roofs of the city. There was a side street that didn't seem quite sure whether it was city or suburb. Among fireproof apartment buildings stood several old frame houses with the cupolas and fretwork of the Seventies. At one of these, the car stopped.

A man lounging on the corner sauntered forward and said softly, "He hasn't left the house, Inspector."

Their footsteps sounded hollow on the wooden porch. The door was opened by a shapeless, blowsy woman wearing a bungalow apron.

"Leach? Sure, he's my boarder. Second floor front. But I don't know if he's up yet."

"Didn't you see in the papers that he was wanted as a witness in the Jocelyn case?" demanded Foyle.

"Papers? Say, mister, I don't get time to read the papers!

188

What with Baby teething, and little Sammy getting home from school so early, and all my washing and baking and—"

"Don't you get radio news?"

"We use to. But the radio's broke now, and—"

Basil and Foyle mounted the stairs with Duff. Foyle rapped smartly on the door.

A drowsy voice called out, "Didn't I tell you I wanted to sleep late?"

Foyle's only answer was another rap.

"Ah, all right!"

There was a sound of bare feet padding across a wooden floor and the door was pulled open.

"My God!" cried the young man and tried to shut it again.

But Foyle thrust his way in, the others following. Mr Philip Leach was scarcely in a condition to receive visitors. He was clad in a pair of rumpled, mauve silk pyjamas. He had not shaved for several days. His hair was tousled, his eyes bloodshot and gummy with sleep.

"Wha' the devil…" he began.

Foyle planted himself in an armchair, with a hand on either knee. "I'm Inspector Foyle from Police Headquarters. This is Dr Willing of the district attorney's office. You know why we're here, young man!"

"But I—"

"I can swallow just so much!" barked Foyle. "Don't tell me *you* don't read the papers!"

"On my word, I haven't seen a paper for the last eight days."

"Then what in hell have you been doing?"

"Getting drunk," returned Mr Leach with disarming simplicity. "Why?"

Leach's eyes narrowed. "It's a way we have in the news-paper game."

"I've never known a successful newspaper man who made a habit of drunkenness!"

"Then you can see the advantage of being an unsuccessful newspaper man," drawled Leach.

Foyle leaned forward impatiently. "Do you mean to tell me you've been in this room since last Wednesday without seeing a single newspaper?"

"Absolutely!"

"Then…" The Inspector was watching him closely.

"You haven't heard anything about the murder of Kitty Jocelyn?"

"Kitty!"

He slumped to the floor.

They lifted the inert body to a wicker couch. Basil bent the head below the knees.

"I never thought he'd take it like that," muttered Foyle.

Leach opened his eyes. Before Foyle could out the ques-tion, he had answered it.

"She was going to be my wife." His voice was dull and slow. "We were going to be married the day after her coming-out party. And now…"

It came to Basil that these were the first tears that had been shed for Kitty's death.

"Mrs Jocelyn said nothing about all this!" snapped Foyle.

"She knew nothing about it. We were running away."

He lifted stricken eyes. "How did it happen?"

Foyle returned the look for a long moment. "Perhaps you can tell us."

"I?" Leach stared. "But I haven't seen Kitty since the dance. I've been here all the time."

"Getting drunk — all the time?"

"And sleeping it off — and working on a novel."

"Then you didn't know that Kitty Jocelyn was dead until we told you?"

"Good God, no! How many times must I tell you?"

Like most psychologists, Basil had little faith in anything that resembled third-degree methods.

"If we want a coherent statement from Mr Leach I think we'd better allow him to take a cold shower and dress. Perhaps his landlady will send up some black coffee."

Foyle looked at Basil quizzically. "Well that's not exactly the way we do things at Headquarters, but I guess you're the doctor this time!"

Shaved and dressed, Leach didn't look the same man. His features were regular and pleasing. There was a natural wave in his chestnut hair that a Hollywood actor would have envied. His brown suit and brown calf shoes were of the best quality and he was not entirely unaware of the fact that he had a slim figure and a neat foot to show them off. He seemed to have recovered his self-possession.

He picked up a wristwatch with a pigskin strap that lay on top of a portable typewriter.

"It must be later than six!"

"It's nearly eleven," replied Basil.

"Forgot to wind it again!" Leach repaired the omission, gave the watch a shake for good measure, and fastened it to his wrist.

"Have a spot?" He held up a bottle of whisky.

"No, thanks. And I prescribed black coffee."

"I never obey doctor's orders." Leach opened the door of a kitchenette, brought out a raw egg and a bottle of catsup, and proceeded to mix himself a pick-me-up with the competence of long practice.

"Well, when you're quite ready, Mister Leach, I'd like to know just why you're hiding here in Washington Heights," remarked Foyle, with laborious sarcasm. "We've been combing all the hot spots and big hotels for you."

"And you never thought of looking way out here?" Leach smiled as he tossed the eggshells into the sink. "I'm not hiding. I live here because I get plenty for my money — two big rooms, a bath and kitchenette, a view and plenty of light and air. If I were farther downtown, on my salary, I'd have to live in a miniature edition of the Black Hole of Calcutta, and I'd be interrupted every time I tried to work on my novel by the phone ringing and people dropping in. Here I have no telephone, and no one knows this address. I don't miss invitations because I'm at my club every morning and at my office every afternoon."

"Well, I'm afraid you won't be there again very soon," remarked Foyle. "Your managing editor told me you were fired."

"Did he?" Leach sipped his unpalatable drink with a wry face and added a little more whisky.

"It doesn't seem to worry you much?"

"Oh, no. They'll take me back. They always do. I've been fired five times altogether, but each time they find they can't get anybody else so cheap who has all the dope I have."

"I'd go easy on that whisky if I were you. Just what is your salary?"

"Fifty. I'm not like the big guns who get their stuff syndicated. I'm just a local space-filler."

"You dress on that?"

Leach smiled. "No. A friend lent me credit at his tailor for this suit. I don't know where the next one's coming from. As for the shoes…" He contemplated his burnished boot tips, "I gave the bootmaker a puff in my column."

"Wasn't it rather reckless to plan marriage with a girl of luxurious tastes on fifty a week?" suggested Basil.

"In a way. But, of course, Kitty had something of her own."

"You're wrong." Foyle's gaze was penetrating. "She hadn't a cent."

"But… that's impossible!" Leach gaped at him. "I mean… she must have had something. That house and the coming-out party and — and the way she was publicised."

"All part of the game," said Foyle, bluntly.

"Game?"

"Rhoda Jocelyn's game. She wanted her stepdaughter to marry well, so she got Edgar Jocelyn to pay for the coming-out party. It was a gamble. A speculation. Neither Rhoda nor Kitty had any money left. But, according to Rhoda, the girl herself didn't realise that."

"No, she didn't."

"And neither did you?"

Leach coloured. "It wouldn't have made any difference if I had!"

"Perhaps you have relatives who would have helped you out if you had married Kitty?"

Leach refilled his empty glass with neat whisky and drank it at one gulp.

"Nothing like that. My father was a Cleveland banker. The police out there will tell you he shot himself after the Wall Street crash of 1929, so I might as well tell you now. I was in my junior year at college and of course I had to leave. I came to New York determined to be a novelist. Not a bestseller. The real McCoy. Dostoevsky and all that… But I didn't click. Then I tried to write hooey — business stories, love stories, action stories — the 'folk prose of Western democracy'. But I couldn't even sell that. I was in the position of the man who decided to sell his soul to the Devil, only to find that the Devil wouldn't have his anaemic little soul at any price. If there's anything more humiliating than deciding to barter your honour only to find there aren't any takers, I don't know what it is. There I was — betraying every ideal I had — and not making one red cent out of it! I barged into an ex-speak one night to drown my sorrows and whom should I see but an old college pal, a New York fellow. He didn't know how hard up I was. He thought I'd just blown in from Cleveland. So he introduced me to all his friends and they began inviting me right and left. I accepted all bids because each one meant a free feed. Suddenly, it dawned on me that there might be money in gossip writing. I dashed off something, took it into a news-paper office and the rest is just another success story."

"I thought you used a typewriter," remarked Inspector Foyle. His disapproval of Mr Leach was patent.

But Basil perceived the bitter sense of failure under the flippancy that was obviously Leach's stock in trade — the coin in which he paid for "free feeds" and "loans" of credit at a tailor.

"When did you first meet Kitty Jocelyn?" asked Basil.

"Last summer. Ted Aldrich, the polo player, took me over to Burlingham as his guest, and we met Kitty on the boat coming home. She and I were engaged, secretly, before the voyage was over. It could never have happened on shore, for Rhoda Jocelyn used to watch Kitty like a hawk. But Rhoda and Victorine and that fat pig, Pasquale, were all seasick, so they didn't know what was happening. We didn't tell anybody —

we knew it wasn't any use. Rhoda was full of ambitions for Kitty."

"Miss Jocelyn was poisoned by a cocktail she drank the afternoon of the dance and—"

"Poisoned! A cocktail? Good God! Do you mean Kitty was actually poisoned at the Jocelyn house when I was there?"

"Exactly. What can you tell us about that cocktail party?"

It was some moments before Leach pulled himself together. Then he answered: "I was feeling pretty blue that day. I'd struck a snag in my work on the novel that morning, and I felt like burning the manuscript and jumping in the river. When I got to the Jocelyns', I found Kitty was pretty miserable herself. We were out of hearing of the others for a few moments and she said to me, 'Rhoda really believes I'm going to marry Danine, and she's so terribly in earnest. She frightens me.'

"We'd planned to get married when my novel was done. But I saw the situation was getting on her nerves. So I said, 'Why not elope tonight right in the middle of the dance?' I'd just had four cocktails and I suppose that made me reckless. I told her I'd be at the 79th Street entrance to the park with a car at 11 pm and wait until she came. She wasn't sure just when she could slip away — probably not until midnight. She was to leave the house as soon as the crowd at the dance was big enough to cover her departure. Then we were going to drive down to Washington — that seems to be the only place left now where you can get married in a hurry.

"When I left the Jocelyn house, I had to go downtown to see the old man — I mean, my editor. After that I got dinner at a restaurant and borrowed Tony Belcher's Buick sedan. I reached the 79th Street entrance to the park at 10:55, and my watch was all right that time, because the old man had grouched about my being late for my appointment with him, and he'd made me set my watch by the office clock that's regulated by radio. So there I was on the dot — and Kitty never turned up at all!

"At 3 am, I decided that either she was ill, or Rhoda had found out about our plan and made trouble. Fortunately, I'd kept my card of invitation to the dance. I drove out here, changed into evening things, and then went downtown again to the Jocelyn house. It was ablaze with lights and you could hear the dance music in the street. I went inside and there was Kitty dancing and looking perfectly well and completely unworried. When she saw me, she smiled — just as if nothing had happened.

"My first feeling was relief. I really was glad to see she was all right. But the next minute I was furious at the way she'd stood me up. Four solid hours I'd waited for her and it was as cold as the Ice Age that night. I went to the bar and had a couple of drinks. Perhaps I had more than a couple. Then I cut in on her — just to see what she'd say. Believe it or not, she never even attempted to apologise or explain! She was gay and carefree and talked about impersonal things.

"By that time I was too dazed — or too drunk — to be angry. I got her alone in a corner of the library and tried to ask her what had happened, but she wouldn't listen to me! The minute I put my arm around her she pushed me away. That was too much. I left her and I left the house. I could guess what had happened. Rhoda had wormed everything out of her — somehow — and persuaded her to break the engagement. Kitty was weak enough to let herself be persuaded and this was her charming way of doing it!

"Nothing seemed to matter much then. I didn't even bother to turn in my story on the dance at the office. I came home here and…well…I got drunk in earnest and slept it off and worked on my novel and got drunk again. And I've been here ever since. God, it's awful to think that the last time I saw Kitty we quarrelled."

Basil broke the silence.

"Did it never occur to you that the girl at the dance was not Kitty Jocelyn?"

"What?!"

Again Foyle told the tale of Ann's impersonation.

"Then… Kitty did keep her word! She did try to meet me — even though she was ill. And all the time I was waiting for her, she was dying only a few yards away."

"She must have planned the impersonation from the first as cover for her elopement with you," said Basil. "That's why she wore Ann's clothes when she left the house instead of her own. She evidently had no idea how seriously ill she was. According to Victorine, Kitty, like Rhoda, believed it was just another touch of her recurrent malaria. Her talk with you the afternoon of the dance shows she was afraid of Rhoda's scheming, and determined to leave the house that night if she possibly could. The effort used up her last reserve of strength. She must have collapsed when she got as far as 78th Street and Fifth where her body was found. At that hour, on such a stormy night, the pavement beside the park would be empty, and the snow would soon cover her."

Leach buried his face in his hands.

"If I hadn't been half drunk when I danced with her, I would have seen through that impersonation — I know I would. I knew every line of Kitty's face by heart."

"What about Danine?" Foyle looked at Basil. "He wasn't tight, but he was taken in by the impersonation."

Basil nodded. "I've been wondering for some time if Danine was quite as much in love with Kitty as he claims."

Leach looked from one to the other.

"If Danine didn't love her why was he pestering her to marry him?"

"Did he ever ask her directly?" inquired Basil.

"I believe not. She kept him at arm's length. But everybody thought he wanted to marry her. Rhoda was sure of it."

"Do you know of anyone who had reason to hate Kitty?"

"No one could have hated her. Of course I always had a feeling that Mrs Jowett didn't like her. But I think that was just because Mrs Jowett is a stuffy old thing and Kitty was young and gay."

"One more thing. Do you recognise this?"

Foyle extended the palm of his hand. On it lay the diamond ring.

"Why, that's my mother's engagement ring!"

"Sure?"

"Of course I'm sure." Leach examined it. "I'd know that little V-shaped scratch on the side anywhere. I gave the ring to Kitty. She couldn't wear it publicly, but she kept it in her purse. Where did you get it?"

"We found it in Pasquale's rooms."

"In *Pasquale's* rooms?" Leach looked utterly astonished. "But Kitty would never go there! She didn't like him. Nobody liked him but Rhoda. I — I don't understand."

Outside again, on the rickety porch, Foyle sighed heavily.

"D'ye suppose he was acting when he pretended he didn't know Kitty was hard up? A fortune hunter might poison a girl to get rid of her if he believed she was an heiress, and then found out a bit too late that she was a fortune hunter herself."

"He might. But it would be so much less risky to break the engagement."

"Lord! What next?" muttered Foyle.

The question was answered when they entered his office.

"Say, chief!" cried a policeman in uniform. "Word's just come in from the 19th Precinc' that they pinched a young feller last night for drunk 'n' disorderly 'n' assaultin' an officer 'n' they found he had two menu cards on him engraved in French — real engravin' not printin' 'n' there wasn't no restaurant name. Justa funny-lookin' thing like a unicorn 'n' a date — same date as Kitty Jocelyn's coming-out party. One o' the boys hopped round to the office o' the caterer the Jocelyns had 'n' sure enough, he identified the cards as two o' the menus used for supper at the Jocelyn dance."

"Re-enter the gate-crasher!" cried Basil.

"What name did this bird give the boys at the Precinct station?" demanded Foyle.

The policeman looked a little embarrassed. "Well, chief, he said his name was Adolf Hitler."

20

VIGNETTES

The man brought into Foyle's office thirty minutes later was young, tall, and gaunt. He wore evening clothes, but one trouser leg was torn at thc knee, the whole suit was grey with dust, and the bow of his white tie had come undone. His hair was mussed, his lower lip cut, and he sported a black eye.

Foyle regarded him for a moment.

"Well, Herr Hitler, just what were you doing at the Jocelyn house the night of Kitty Jocelyn's coming-out party?"

"So that's it!" The young man sat down without asking permission. "I suppose you found the menu cards in my pocket an' recognised the Jocelyn crest? Did you notice it violates two laws of heraldry? The al' grandfather must've got one of these paid genealogists to fake it for him."

"Crest? Oh, you mean that unicorn thing? No, it was the date that put us wise. Lissen, young feller, I don't want any cracks outta you. This is a murder case and it's serious. What's your real name?"

"I don't believe my name'll convey much to the police, Inspector. It happens to be Elmer Judson."

"Why did you crash the Jocelyn party?"

The young man smiled. "Because I wanted somethin' to eat."

"Something to — *eat*?"

Of all possible explanations, Foyle had not expected this.

"Precisely. Somethin' to eat. Sordid but necessary. I hope to be an anthropologist someday. At the moment I'm workin' my way through Columbia, by servin' as night clerk in a small Broadway hotel — the Miramar. I earn enough for rent, tuition fees, an' books. Unfortunately there remains the somewhat pressin' problem of food. An' that's how I've solved it — by crashin' swell parties.

"I'm required to wear evenin' dress at the Miramar, an' I'm on duty there from 6 pm to 2 am. That lets me out just in time for supper. Durin' the season, I live on the fat o' the land. I believe one of the government departments in Washington has spent considerable time and money in workin' out a series of 'balanced diets' for the poor. You know, margarine instead of butter, meat every other day, and tomatoes instead of oranges. But, poor as I may be, I've been able to enjoy the luxury of an unbalanced diet all winter. The only trouble is I'm beginnin' to get a little tired of caviar, pheasant, terrapin, an' *foie gras*. I'd give anythin' for a dish of corned beef an' cabbage."

"Why did you take those two menu cards?" demanded the Inspector.

"One of the boys at Columbia told me I was only able to get away with gate-crashin' because parties are given in hotels nowadays. I bet this fellow a week's salary I'd crash a party in a private house. I was to bring him a supper menu card in order to prove I'd actually been there."

"How did you get in to the Jocelyn house?" asked Basil.

"I got the afternoon an' evenin' off. Then I hid my glad rags under an old raincoat, took a bunch of red roses that had been used to decorate the lobby of the Miramar, an' went round to the Jocelyns' about four in the afternoon. The red carpet was down already, there were several delivery wagons at the tradesmen's entrance, an' all sorts of fellows goin' in and out — florists, caterers, messenger boys an' so on. It was as easy as pie to follow the crowd down the stone steps into a basement kitchen. I saw a fellow with a chef's cap on, an' I waved the roses in front of him an' said, 'Where do these go, brother?' He glared at me an' answered, 'Upstairs, of course!' So I trotted upstairs with a messenger boy who was totin' a bunch of gardenias, an' he says, 'This way, buddy,' an' takes me into the biggest private ballroom I ever saw outside the movies. There were more florists there drapin' flowers all over the place, an' everybody was too busy to notice me particularly, so I shoved the roses in a corner, an' beat it upstairs to the next floor. "It was really too easy. I found an unused room an' camped out there. The time passed quickly because I had a bar of chocolate in my pocket, an' a pamphlet on the derivation of the levirate from fraternal polyandry among the Kuki-Lushai tribes of North East India. Around 3 am, when I judged the party would be well under way, I slicked down my hair with a pocket comb, lit a cigarette, an' strolled out into the hall, tryin' to look as if I owned the place."

"And no one noticed you until you got downstairs?"

"Well, I had one narrow squeak. I'd hardly taken a dozen steps when another door opened a little way down the corridor an' a fat, pasty-faced fellow came out into the hall. I thought my goose was cooked. But he seemed to be as scared of me as

I was of him! His face went sort of greenish an' then he said somethin' about Miss Jocelyn havin' asked him to get her a wrap an' that was why he'd been in her suite. I couldn't help sayin', 'Where's the wrap?' An' then he looked sicker than ever an' said he couldn't find it. It never seemed to occur to him I was a gate-crasher.

"I got downstairs without meetin' anyone else, an' made a beeline for the supper room. Gosh, it was like somethin' in a dream! Roses an' strawberries on every table an' outside icicles on the lamp posts an' men shovelling snow. I grabbed two menu cards for good measure. Then I drifted into the ballroom an' said to a guy beside me, 'Which gal is this Kitty Jocelyn anyway?' An' he said, 'I don't know her from Eve. I'm just a name on Mrs Jowett's "bachelor list"!'

"Just then a bird with a dead pan came up an' said, 'Please step this way, sir,' an' before I knew what was happenin' he'd got me into a little room with a grey-haired dame an' she was onto my bein' a gate-crasher somehow, an' she began to threaten me with the police. I was gettin' the wind up, when the door opened an' in walked Fatty — the pasty-faced sneak I'd met in the hall upstairs.

"Boy, was he scared when he saw me! He thought I was goin' to give him away! He told this dame — Mrs Jowett, he called her — to let me go pronto, an' she looked down her nose, an' said: 'Really, Mr Pasquale.' I looked him in the eye an' said: 'What about these supper menu cards, ol' fruit? Do I keep them?' He positively twittered, 'By all means,' he was so anxious to get rid of me. I shoved 'em back in my pocket an' forgot all about 'em after I'd shown 'em to the fellow I had the bet with, an' that's why you found 'em there."

"Why didn't you come forward with this story when Kitty

Jocelyn's murder was reported in the newspapers?" snapped Foyle.

"We-ell, would you have done that in my place, Inspector?" The young man started to smile and then remembered his cut lip. "Somehow I've a hunch the big bugs at the university wouldn't be any too pleased about my gate-crashin'. I might even be shot out on my ear for givin' the Alma Mater a bad name. An' I knew you had no way of tracin' me. You'd never have caught me at all if I hadn't been fool enough to keep those menu cards in my pocket an' drink some champagne on an empty stomach at a dance at the Ritz last night, an' there's nothin' I can do to help you. I don't know a thing about the murder."

"That's what you say." Foyle's voice was grim. "But there's nothing to prove your story, is there?"

The young man thought a moment. "There's one thing. If you'll look under the mattress in the bedroom farthest from the stairs on the third floor, you'll find an old raincoat. I had to leave it when I went downstairs. I'd like it back when you're through with it."

After the gate-crasher had gone, Foyle took out one of his blue and white handkerchiefs and wiped his forehead.

"I'm getting pretty tired of these bright young things, to say nothing of the bright old things. It would be a relief to talk to a plain, old-fashioned cracksman, or even a gunman. But I'm afraid we'll have to have another little chat with Rhoda and Pasquale."

RHODA JOCELYN GLANCED about Foyle's rather dingy office with impersonal curiosity. Her hand was entirely steady as she took a cigarette from a sandalwood case. "I see you have found your cigarette case." Basil brought out his lighter.

"Oh, this isn't the one I lost!" She paused, the unlighted cigarette between her fingers. "How odd you should remember a little thing like that!"

"Did you ever find the one you lost?"

"No. And I've looked for it thoroughly because I should be able to get several hundred for it and—" she smiled, "I need hardly tell you that would be useful at the moment. But have you called me all the way down here just to ask me about my cigarette case?"

"No, ma'am." Foyle looked at her accusingly. "We've found Philip Leach."

"Oh." Rhoda regarded the tip of her cigarette with undivided attention. Then she smiled again — the fatalistic smile of a gambler who accepts a loss without whining.

"Very well, Inspector. I'll answer your questions before you ask them. When Kitty first disappeared, I felt certain she had seized the chance the impersonation gave her to run away with Phil. Those children believed they had succeeded in keeping their little affair a secret. But I'm not quite so stupid as all that. They gave themselves away to me every time they looked at each other. That explains everything, doesn't it? Instead of sending private detectives to look for Kitty at the hospitals and mortuaries, I sent them to find Phil Leach — before the wedding if possible. If not — well, then there would have been nothing for it but an annulment or a divorce. Unfortunately, the detectives I engaged were unable to find any trace of Phil. But it wasn't until you came to the house that I seriously considered the possibility Kitty might be dead."

"Why didn't you tell us then that you had believed Kitty was with Leach when she first disappeared?"

"I wasn't at all sure that you were speaking the truth when you said Kitty was dead, and as long as she was alive, I wanted to keep her infatuation with Phil a secret, so that Danine would not hear of it and lose interest in her, or become jealous, or anything tedious like that. So I told you a tale about believing Kitty had wandered into the street suffering from loss of memory — and I really think I did it rather well considering it was all on the spur of the moment."

Foyle grunted. "That's pretty near perjury, Mrs Jocelyn!"

"Nonsense, Inspector. I wasn't under oath."

Basil smiled at Foyle. "In those circumstances, it scarcely seems worthwhile to go on questioning Mrs Jocelyn, does it? And yet there are several things I'd like to know."

"Such as?" Rhoda looked at him with unruffled good humour.

"Did you tell Ann Claude that Leach was a philanderer so she would not take him seriously if he made love to her when she was impersonating Kitty?"

"Naturally. I had to prepare Ann somehow, or she might have given everything away when Phil made love to her. I doubt if she would have been willing to play such a trick on Phil if she'd known he was seriously in love with Kitty."

"Yet Kitty herself was willing to trick him?"

"Oh, no, I don't believe she ever intended the impersonation to deceive Phil. That's why she did nothing herself to prepare Ann for Phil's love-making. I suppose Kitty thought she and Phil would be miles away on their elopement when Ann was playing Kitty's part at the dance. Unfortunately, I didn't suspect any of this until Kitty disappeared."

"We only have your word for that, Mrs Jocelyn! How do we know you didn't plan from the first to poison Kitty and force Ann to take her place permanently? Ann was not entangled with Leach. By threatening to have her declared insane, you might have coerced her into marrying Danine under Kitty's name so you could get your hands on some of his money!"

"Must you bellow, Inspector?"

"Maybe that's the real reason you didn't tell us about Kitty's affair with Leach. You knew that the fact Kitty wanted to marry Leach instead of Danine gave you a motive for murdering Kitty and putting Ann in her place for good. Maybe that's what Pasquale was thinking about when he accused you of murdering Kitty that first evening we saw you. Maybe all this impersonation business was just your alibi. You could never be publicly accused of murdering Kitty if everyone thought she was still alive. They would think just that with Ann taking her place, and you knew that there was no one who cared whether Ann disappeared or not. Maybe it was really you who induced Kitty to leave the house wearing Ann's clothes after she was poisoned. That's a new twist to murder — getting the corpse to disguise and remove itself before the actual moment of death."

Rhoda crushed out her cigarette in Foyle's ash tray.

"That would do as a plot for a Hollywood scenario, if it weren't just a little bit too melodramatic. The trend is toward realism nowadays, even in Hollywood. I had no need of such an elaborate intrigue to rid Kitty of Phil Leach. I need only have told Phil that she was penniless, and the affair would have settled itself."

Foyle looked helplessly at Basil. Rhoda was taking full advantage of the fact that her name protected her from the more rigorous methods of questioning.

"You didn't think it necessary to warn Ann that Danine

might make love to her when she was impersonating Kitty?" asked Basil.

"A man of Danine's nationality and age would not make love to a girl in Kitty's position unless he were engaged to her."

"And yet he did so at the dance, according to Ann Claude. Can you account for that?"

"No, unless… Are you quite sure Ann's testimony can be relied on?"

Her smile annoyed Basil. He carried the war into Africa.

"Are you aware that Mr Pasquale takes morphine?"

The lipstick stain on her mouth stood out so vividly that he knew she had turned pale under her mask of powder.

"I — I was never sure…"

"Perhaps you didn't want to be sure?"

"Perhaps."

"Has it occurred to you that he may have poisoned Kitty without your knowing it?"

"Luis?" Her breath came faster. "Of course not! Why should he?"

"Do you know if Ann sent him to Kitty's room to get a wrap while she was impersonating Kitty at the dance?"

"What would Ann want with a wrap?" Rhoda's voice was almost shrill. "She was dancing. The house is well heated. There is no garden."

"Then why did Pasquale go to Kitty's suite the night of the dance?"

"I don't know."

"Could Kitty herself have asked him for a wrap?"

"Kitty had a fever. She kept throwing off the bed clothes because she was so warm. And she was in Ann's room where there were plenty of wraps."

Basil smiled. "Mr Pasquale is evidently not as accomplished a liar as you, Mrs Jocelyn. He was seen by a witness coming-out of Kitty's suite during the dance. He volunteered the improbable explanation that Kitty had sent him there to get a wrap which he had failed to find. Kitty's suite was empty then, wasn't it?"

"Yes."

"Have you any idea why this ring, which Leach gave to Kitty, should have been found in Pasquale's rooms over the coach house?"

Rhoda stared at the ring in Basil's hand as if it had been a snake.

"I don't believe it! She wouldn't have dared!"

"Who wouldn't have dared?"

A deep flame spread under Rhoda's face powder. But she remained silent.

"Could Kitty have visited Pasquale secretly? Perhaps she was not such a child as you thought."

"It's impossible! Ridiculous!" cried Rhoda. But her hands trembled as they lay in her lap.

"Are you quite sure now that you can't tell us what Pasquale was doing in Kitty's suite the night of the dance?"

"I would tell you if I knew. But I don't."

When Rhoda had gone, Foyle said, "You got under her skin all right, doc, but what she sees in that pale, fat slug beats me!"

"Perhaps it's a form of perversion," suggested Basil. "Like those morbid people who enjoy the taste of rotten fruit. Most sexual excitants are arbitrary, you know — largely a matter of association."

"Where is Pasquale now?" demanded Foyle.

Duff consulted a notebook. "The party in question was last

seen twenty minutes ago entering the Viviane Galleries on 59th Street," he announced.

"Okay," Foyle turned to his desk, piled high with reports on other cases. "Next time Mullens phones in tell him to bring Pasquale down here for questioning."

Outside the building, Basil hailed a taxi. "The Viviane Galleries — 59th Street."

2 1

ROUGH SKETCH

The Viviane Galleries were just off Fifth Avenue. One show window contained a Rembrandt sepia drawing; the other, a portrait of the English 18th century school, with a name in black letters on the gilt frame: *Mr Heron of Heron*. An inconspicuous placard proclaimed:

EXHIBITION OF PAINTINGS
by
Sir JOSHUA REYNOLDS
And Other Artists of His Period
November—December

Basil studied the youthful, arrogant face of Mr Heron.

Every thickness and shadow was recorded with painstaking naturalism. The artist's sole purpose had been the accurate mimicry of a three-dimensional world in a two dimensional medium. The technique was as different from the emotional symbolism of the surrealist school as prose from poetry. Basil remembered having heard that Viviane was one of those ghouls who never exhibit the work of a living artist. Only after death had limited a painter's production and given his work a scarcity value could he hope for the honour of a show at Viviane's. The gallery catered to millionaires who thought art a much smarter hobby than newspapers or cancer research, and, if Viviane had had his way, promising young artists would have been "ploughed under" with some humane lethal gas the moment they became at all famous.

Basil was on the point of turning away when the door opened and Pasquale came out. His long, fur-collared overcoat was unfastened. He wore a Homburg hat of soft, black Viennese plush, and carried a flat, oblong parcel wrapped in brown paper.

"Good morning," said Basil. "I didn't know you were an amateur of Reynolds."

Pasquale did not look as if it were a pleasant surprise. Even his moist, red lips lost colour. His broad throat rippled as he swallowed and gasped and swallowed again. Then he took to his heels and ran toward Madison Avenue.

Pedestrians turned to see a stout, young man tearing down the street clasping a brown paper parcel to his bosom while a heavy overcoat bellied out behind him. When Basil caught up with him, he was panting as if he had run five hundred yards instead of fifty. But panic had given him an unintelligent courage. His right fist shot out wildly in the direction of Basil's jaw. Basil dodged neatly and caught Pasquale with a light blow in the stomach. He collapsed on all fours. His hat fell off and rolled in one direction, his package toppled in another. Something fell out of his breast pocket into the dirty snow with a soft plop.

Basil picked it up. It was a woman's platinum cigarette

case inlaid with slivers of dark sapphire — an expensive trifle that did not look expensive.

"So this is the cigarette case that Rhoda Jocelyn lost!" cried Basil.

Pasquale looked at him sullenly and announced, "I'm going to be sick."

"You brutal murderer!" A middle-aged female in low-heeled shoes constituted herself a one-woman League of Nations. She was shaking an umbrella in Basil's face. "You were the aggressor! I saw you chasing the poor man down the street! Officer, arrest this bully!"

A uniformed traffic policeman pushed his way through the little crowd that was gathering.

"I am Dr Willing of the district attorney's office…" began Basil.

"Yeah?" responded the policeman with indurated scepticism.

"I am a psychiatrist…"

"An' I suppose ye was just psycho-analysing' this poor guy? Lissen. Ye're charged with assault—"

"It's okay, Rooney. He is Dr Willing."

Mullens, the man who had been shadowing Pasquale, came up puffing and blowing. He was not built for a sprint and he had been watching the Viviane Galleries from the other side of the street.

When Basil entered Foyle's office, he was carrying the brown-paper parcel. He cut the string with a pen knife. Foyle looked over his shoulder and saw a red chalk drawing framed in carved, unpainted wood.

"Unmistakably French and unmistakably 18th century, isn't it?" Basil laid the picture on Foyle's desk and contemplated the group of seductive nudes with insipidly sensual faces, and bodies as sleek as pink and white seals. "Well, I dunno much about art," returned the Inspector. "But I do know the Commissioner will never let me hang up anything like that in my office."

"Oh, I didn't intend it as an ornament for Police Headquarters." Disregarding the succulent display of breast and thigh, Basil dug his knife into a corner of the frame. The two halves split apart, and white powder dribbled onto the Inspector's green blotter.

"Works of art come into the country duty free. You probably remember the hullaballoo in the papers a little while ago when the Customs' officers decided modern sculpture wasn't art and was therefore dutiable. But they would pass any sort of antique automatically. If they looked at this particular one at all, they'd be more likely to notice the picture than the frame. Any male would. And therefore it was a singularly clever way to smuggle dope."

Foyle whistled. "Not the Viviane Galleries!"

"Oh, yes. It would have to be an eminently respectable gallery — quite above suspicion."

"Well, I'll never say anything against psychology again," cried Foyle, in a burst of magnanimity. "What put you onto it, doc?"

"Not psychology this time. Just common sense. When a *sur-réaliste* artist visits an exhibition of painting as purely representational as Reynolds' more than once, there must be some reason for it that has nothing to do with art. Pasquale might go to a Reynolds' exhibition once to scoff, as Blake, the grandfather of *sur-réalisme*, did. But he would never go twice unless he had some other business there, and I knew he couldn't have any ordinary business with the Viviane Galleries, because Viviane never shows the work of a living artist. When I heard Pasquale had gone there a second time, I went to the place to make sure they really were showing Reynolds all during December. I intended to pass my hunch on to you. But just then Pasquale came out, carrying this picture under his arm. When he saw me, he naturally assumed I knew all about it, and had come to catch him with the goods. He lost his head and ran — and I went after him because I was afraid he might really escape."

"We must get after this Viviane place. Who woulda thought it? A highbrow joint like that!" Foyle reached for his telephone and instructed the officer commanding the Narcotic Squad, while Basil soothed his nerves with a cigarette.

"There was something else Pasquale had with him.' Basil laid the cigarette case on the table. "Rhoda Jocelyn's."

The sapphires caught the light from the desk lamp and glittered.

Foyle lifted his eyes to Basil. "Then it wasn't lost?"

"No. Rhoda's losing her cigarette case wasn't a blunder at all — any more than Mrs Jowett's mislaying her glasses."

"And it had nothing to do with Rhoda's smoking too much?" Foyle grinned. "I'm glad you're not always right, doc. I'd be getting one of these inferiority whatd'ye-call-it's if you were. But what did Pasquale want with Rhoda's cigarette case?"

"Suppose we ask him."

When Pasquale saw the cigarette case on Foyle's desk, what fight there was left in him died a natural death.

"Don't tell Rhoda!" Tears stood in his eyes. "She'd never understand!"

"Why did you steal it?" demanded Foyle.

"It wasn't really stealing, you know." Pasquale looked at

the Inspector reproachfully. "She often said everything she had was mine."

"Then why did you take it without telling her?"

"I can't paint without morphine and it costs a lot. I wasn't sure Rhoda would be willing to spend money for it, so I never told her. At first, in Cannes, she gave me a bit of money now and then, and her friends bought my paintings at good rates. But Rhoda hadn't as many friends in New York as in Europe. Those she had, didn't seem to want my paintings. And somehow I just didn't feel much like painting over here. I felt crushed by the crude materialism of the American environment. Rhoda herself was running short of money and she said I'd have to wait until Kitty married Danine before I got any more. She kept saying I didn't need money because I could eat at her house and live rent free over her garage. As if food and a roof were all that an artist needs!"

Pasquale's calf-like brown eyes were wistful. "Morphine is more expensive in New York than Cannes, but I had to have it, so I began taking things. There were a lot of little knickknacks in that big house that had a certain money value — things that no one would miss particularly, like gold and quartz push buttons for bells and electric lights. But I only got enough to buy one ounce and that doesn't last me very long — especially when it's diluted with bicarbonate of soda, as it is at Viviane's. The night of Kitty's dance I had a real chance to get something valuable because everyone was too busy to notice what I was doing. I slipped into Rhoda's suite and took the cigarette case. Then I went into Kitty's rooms and took that diamond ring you found in my room later. Rhoda's always losing things like cigarette cases, and I didn't think Kitty would miss the ring because I'd never seen her wear it. It was just loose in one of her purses with a lot of other things.

"After you pocketed the ring, I took the cigarette case to Viviane. I knew I was being watched, but I didn't think a policeman would see anything suspicious in an artist visiting an art gallery. That devil, Viviane, wouldn't take the case. He said I'd have to pawn it or sell it and bring him the money. But I didn't dare sell it or take it to a pawnshop while I was being watched by the police.

"For days I suffered the tortures of the damned. I didn't know any other place in New York where I could get morphine. This afternoon I went back to Viviane's and said, 'There's a detective outside trailing me. If you don't give me the stuff at once I'll go outside and tell him you're a dope peddler.' If it hadn't been for the detective waiting for me to come out, I think Viviane would have killed me. He gave me a framed picture and told me there was an ounce in the frame. Even then he wouldn't take the cigarette case — too risky, he said. It's obviously a woman's case and that was what made him so wary. That and the fact that I was mixed up with the Jocelyn murder. If I testify against him now, you won't send me to prison, will you? I really think prison life would kill me! An artist's senses are so much more delicately adjusted than those of ordinary man that he can't stand the things they can, and he ought not to be judged by the same moral laws."

"Mebbe," countered the Inspector in an arid voice. "But it ain't so in the penal code o' this state."

"Have you ever studied chemistry, Mr Pasquale?" inquired Basil.

"No. Why do you ask?"

"I merely wondered if you drank half of Kitty's cocktail deliberately, because you knew beforehand that the morphine habit would make you immune to thermol?"

"How could I have been absolutely sure beforehand that

217

morphine would make me immune?" Pasquale's voice rose to a scream of petulance. "You know, I wouldn't take a chance like that. My life is not my own to risk — it belongs to posterity. Why do you keep hounding me with these ghastly insinuations?" His full, lower lip trembled. "If you must have a victim, go after Nicholas Danine! Ask him why he's broken his rule about never talking to reporters or being photographed! Ask him why he goes round telling everyone he was in love with Kitty!"

"Well, wasn't he?" barked Foyle.

"I thought so when we were all at Cannes, and so did Rhoda. But I'm not so sure now. I suppose you noticed that Danine never said anything about *marrying* Kitty until she was dead, and Rhoda couldn't call his bluff?"

Foyle was getting beyond his depth. "You mean he was gone on Kitty, but it wasn't on the up and up?"

"No. To use your own quaint dialect, Inspector, I mean that he was not 'gone' on her at all."

"Never mind my dialect. Why did he come to America if it wasn't to be with Kitty?"

"Ah!" Pasquale's smile was suddenly sly. "I'll give you a little hint. A week or so before Kitty's dance, Rhoda and I went to the Waldorf for supper. We didn't leave until late. The streets were deserted except for one or two cars — and one of them was at the entrance to the tower apartments where Danine has been staying. There was a man in the car whom I knew by sight — Colonel Felipe Esteban y Cordoba, a South American diplomat well known in Europe."

"So what?"

"Must I do all your thinking for you? Isn't it possible that Danine's real reason for coming to America was to sell the South American Colonel a secret formula for some new gas or explosive? If he came to see Danine openly where everyone knows him, a rival government might hear of it and employ some spy to steal the formula."

"The heavily veiled blonde with an accent?" growled Foyle. "Or the man in the suit?"

Pasquale was nettled. "International spies do exist."

"So do research chemists. What country would employ a spy to steal a formula nowadays, when a first-class chemist can reproduce a gas or explosive soon after the other fellow starts using it?"

"But time counts in war," remarked Basil. "The Colonel might try to hide the very existence of the thing by getting Danine to stage negotiations in New York, where he's not so well known, and can see him without attracting attention."

"And where does Kitty Jocelyn come in?"

"Well…" Pasquale contemplated his pinkly varnished nails. "Danine had to have some other apparent reason for coming to America, hadn't he? Suppose Kitty was a sort of camouflage? Balzac's '*femme-écran*' used to screen a business deal instead of another love affair? Suppose Danine broke his rule about never being interviewed or photographed because he wanted everyone to know about his alleged affair with Kitty? She's been quite as useful to him dead as alive. Perhaps more useful. The Occidental News Service sent out a story about his offering a reward for Kitty's murderer. It was illustrated with a radio photograph of Inspector Foyle leaving the Hotel Waldorf after a conference with ML Danine. The Occidental serves a lot of South American newspapers."

"Hmm," Foyle was growing interested. "Sure this guy you saw was Colonel Esteban what's-his-name?"

"Oh, yes. I was born in San Fernando. I've known Colonel Esteban by sight ever since I was a boy."

. . .

WHEN PASQUALE WAS LED AWAY, Foyle looked at Basil. "If we'd got that tip from any other witness, I'd've taken it seriously, but somehow — Pasquale? What do you make of it, doc?"

"I hardly know. I should have thought that a man like Nicholas Danine would be able to keep the existence of a formula secret without such intricate precautions. He bears no resemblance to the soft-headed hero of fiction who goes home to dinner with the first pick-up in the hotel bar when he is carrying the plans for the new submarine in his breast pocket. He had only to ask for a little discreet police protection and his formula would have been as safe as it could be. Why was it necessary to come to America and deceive Kitty and Rhoda?"

"Search me! I've been wondering why Pasquale should lose the ring he stole and not the cigarette case."

"Possibly because the ring was more incriminating. It had been stolen from a murdered girl. His cautious subconscious seems to have got rid of it as soon as he learned Kitty had been murdered."

Foyle pondered. "This blunder business hasn't got us anywhere so far."

"No, and yet — I have a — well, call it a hunch, that the key to the mystery lies in one of the blunders we have discussed already."

The telephone rang.

"Hello? What? Missed him!" The Inspector was terrible to behold. "You — you—"

He slammed the instrument back into its cradle. "Danine's given us the slip!" he roared. "He got in a big car with his secretary, and that very fellow Pasquale was talking about —

Colonel Esteban. The prize bonehead I had tailing him hopped a taxi and lost sight of them in a traffic jam within a block of the Holland Tunnel. He called the hotel — but they say they don't know where Danine has gone, though he kept his rooms there, and left Sergei in possession."

"The Holland Tunnel," Basil repeated. "And the American Shell Company has a plant in New Jersey."

"Oh, Lord, that's so!" Foyle groaned. "That plant is a regular fortress with a garrison of company guards and enough political influence to gum the works. If he's gone to earth there, we'll never see him again. You can't get the better of a guy with all that dough. He hasn't any weak points!"

"Everybody has at least one weak point."

"Yeah? What's Danine's?"

"Cruelty. I think it's about time I had an interview with Sergei."

"Danine wouldn't leave Sergei behind if he knew anything."

"Everyone makes a mistake now and then. Danine's mistake is his contempt for worms. He's forgotten that they turn sometimes."

"Well," Foyle rose. "We'd better take Duff and—"

"I don't want Duff. I don't even want you. My only chance of making Sergei talk depends on my seeing him alone."

BASIL DINED COMFORTABLY AT HOME. If Danine had gone as far as the American Shell Company's plant in New Jersey, he would not be back until morning, and Basil did not wish to disturb Sergei's dinner hour. The slightest discourtesy would be a tactical error.

After dinner, he killed time by glancing at the evening

paper. A chatty, syndicated article about the "dubious science of psychology" informed him that neurosis was found only among the pampered rich, and that poverty, insecurity, and hard work were the best cures for so-called nervous diseases. He recalled the procession of anxiety neuroses due to economic worry that passed through the psychiatric clinic of his hospital and wondered where the writers of chatty, syndicated articles get their information. Then his eye fell on the stop press news:

Stanton, NJ, Dec 16 — (by Occidental News Service). Three men were killed and five were injured this morning when an explosion occurred at the American Shell Company's testing grounds near here today. Windows were broken within a radius of six miles, and one of the company's buildings was destroyed by fire. The manager told reporters that life pensions will be paid to the disabled men, and ample compensation to relatives of the dead...

There was a suave reticence about the whole thing that suggested a highly paid public relations counsel in the background.

Basil walked up Park Avenue past Grand Central until he came to the Waldorf.

Sergei opened the door of the apartment himself. His face was sullen; his hair untidy; but he was clad in a dressing gown of heavy black silk, handsome enough for Danine himself.

"Good evening." Basil spoke in Russian. "May I come in?"

Sergei gaped and blinked at him. He entered and shut the door.

"I want to talk with you, Sergei. Shall we go into the drawing room?"

Basil led the way and Sergei followed. A single reading lamp was lighted. Beside it stood an armchair and a low table set with cigars and liqueurs. Evidently Sergei had been making himself comfortable in Danine's absence.

"So you speak Russian?" he murmured.

"My grandfather was Vassily Krasnoy, the composer."

Sergei's face lighted with interest. His surly manner changed suddenly to one of easy cordiality. "No, really? When I was a young man I often heard Krasnoy conduct his own symphonies. A gifted man, they said, but dangerous. A rebel in politics as in music."

"I remember him as a terrifying old autocrat," answered Basil with a grin. "I can just remember kissing his hand when I was four years old."

The light faded slowly from Sergei's face. "You are Krasnoy's grandson — and we meet here." His pale blue eyes wandered around the room and came to rest at last on Basil. "I do not understand. You look very American to me."

"I am. My father was American, and I was brought up over here."

"You speak Russian," Sergei reiterated. "Then you must have understood everything that was said the other day?"

"Everything. Tell me, just what relation are you to Nicholas Danine?"

The stillness was troubled only by the distant rumble of traffic. Then Sergei said, "How did you know?"

"There's a certain resemblance — allowing for the difference in age. You have Danine's eyes. And I was struck by the similarity of surnames — Danine and Radanine. His manner toward you told me the rest. Only family hate can be so intemperate. It's like family love — quite uninhibited."

A spasm of distress crossed Sergei's face.

Basil went on, "Your hands are scarcely the hands of a peasant or worker, and you speak English remarkably well. Where did you learn it?"

"I had an English governess, and I was at Oxford for a year."

"Are you Danine's cousin? Or, perhaps, his elder brother?"

Sergei shook his head. "I am his father."

22

FAMILY PORTRAITS

"His — father!" Basil knew only too well the Victorian respect a Russian of the old school expected from sons and grandsons.

"It should not be difficult to understand." Sergei smiled. "After all, why shouldn't I tell you? But first have some of this cognac. As a member of the family, I feel at liberty to offer it to you."

He filled a glass and handed it to Basil, his dignity quaintly blended with humour.

"Nicholas Danine is my bastard son," he went on, calmly. "Have you never heard that in Russia of the 18th century there was a custom that a bastard should take his father's name without the first syllable? Like other old traditions, it lingered in some of the more backward country districts until the end of the 19th century. As I told you, my full name is Sergei Piotrovitch Radanine. Therefore, my illegitimate son, Nicholas, was known in his native village by the last two syllables — Danine. It is characteristic of him to cling to that badge of bastardy when he could easily have changed his name a dozen times in after life. He luxuriates in his bitterness."

"I'm beginning to understand," said Basil, slowly. "But how did you ever come to enter his employ?"

"The war made Nicholas rich, and the revolution ruined me," Sergei spoke with fatalistic detachment. "I was once a landowner and a captain of the Chevalier Guards. We met, as he told you, in Nice. What a meeting! I, the father, poor and old and broken. He, the bastard son, rich and successful. It is comparatively rare in life for the tables to be turned so suddenly and so completely.

"When he was born, I provided for his mother, a peasant girl, according to her station in life. I thought I had acted generously. I didn't realise what he has since taught me, that nothing is more galling than having to be grateful to someone who has done you a wrong. He has given me every material comfort — food, clothes, shelter, and high wages. But on one condition — that I should be a servant to him, my own son. How could I refuse? I need hardly tell you how difficult it is for a man of my age, a friendless alien without commercial training, to get a job of any sort anywhere. My discomfort is purely mental — the humiliation of being a servant to my own son, just as in Danine's boyhood his discomfort was purely mental — the humiliation of bastardy. You heard the way he speaks to me? He is slaking a hatred that went thirsty for many years! How he enjoyed himself when he told you that Russians of my class were 'lazy, stupid, and superstitious'. Of course he meant Russians of the former ruling class, which he hates. But he knew you would think he meant Russians of the servant class and he thoroughly enjoyed the joke on you, and on me. Really, he is a remarkable man. I am almost proud to be his father…

"When he was about twelve years old, he ran away from his mother's village. How he managed to live after he ran away, I don't know, for he had no money. But he picked up some sort of education somehow and he made money. I've been told he got his first real start in Paris renting slum houses to brothel keepers.

"He has no pity. Every day he finds some new way of humiliating me. He knows I am too lazy or two cowardly to leave him and try to get another job. He knows I could not get another so well paid. He knows that I have gone without food and shelter and that now I will endure almost anything for their sake. He is cruel, but it is I who made him cruel."

"Hardly that." Basil tried to soothe him. "Cruelty is the oldest biological trait. We don't make each other cruel — we're born that way, and it takes years of training in childhood to make any of us humanly kind."

"Yes, and I deprived him of that training. His childhood was not normal, and I was the one to blame."

Basil set down the glass he had been holding. "Captain Radanine—" he began.

"Oh, do go on saying 'Sergei'. Anything else sounds unnatural now. And I've told you so much, I'm really beginning to regard you as an old friend."

Basil smiled. "That only makes it more difficult for me. Your situation is so bizarre, I'm afraid I can't ask you the questions I planned to ask."·

"What questions?"

"You probably know more about Danine than anyone else in the world. Do you believe that he loved Kitty Jocelyn enough to murder her if he discovered that she loved someone else?"

Sergei shook his head.

"Why not?" asked Basil. "He gave every evidence of being greatly attracted to her, didn't he?"

Sergei's blue eyes filmed over as if he were looking at something far away. "You came here this evening because you thought I hated Danine enough to spy on him."

"It never occurred to me you were his father."

"Naturally. That would not occur to any normal person. Only an abnormal mind like Danine's could have devised such a situation."

For a while he was silent, sipping his brandy. Basil did not hurry him.

"Do you know," he said at last, "you are the first person who has spoken to me as if I were a human being for years! And you are the first person I've been able to speak to without reserve. I suppose it will help your investigation of this case if I throw a little light on Danine's real attitude toward Kitty?"

"It most certainly will — if you can do so."

"I believe I can. After all, I have no great feeling of loyalty to my employer." His smile was edged with irony. "Wait!"

Sergei left the room and returned carrying a box of mahogany red leather tooled in gilt, with the Imperial Russian eagle. It was cracked and shabby, but it looked like an official dispatch case.

"Danine is very careful to destroy all his private letters and papers when he is through with them," said Sergei. "But I have exceptional opportunities. I have been collecting scraps of paper from his desk and the pockets of clothes he gives me to press. He is a man of many secrets, and if I were to find anything of real value that I could hold over his head he might be induced to give me a pension and let me go back to my family. I suppose you think this is unbelievably shocking. What is the ugly English word? Blackmail! A thing no gentleman would ever stoop to: Well, I am no longer a gentleman and that is very convenient."

Sergei unlocked the leather box with a small key. It contained an extraordinary collection of unrelated odds and ends. A Russian blackmailer would be unsystematic, thought Basil. There were telegrams, business letters, social notes and memoranda. Sergei fished among them until he found a sheet of pale green notepaper with a dark green border. Diagonally, across one corner, was printed the name *Suzy* in facsimile handwriting, also dark green. It was covered with fine, spidery handwriting and the words were French.

"I suppose this is from Mademoiselle Suzy Comminges of the Théâtre d'Harlequin?" asked Basil.

"Oh, you know that much? Then read the letter. It was received yesterday."

The fragment began abruptly:

... and how I laughed at your description of the way this incredible Madame Jocelyn has pursued you and dangled her blatant stepdaughter before your nose! Her subterfuges are so threadbare! Her contortions to make you believe the poor girl an heiress are worthy an acrobat! Truly, my friend, I do not see how you preserve your grave face in such circumstances of comedy!

Well, I, too, can act off the stage. Ambrosine d'Eze came to see me the other day and to tell me with infinite delicacy that she was so sorry to hear that you had left me and were going to marry a young American — an heiress, isn't it? Like you, with the reporters, I pulled long face and sighed and shrugged and said: 'Ah, these men!' and so on — like a deserted woman. How furious she will be, poor child, when

you return and we are seen together again. My very dear one
please make it soon! She does so miss you
   — Your, Suzy.

Basil laid down the sheet of green paper. "What business had Danine in America that required such exceptional secrecy?"

Sergei shrugged. "I know nothing of business. It is quite useless to ask me."

Basil could not help smiling. "A knowledge of business is very useful to a blackmailer," he pointed out.

"I dare say, but, after all, I am an amateur, my friend, not a professional."

"May I look at the rest?"

"But certainly!"

Basil took the dispatch box on his knees and sorted the amazing collection of odds and ends with academic method. A sheet of thin, white foolscap floated to the floor. Basil picked it up. It was covered with typewriting mimeographed in purple ink and it seemed to be part of a report made by experts, who had been testing a new explosive, to the directors of the American Shell Company, in which Danine was a shareholder. It also was a fragment and began abruptly:

... Without wishing to be unduly optimistic, we feel safe in affirming that PD 30/60 is the ideal explosive — the formula for which the inventors of the civilised world have searched so long and so patiently. The commercial possibilities of the invention are most satisfactory. It is cheap to manufacture and, as we and our foreign affiliates have exclusive knowledge of the formula, we are in a position to secure a reasonable profit on all sales for some time to come.

The typewriting ended at this point, but someone had written a note on the margin in ink:

As the law stands, shipments of PD 30/60 can be exported from the US until the President proclaims a state of war in South America. It is to be sincerely hoped that no ill-timed legislation will hamper this gratifying expansion of our international trade and I recommend strengthening our lobby in Washington by every means available. When the minister Montenriquez placed his order for PD 30/60, he…

Basil frowned. Was it a clerical error? It was Colonel Esteban y Cordoba whom Pasquale had seen with Danine. It was he who had driven away with Danine that morning, according to the police. Basil felt certain that Danine had taken Esteban to the American Shell Company's plant in order to demonstrate the new explosive to him. The accident reported in the evening paper had occurred at the testing grounds. It all hung together — except for one thing. This report spoke of *Montenriquez* as the purchaser of PD 30/60.

Suddenly Basil struck the table with his hand. "I have it! How obvious it is once you have the clue!"

Sergei stared. "You are more clever than I if you can make anything out of that report. I went to some trouble to get it, but once I had it, I thought it was just a routine report of no value as a secret."

"And you a former officer of the Chevalier Guards!" exclaimed Basil. "Did you never hear of the cordite scandal? It's the oldest and most famous trick of the munition industry's super-salesmen selling a secret formula to both sides at the same time. Russians and English both paid handsomely for the secret of cordite in the 19th century.

"It's not Esteban who is insisting on secrecy, but Danine himself. And it isn't the formula he wants to keep secret, but *the sale of the formula to both sides*. Danine is not afraid that the secret will be stolen by international spies and sold to Montenriquez before he can complete negotiations with Esteban for the simple reason that he has already sold it to Montenriquez himself!

"That is why Danine was willing to go to almost any lengths to ensure absolute secrecy for his deal with Esteban. He chose America, an ostentatiously neutral country, as the scene of negotiations and he paraded his devotion to Kitty publicly in order to provide the insatiable newspapers with an explanation for his sudden visit to America. He even tried to make love to Kitty at the dance, so she, too, would be deceived and act her part in the farce convincingly. Nothing must be published that could rouse suspicion in either Esteban or Montenriquez. The Esteban orders will be filled by one company, the Montenriquez orders by another, and few people will realise there is any link between the two companies — except for the fact that Danine happens to be a shareholder in both."

"Then — that paper is valuable?"

In his excitement, Basil had almost forgotten Sergei. "Yes." He folded it up with the letter from Suzy Comminges and put them together in his breast pocket. "It is so valuable that if you had tried to blackmail Danine with it, you would have been in considerable personal danger."

He hesitated. If he had been dealing with anyone else, he would have offered to buy the papers he had taken.

But though Sergei had confessed to attempted blackmail with engaging frankness, Basil knew he would regard such an offer from anyone but Danine as insulting.

"You have been a real help to me," said Basil, finally. "Here is my address. I'm always glad of a chance to talk about Russia."

In the morning, Inspector Foyle had only one comment to make on the letter from Suzy Comminges, when Basil laid it on his desk. "The old humbug!"

"Danine would not have dared to play such a trick on a real heiress," mused Basil. "But Kitty was made for his purpose with her beauty, her scheming stepmother, and her secret poverty, which he had discovered."

"You said it, doc. I thought he was crowdin' the mourners a bit when I got that cable from Scotland Yard saying he'd been playing round with this Suzy What'sHer-Name this autumn — after he met Kitty last summer. His face was sad enough that first day he came to Sobel's office and talked about Kitty's death, but I noticed his shoulders had quite a jaunty swing. Didn't Lambert say thermol was used in making Shellite?"

"He did. The 'P' probably stands for picric acid, and the 'D' for di-nitro-phenol, or thermol. There's evidently 30% of one and 60% of the other and then 10% of some third ingredient so secret it isn't indicated. Even if Danine didn't bring any chemicals with him from Europe, he has had access to thermol all along in the laboratories of the Not-So-American Shell Company."

As Basil entered his own office, a few moments later, Sobel's secretary accosted him. "The DA's asking for you. Edgar Jocelyn is with him now."

23

ILLUMINATED MS CIRCA 1930–40

E dgar Jocelyn was pacing the floor.

"This is Dr Willing," explained Sobel. "He is a psychiatrist with experience of law and criminology. He really knows more about the case than I do and I'm sure he'll do anything he can for you."

"Perhaps you will come into my office?" suggested Basil.

"Very well," Edgar Jocelyn was obviously in a bad temper. "This is my lawyer, Mr Gillespie." He nodded toward a tall, bleak individual, who made no effort to hide his passive disapproval of the whole scene.

Basil led them down the corridor.

"See here, Dr Willing," Edgar burst out as soon as they were alone. "Am I under suspicion for the murder of my niece?"

"You are no more under suspicion than everyone else who was at that cocktail party," answered Basil.

Edgar's bushy black brows drew sharply together. "Well, I call it damnable, sir! Damnable!" he snapped. "Here I am a respectable citizen and taxpayer being followed about by a greasy detective as if I were a common criminal! I've complained to Inspector Foyle and the Police Commissioner, but I'm still being followed and I resent it! I want to go to the Bahamas. I always go at this time of year. Are you going to make any difficulties about my leaving the city?"

Basil had noticed how suddenly suspects in a case discover pressing engagements elsewhere. First Danine and now Edgar Jocelyn. Was it guilt in either case? Or merely panic?

"I'm afraid it will be impossible," said Basil, as soothingly as he could.

"Then I'm to hang round New York indefinitely while you and the police dawdle over the case? I thought you psychiatrists had lie detectors! Why don't you test me with one and prove my innocence that way?"

"I have no lie detector here," answered Basil. "Of course, there is the free association time test," he added.

"Well, if I take this test of yours, can I go to the Bahamas?"

"It's not my test. It's Jung's," returned Basil. "And I can't promise anything about the Bahamas. But you would help our investigation by taking it."

"Really, Jocelyn, do you think it prudent?" pleaded Gillespie.

Edgar laid his hat and gloves on the table, and then removed his overcoat. "What do I have to do?"

"Please sit down and wait a few minutes."

Basil hurried into the outer office and prepared a list of one hundred words with the aid of his stenographer. Then he came back to his own office and began adjusting a rather complex mechanism.

"As each stimulus word is shown on this Ach-card exposure apparatus, you are to answer with the first reaction word that comes into your mind — no matter what it is. The machine is placed in an electric circuit controlled by a lip key and attached to a chronoscope. The exposure of the stimulus word completes the circuit and starts the chronoscope. Your spoken reaction word breaks the circuit and stops the chronoscope. In that way, the chronoscope records exactly the time you take to reply in 1000ths of a second.

"If any of your reaction words come more slowly than your average reaction time, it will mean one of two things: either you have repressed the first word that came into your mind and substituted another with intent to deceive, or the stimulus word had some special emotional significance for you. You will be unable to control your reaction time consciously because no one is conscious of a hesitation that lasts only a few 1000ths of a second. Studying such an infinitesimal time-reaction is like getting a microscopic view of the thought process. The consciousness cannot perceive a very minute portion of time, just as the naked eye cannot perceive a very minute portion of matter."

"Diabolical!" said Gillespie.

As Basil placed a chair for Edgar, he wondered if he were "diabolical". For he had not told either of them the real purpose of this test. One way to ascertain a man's knowledge of any given subject, such as chemistry, is to find out what words he associates spontaneously with its technical terms.

"There's something decidedly unsportsmanlike about the whole procedure," Gillespie was saying.

"Well, it's less painful than the third degree," Basil reminded him. "And more accurate."

"I've got a perfectly clear conscience!" Edgar grasped both arms of his chair and glared at the apparatus. "I'm not afraid — let's get on with it, Dr Willing."

Basil switched on the current. The stimulus words began to

flash into view. Edgar responded brusquely, as, a man who wants to get an unpleasant business finished.

"Solvent."

"Bankrupt!"

"Volatile."

"Fade!"

"Ester."

"Rachel!"

"Reduce."

"Scales!"

"Oil."

"Stock!"

"Isomer."

"I don't know what that means. Archaic, isn't it?"

"The other words are simpler. But please don't stop to comment." Basil readjusted the mechanism and the test went on:

"Poison."

"Upon my word!" cried Gillespie. "This is ridiculous! Unless Dr Willing and the district attorney agree to regard the entire communication as privileged…"

"If there are any more interruptions I will not continue this test," exclaimed Basil.

"I know what I'm about, Gillespie," insisted Edgar. The lawyer returned to his first attitude of passive disapproval, until 100 reaction words had been recorded. "Thank you, Mr Jocelyn," said Basil. "I will analyse this test as soon as possible."

"Analyse it?" Edgar looked as if he were only just beginning to realise the possibilities latent in such a test. "Well, I only hope some good will come of all this mumbo-jumbo!"

As soon as he was alone, Basil made a preliminary analysis, and the result was so interesting that he decided to take it to Foyle at once.

The sound of a woman sobbing came from Foyle's office. Basil rapped on the door and it was opened by Duff. Foyle sat behind his desk. In front of him were two chairs occupied by Sergeant Samson and Minna Hagen. Samson leaned forward, something ugly and primitive in his eyes. "Come on! Spill it! We got the goods on you, toots, an' you're gonna burn! Your fingerprints was on that Sveltis bottle. Poison is a woman's weapon. You hated Kitty Jocelyn. She had everything you hadn't — fine clothes, good times, boyfriends. You done it!"

"I didn't...I didn't...I didn't!" sobbed Minna, with the peculiar obstinacy of the weak.

Basil recalled how considerately Rhoda Jocelyn had been questioned. He walked over to Samson.

"That's enough, Sergeant."

"Now, doc—" began Foyle in a conciliatory tone.

"I can tell you why Minna Hagen's fingerprints were on that Sveltis bottle," said Basil. "But I prefer to do so without the assistance of Sergeant Samson."

Samson looked at Foyle, and Foyle said, "Better go."

Basil sat down in the chair that Samson had left. "No one suspects you of murder."

Minna stared at him, lips parted, tears drying on her plump, pink cheeks.

"But you took the Sveltis tablets from the bottle in Mrs Jocelyn's bathroom cupboard."

"You — you know?"

"Yes."

"I d-didn't mean any harm!" she wailed. "I only took one at a time and I never meant to take so many. I found the bottle in the scrap basket in Mrs Jocelyn's sitting room the day it

238

came. I thought Mrs Jocelyn or Miss Kitty must have thrown it out by mistake — a b-beautiful new bottle like that with a yellow silk tassel and full to the b-brim. So I put it in her bathroom cupboard. And then — I saw what it said on the bottle, and I'm so horribly f-fat! Everybody laughs at me, so I-I took one. And the next day I took another and Mrs Jocelyn never said anything about it. I guess she used the little refrigerator in the bathroom more than she did the cupboard. And then, before I knew it, I'd taken half the bottle. I did so want to be like Miss Kitty! She was lovely — just like a b-boy!"

"Why didn't you tell the police all this when they questioned you about your fingerprints on the bottle?"

"I saw in the papers that Miss Kitty had been poisoned with Sveltis and I was sure the cops were trying to frame me the way they frame people in the movies, and I made up my mind I'd never let on about taking those tablets no matter what they did to me." She gulped. "Are you — are you g-going to arrest me now?"

"What for?"

"F-For stealing the Sveltis tablets?"

"No." Basil smiled. "You've had a lucky escape — in more ways than one. You would have fallen ill, if you had taken too many of those tablets at one time. You might even have gone blind or died."

Minna's eyes were round with horror. "I suppose it was too good to be true. All that stuff about keeping slim without diet or exercise."

"You must get exercise in your work. Perhaps you're a little too fond of soft drinks and sweet desserts?"

"No, I'm not. But I do like a chocolate malted now and then. And I'm rather fond of pie, especially lemon pie with whipped cream."

"How did you get onto it, doc?" asked Foyle, after Minna had gone.

"By applying another theory." Basil spoke lightly. "I asked myself what human type would react by theft to the stimulus of these Sveltis tablets? The answer was someone who was over-weight, someone who couldn't afford to buy Sveltis, someone with access to Rhoda Jocelyn's bathroom, someone who wasn't very intelligent and couldn't resist the suggestive power of slogans and the lure of a handsome, modernistic bottle. Only one person met all these requirements — Minna Hagen, the housemaid whose fingerprints were found on the bottle, who had a high colour and who complained that her food tasted bad. You doubtless recall Lambert's telling us that small daily doses of thermol cause a high colour and an impaired sense of taste? Of course it was the yellow tassel of the Sveltis bottle dangling out of your own coat pocket that frightened her that first evening we questioned her in the Murillo Room. She thought we'd found out all about her stealing."

"Say, that works out pretty neat," admitted Foyle.

Basil dropped his bantering manner. "It only remains to apply the same method of deduction to the murder."

Foyle looked up. "You mean — Kitty Jocelyn was the stimulus?"

"And the murder was the reaction. Which of our suspects would react to such a stimulus with murder?"

"Do you mean who would profit by such a murder? We've been using that method to solve crimes for years!"

"No, not whom does this crime benefit. What psycholog-ical type would be gratified emotionally by this type of crime? The modern theory is that all crime is committed primarily for emotional gratification. When there's an element of gain, it's secondary — the occasion rather than the cause of the crime."

"You can't teach an old dog new tricks!" Foyle rose heavily. "You know I don't like Samson and his rough stuff any better than you do. But it's the only way I know to make a stubborn witness talk... What's this?"

"A report of Edgar Jocelyn's association test." Basil explained what he had been doing. "When I analysed it, I found that Edgar reacted to all the chemical words at rates closely approximating his own average rate of association time. That means he didn't try to deceive me when he responded to those chemical words. He really does associate *solvent* with *bankrupt* and *reduce* with *scales*."

"And I suppose that means he was telling the truth when he said he was a businessman and not a chemist?"

"Evidently. A chemist's first reaction to the word *solvent* would almost certainly be associated with chemical solubility. Edgar automatically assumed the financial meaning of the word as shown by his response *bankrupt*. A chemist would most likely associate the word *reduce* with the deoxidising process. Edgar associated it with slimming and the word *scales*. A chemist would be liable to think of *oil* as a noun and a chemical classification. Edgar took oil as an adjective and reacted with *stock* — a typical businessman's reaction. He even mistook the common chemical term *ester* for a misspelling of the proper name *Esther* and reacted with *Rachel*. It was the same throughout a list of words that included fifty chemical terms, with only one exception — *volatile*. That word would suggest human frivolity and fickleness to most laymen, but Edgar assumed the chemical meaning and associated the word with *fade* — the fading of cloth dyed with a volatile substance. Apparently his chemical knowledge is limited to a smattering of dye trade terms he's picked up in his business. That is how he was able to recognise thermol as an intermediate for Sulphur Black."

"As far as it goes, that sort of lets him out, doesn't it?" mused Foyle. "For the murderer must have known enough about either chemistry or medicine to know that thermol was the basis of Sveltis. As you've said all along, he must have counted on Kitty's endorsement of Sveltis to cover up the murder. Still — I wish that lawyer hadn't interrupted when you tried to get Edgar's reaction to poison."

Foyle studied the report for a moment, and then thrust it into his pocket. "I'll read it at luncheon. Want to come with me?"

"Not just now."

Basil was looking at the incongruous objects strewn on Foyle's desk. If he had not known they were the exhibits in the Jocelyn case, he might have suspected the Inspector of raiding a junk shop:

A red chalk drawing with a split frame of carved,
unpainted wood.
A woman's platinum cigarette case ornamented with
slivers of dark sapphire.
A platinum ring set with a rose diamond.
A half empty bottle of Sveltis.
A filthy old khaki raincoat.

"It was just where he said it was," explained Foyle. "Under the mattress in the bedroom farthest from the stairs on the third floor."

"He?"

"Elmer Judson. The gate-crasher."

A dirty, dog-eared fiction magazine with Kitty's
endorsement of Sveltis on the back cover.
Photographs of Kitty Jocelyn's dead body and rooms in
the Jocelyn house.
Letters, bills, invitations, and advertisements addressed
to Kitty and taken from her desk by the police.
A huge file of typewritten manuscript — statements of
witnesses and reports of detectives making up the offi-
cial police record of the case.

"I'd like to go over that file again while you're at luncheon," said Basil.

"Help yourself! I'm sick of it." Foyle reached for his overcoat and hat. "If you want anything else Duff will be in the outer office. So long!"

Basil didn't mind the continuous murmur of traffic, any more than he would have minded the rhythmic beat of surf at the seashore. Blended in an orchestral rumble, individual sounds lose their power to invade consciousness. He sat at Foyle's desk, and studied each of the exhibits in turn. Then he took up the file of manuscript. "If only I knew what to leave out!" he thought. "All design is an algebraic process. If I could see which facts cancel each other, then whatever remained would be the pattern of the murder and the murderer."

Carefully, he read every word, as if the story were new to him, and he didn't know what was coming next. When he had finished he turned back to the exhibits on the desk and it was then he noticed something in the evidence he had not noticed before. Such a small thing! No wonder he and Foyle had missed it every time they went over the file of the case.

"Just an accident..." he reassured himself. But, "*No individual human act is ever accidental*."

Again he flipped over the pages of the bulky manuscript, paused, re-read a page, and frowned. Was this the "message in code" he had been looking for? The answer came in a flash of illumination as sudden as lightning. Murderers outwardly normal were well known to forensic psychiatry. The signs of abnormality were slight enough to escape their closest friends for years. And self-possession was always a marked trait in poisoners.

"But it can't be — it mustn't be!" He was startled to find he had spoken aloud.

Up to this moment, he had been sustained by intellectual curiosity. The mystery had seemed more important than the murder. It had challenged him like a problem in chess or mathematics.

But now that it was no longer a mystery, he realised to the full that neither was it a game played with senseless pieces, nor a problem living only in the mind of a mathematician. He was dealing with human beings like himself who could feel and hope, think and suffer.

24

MONTAGE

Duff looked at Basil curiously as he entered the outer
office. Something of his feelings must have shown in
his face. He asked Duff to call Ann Claude on the telephone.
"You remember saying that the room was close and stuffy on
the day of the cocktail party?"

"Why, yes." Ann's voice was puzzled. "There were so
many sweet-scented flowers it was quite heady, and Mrs
Jowett asked Gregg to open a window."

"Was that before or after Gregg announced Philip Leach?"

"Let me see. I think it was just before. Yes, I'm sure it was.
I remember there was a draft from the open window as Phil
came through the doorway."

Basil left Headquarters and took a taxi to the public library
at 42nd Street. Downstairs in the newspaper room he accosted
a pallid boy in shirt sleeves.

"The *Times* for this year? On that shelf. Help yerself. Naw!
We ain't got nobody to help lift 'em down!"

Basil spent a strenuous hour carrying huge bound files to a

readers' table. He went steadily through the last eight months reading a section of the paper he usually neglected — the society page.

Oct 8 — *Latest studio portrait of Miss Katherine Jocelyn who will be presented to society in December at a dance to be given by her stepmother, Mrs Gerald Jocelyn.*

Nov 16 — *Among those who reached New York yesterday on the* Queen Mary *were Elmer Burton Berry of Chicago, Mr and Mrs Dallas Dillingham of Boston, Mrs Gerald Jocelyn of New York and Paris, and her stepdaughter, Miss Katherine Jocelyn. Also on board were Mauritz Schurr, Austrian welterweight, Luis Pasquale, artist, and Lisa Ginette, fashion editor.*

Dec 1 — *Mr Nicholas Danine entertained a small party of friends at dinner yesterday evening. His guests included Mrs Gerald Jocelyn, her stepdaughter, Miss Katherine Jocelyn, and Mr Philip Leach.*

Dec 4 — *Among prominent people taking part in the historical pageant at the Third Empire Ball to be given Jan 8th for the benefit of Chinese war orphans, are Mrs Lawrence Devereux who will play the Empress Eugénie, Edgar Jocelyn who takes the part of Napoleon III, and his niece, Miss Katherine Jocelyn, who will appear as the beautiful Countess de Castiglione...*

Dec 12 — *Miss Lilian Hope will take the part of the Countess de Castiglione in the historical pageant to be given on Jan 8th for the benefit of Chinese war orphans. Miss Katherine*

Jocelyn, whose coming-out dance took place two days ago, has given up the part for reasons of health...

Basil shivered a little as he realised that Kitty was dead when that paragraph appeared in print. "*Reasons of health...*" But, of course, the moment Kitty disappeared Rhoda would cancel all immediate engagements.

He went upstairs to the magazine room. "Have you any magazines devoted to — er — fashion and society?"

The librarian brought him a number of highly glazed magazines, in which it was impossible to tell the articles from the advertisements. There were photographs of Kitty Jocelyn all through the spring and summer issues. A few paragraphs proclaimed her sojourn in Cannes and her arrival in America. But the first paragraphs of any length devoted to her had been published in November over the signature "Lowell Cabot":

According to all rumours, the Jocelyn ball next month will be something quite out of the ordinary...

Basil smiled grimly.

It will be Kitty Jocelyn's first real public appearance in this country. Those who saw her in Cannes last summer are prophesying that she will be the most beautiful debutante of the coming season. Kitty — her real name is Katherine, but everyone calls her Kitty — is tall and excessively slender. Her grey eyes are startlingly pale under black brows and lashes. Her hair is black; her skin the creamy tone of fresh-cut pith, which makes a perfect background for the famous Jocelyn pearls.

There was something peculiarly grisly about that present tense. But Basil ploughed on until he had read every published reference to Kitty Jocelyn that the library afforded. When he had finished, he sat still, watching the pigeons strutting in the paved yard outside.

One by one details fell neatly into place, like a process of crystallisation. What had been a shapeless, unorganised mass, was becoming a pattern. It was hard to realise that his own mind was doing the trick. It seemed as if the facts had begun to move and arrange themselves while he sat passive, watching them...

His body was tired by this time, but his mind refused to let him rest. He returned the pile of glossy fashion magazines and went out into the early winter twilight. He hailed a cruising taxi and gave the address of the Bureau of Records.

"I want to see the death certificate of Jane Jowett. She died last May."

In a few moments he was looking at a printed form filled in with rather untidy handwriting:

Cause of death: hyperpyrexia.
Contributory cause of death: patent nostrum containing hydroxy di-nitro-benzene 1, 2, 4.

Basil made a note of the doctor's name and took another taxi uptown to a private hospital. He sent in his card with a scribbled message to the house surgeon. A fussy, voluble little man came bustling into the anteroom. "Dr Willing? How do you do! I remember the case quite well. It had some most instructive features." He spoke with a certain pride. "I was fascinated by the sudden, board-like heat *rigor*, but there was no autopsy, because it was such a clear case. What is it you wish to know?"

"The trade name of the patent nostrum."

"What?" The house surgeon had been expecting a purely medical question. He looked at Basil curiously, then rang for his secretary and asked for a file.

"You don't read magazines, do you?" asked Basil.

"Magazines? Oh, yes! I'm a subscriber to *Biometrika* and *JAMA* and the *Lancet* and—"

The secretary returned with the file. The doctor adjusted his glasses and chuckled. "The names these fellows think up! Believe it or not, it was actually called Sveltis."

"The name Sveltis was not published in the newspapers at the time?"

"No." The doctor chuckled again. "The Sveltis Company saw to that!"

"And when the Jocelyn case appeared in the papers, it didn't occur to you to connect the two?"

The doctor was startled. "Good God, no! You don't mean — it couldn't be she was — murdered?"

Basil didn't wait for explanations. But it was nearly dark by the time he reached the too-exquisite offices of the De Luxe Advertising Agency. An onyx clock informed him that it was 4:45. A beautiful young man in a double-breasted waistcoat welcomed him with the relentless cordiality peculiar to salesmen and advertising men.

"When you arranged those endorsements of Kitty Jocelyn's did you deal with her personally?"

"The first time we got her address through a Paris dressmaking house. After that we always dealt with her personally. I say, you know this Jocelyn murder is making a lot of money for us!"

"How?"

"New contract with the Sveltis Company. They're spending fifty grand on an educational campaign, to counteract the adverse publicity."

"Did you say — 'educational'?"

"Well — you know what I mean."

"I'm afraid I do." Basil rose. A sudden thought occurred to him. "Did anyone else endorse Sveltis?"

"Oh, yes. Kitty Jocelyn was the first, but there were a dozen girls on the list altogether. Each one from a different part of the country."

"May I have a list for the district attorney?"

"Certainly. We're always delighted to co-operate with the authorities. But I do hope… I mean to say… I'm sure you'll understand that we don't want the name of our firm involved in anything the least bit — well — unpleasant, don't you know. We…"

The young man's voice trailed away. Basil was frowning at the list of names. There was one he recognised:

Boston — Isobel Archer.

"WHY ARE you so certain there will be another murder tonight?" Sobel's face was hidden in the shadow cast by his lighted desk lamp, but his voice was anxious. It would not be a popular prosecution — too much sympathy with the defendant.

"Because the conditions are exactly the same tonight as they were the night Kitty Jocelyn was murdered," explained Basil. "And criminals tend to repeat the same crime automatically under the same external conditions."

"But no sane criminal would repeat the same crime in the same way."

"Is there such a thing as a sane crime, or a sane criminal?" returned Basil. "Even when there's a logical motive, a criminal shows the tendency to repeat his crime in the same way indefinitely. You know as well as I do that professional criminals are such slaves of habit and tradition that the police learn to identify the individual criminal by the technique of his crime. That's *automatism* —a recognised symptom of mental debility. Poisoners show it particularly by using the same poison over and over again. We are dealing with a poisoner tonight. And there is no antidote for thermol."

"But I thought morphine—"

"Only when you take it in advance over a long period. If you take it for the first time after a fatal dose of thermol it doesn't do the slightest good."

"Then you should have warned the Archers!"

"I did. The moment I heard that Isobel Archer had endorsed Sveltis last spring, I telephoned Archer and tried to make him understand the danger she was facing. He finally promised to keep her from eating or drinking anything. But he wouldn't take any other precautions. He complained that my evidence was *only* psychological, and he has no use for modern psychology."

"The old fool!" Sobel rose. "The sooner we get to the Archers' the better. We'll pick up Foyle on the way."

The Inspector was not easily shocked, but Basil's story seemed to shake him. "I don't like this, doc," he muttered. "It's awful."

"It is," agreed Basil. "Most crimes are due to the failure of the individual to adapt himself to society. But this crime is due to the failure of society to fulfil its obligations to the individual."

25

END-PAPER

Isobel Archer sat at her dressing table studying the flower in her hair. Would it have been better a little more to the left? It was too late to change for the hairdresser had gone and she would not leave such an important decision to her maid. She was surprised to find that her hands were cold and trembling. It was absurd to care so much about the success of her coming-out party.

There was a tap on the door and Clélie came in. "Madame says she thinks it better for you not to have anything before the dance, mademoiselle."

"How silly! I always take black coffee before a party — and I must have it tonight."

"But Madame says—"

"Never mind Aunt Emily. I want it and I'm going to have it!"

Clélie shrugged and went downstairs to the kitchen. The coffee had been started in a small percolator before Mrs Archer told her that Isobel was not to eat or drink anything before the dance. Clélie thought the request unreasonable, and so did Mrs

Archer, judging by her embarrassed manner. It was the old general who had insisted on it so pompously without any explanation. Clélie had no respect for his intelligence and no hesitation about ignoring his orders.

She carried the tray up the back stairs and hurried along the corridor. When she tapped again on Isobel's door, it opened so suddenly she almost dropped the tray. But it wasn't Mrs Archer or the general. It was that old Mrs Jowett who had something to do with the arrangements for the dance at the Ritz this evening. Just what Clélie didn't know, or she might have wondered why Mrs Jowett was not at the hotel now.

"I'll take it, Clélie."

"But, madame, I might just as well—"

"I'll take it."

Clélie handed over the tray and went back to the kitchen.

"Here is your coffee, my dear," said Mrs Jowett. "Shall I pour it out?"

The question was rhetorical. Mrs Jowett had already poured the coffee and was coming toward Isobel with the cup in her hand.

Isobel took it, thinking, *The old girl looks really excited this evening. I should think she'd be used to coming-out parties by this time.*

Aloud she said, "Thank you. Is the gardenia in my hair all right? Or should it be a little more to the left?"

With flushed cheeks and brilliant eyes, Mrs Jowett watched the cup in Isobel's hand.

"Drink your coffee, dear — before it gets cold," she said, softly.

"Did you put in sugar?"

"Oh, yes. Two lumps."

Isobel smiled. "How nice of you to remember that I always

take two lumps! Some people think it's disgusting to put sugar in black coffee, but I don't care, it's too bitter if you don't."

They both heard steps and voices in the corridor. The door flew open, someone dashed at Isobel, and she cried aloud as she felt the hot coffee on her knees through her tulle skirt.

"Smelling-salts — without any smell." Basil disengaged the green glass phial from Mrs Jowett's fingers.

And then her face shivered and changed as a face reflected in water shivers and changes when the water is stirred. From her lips came words that are sometimes heard on the lips of conventional women under anaesthetic.

"I am glad I killed Kitty Jocelyn." She smoothed her skirt and smiled as she said it — the calm, motherly smile that had once made Inspector Foyle think of sunlit farm kitchens and freshly baked bread. She was dictating her confession to Duff — one of the strangest confessions in the records of the Police Department.

"My husband died years ago. Janey — my daughter — was all I had in the world. She was fifteen last May, and she was still as plump and chubby as a child. I knew she worried about it, but I didn't know she was taking Sveltis. She died in convulsions after four hours of torture. She had not taken more than the dose advised in the advertisements, but the doctors told me that the drug was capricious. I kept saying, 'Oh, Janey, why did you do it?' And she answered every time, 'I thought it must be safe if a girl like Kitty Jocelyn said so. She was taking it herself — she said so in the advertisement. And I wanted to look the way she did in the picture, slim and modern.'

"Kitty Jocelyn murdered my daughter just as surely as if she had thrust a knife in Janey's heart. But the newspapers glossed it over as 'accidental death from a patent reducing medicine' without mentioning Kitty or Sveltis by name. I consulted a lawyer and found that I could not institute criminal proceedings against either Kitty or the Sveltis Company. The most I could do was to bring a civil suit for damages. The Sveltis Company actually wrote me offering $20,000 damages. I refused.

"By the same mail, I received a letter from Rhoda Jocelyn, then in Europe, asking me to arrange for the debut of her step-daughter, Kitty, in New York the next winter.

"I was speaking the truth when I told Inspector Foyle that I refused Kitty as a client last May. I only lied about my motive for refusing. It was something of a shock when Rhoda and Kitty walked into my office this autumn and begged me to reconsider. That was the first time I ever saw Kitty and I realised then that she was beautiful — much more beautiful than Janey could ever have become — and I hated her. She was on the threshold of life and love. And Janey was dead. When Rhoda pleaded with me and said, 'Kitty must have her chance in life!' I smiled and thought of Janey who would never have life nor chance nor anything, because of that thoughtless, selfish, shallow girl. They were planning to spend $60,000 on Kitty's party. I had never had a twentieth of that money to spend on Janey all her life. I don't believe I showed my feel-ings even then. I merely said that I didn't care to bring out a girl who had been publicised as sensationally as Kitty.

"And then Kitty laughed and said, 'I suppose you're thinking of Sveltis, the "reducing method of the sophisticate"?'

"I was surprised at the calmness of my own voice as I answered, 'Perhaps I am. Do you really take Sveltis yourself?' She little knew how much depended on her answer. She laughed again and said, 'Of course not!' At that moment, I made up my mind that Kitty Jocelyn should die exactly as Janey had died — by the same poison, her beauty disfigured by the same yellow stain, suffering the same torture for the same long hours. Kitty should be hoisted with her own petard. It could never be proved in court beyond a reasonable doubt that she had not taken an accidental overdose of the stuff she had endorsed. Her death, like Janey's, should be attributed to the 'caprice' of the drug, and her doctors, like Janey should be ghoulishly enthusiastic about her 'instructive' symptoms.

"I only agreed to take charge of Kitty's debut because I knew that would give me a chance to poison her. I only accepted the double fee Rhoda offered because I knew I would need some explanation for having changed my mind about taking charge of Kitty's debut, if the police investigated her death.

"When Rhoda told me that Kitty had suffered from chronic malaria in Europe, I knew that Fate was on my side. After Janey's death, I read everything I could find about thermol and I knew that malaria victims were more susceptible to thermol poisoning than ordinary people. I bought a bottle of Sveltis outside the city limits. I used to assist my husband in his dispensary and I recognised the tablets as those triturate tablets that crumble so easily. I dissolved them in a little water so they would pour smoothly. Like most proprietary drugs, Sveltis is sweetened to make it palatable. There was no danger of Kitty noticing the bitter taste of thermol.

"For nearly six weeks I visualised myself slipping the poison into something Kitty was about to drink, until that daydream became more real than reality to me. My chance came at last the evening before the dance when we were drinking cocktails in the Murillo Room. The air was heavy with the scent of flowers. I complained of closeness and asked Gregg to open a window. That gave me a pretext for taking out the smelling-salts phial and carrying it un-stoppered. The green glass disguised the yellow of the Sveltis solution. Kitty was restless, wandering about the room, glass in hand. When Gregg announced Philip Leach, everyone turned to look at him and Kitty set down her glass three-quarters full. With one twist of my wrist, I emptied the contents of the phial into it. I think it was because I was acting out a daydream that I was able to do it with such swiftness and dexterity. It was like doing something I had practiced for a long time. There was little sense of volition. I watched her drink with the keenest pleasure. She was so unconscious of what was in store for her!

"It came to me then in a blinding flash that it was my duty to poison all the girls who has endorsed Sveltis. Most the of the people who were killed or injured through taking Sveltis were so obscure the newspapers devoted little space to their fate and didn't even mention Sveltis by name. But if all these publicised girls, who had endorsed Sveltis, were to die of thermol poisoning one by one, the newspapers would have to print everything about it, and that would ruin the Sveltis Company, and drive Sveltis from the market. In each case it would be difficult for the police to prove murder, because it would be difficult to prove legally that these girls who were advertised as taking Sveltis never actually touched it and could not have died from accidental overdoses. Kitty was the only one Janey had mentioned by name — indeed Janey died before the other endorsements appeared. But they were all doing as much harm to other people as Kitty had done to Janey.

"Ann Claude's impersonation of Kitty at the dance deceived me completely. I felt no surprise at seeing Kitty alive; I thought Pasquale's mistake in drinking half the poisoned cocktail had saved her from a fatal dose. I had no idea I had succeeded in murdering Kitty until her death was announced in the papers.

"During my interview with Inspector Foyle, I played my part with all the skill at my command, and I still don't see what I can have said or done to rouse suspicion. Of course, I lied when I said I was afraid the Jocelyn murder would ruin me professionally. What did I care for such a profession as mine? It was Janey I worked for — Janey I lived for — and when she died something in me died with her."

"SHE GAVE HERSELF AWAY," Basil explained to Archer, as once again they sat before the fire in Basil's living room. "You remember how she signed her deposition with the name *Catharine Jocelyn* in place of her own — *Caroline Jowett*?"

"I thought that was only a blunder!"

"A blunder has convicted more than one criminal, as I told Foyle early in the case. Hans Gross gives an example similar to Mrs Jowett — a woman who was so excited she could not remember the name of a man who had attacked her. But when she signed her statement, she wrote a man's name instead of her own — quite unconsciously. The police looked up the man and found evidence proving him guilty."

"But Mrs Jowett was herself guilty and she signed the name of her victim!" objected Archer.

"Exactly. And in the course of that first blunder, she made two other blunders — two mistakes in spelling. Kitty's full, Christian name can be spelled in four ways — *Katherine* or *Katharine*, and *Catherine* or *Catharine*. Kitty spelled it with a *K* and an *e* — *Katherine*. All the letters and bills Foyle found in her desk were addressed to *Katherine Jocelyn* and that was the signature on the uncashed cheque in her cheque book. But when Mrs Jowett signed Kitty's name by mistake she spelled it with a *C* and an *a* — *Catharine*.

"I noticed that double error in spelling one day when I was going over the file of the case in Foyle's office. I believed there was some psychological reason for such a triple blunder, because I accept the Freudian hypothesis that no individual human act is ever 'accidental'.

"Mrs Jowett was familiar with the right spelling of Kitty's name for it was under her supervision that paragraphs about Kitty were prepared for the press, and the right spelling — *Katherine* — was used in these. I verified that at the public library. Every published reference to Kitty I could find spelled her name *Katherine* — with just one exception. In the Sveltis advertisement Kitty herself, or the printer, had blundered — why we will never know — and Kitty's endorsement of Sveltis was signed just as Mrs Jowett signed her statement — *Catharine Jocelyn*, with a *C* and an *a*. Yet Mrs Jowett was telling the truth when she said she had nothing to do with the arrangements for that endorsement. I verified that through the De Luxe Advertising Agency.

"Could it be coincidence that she had made the same errors in spelling Kitty's name that occurred in the Sveltis advertisement and nowhere else? Had there been only one error I might have thought so. But two errors, both corresponding to the two in the Sveltis endorsement, seemed too specific to be coincidence. Many a conscious plagiarist has been convicted because he unwittingly repeated the errors in the thing he plagiarised.

"If this were not coincidence, it not only meant that Mrs Jowett was familiar with the Sveltis advertisements. It also meant that she had seen the particular advertisement which carried Kitty's endorsement. And that was something she had gone out of her way to deny when Foyle suggested it to her.

"I could see only one explanation — she was lying. Nothing is more likely to cause a blunder than a lie. When she denied having seen Kitty's Sveltis endorsement, her treacherous hand gave her away by promptly writing Kitty's name in place of her own and *misspelling it exactly as it was misspelled in the Sveltis endorsement*. Her conscious was using the only way it could use — the symbolic way — to tell us that she was lying. A clear case of unconscious confession.

"But why had she lied? Was it one of those unnecessary lies people tell when they are under suspicion — like Edgar Jocelyn's pretence that he had never heard of thermol? Or was she the murderer, and was her knowledge of Kitty's Sveltis endorsement, which she had denied, one link in a possible chain of evidence against her? Was her conscience trying to tell us that, too, in its roundabout way?

"*Impossible!* I thought at first. *You don't develop a deliberately murderous hatred for someone you've only known six weeks and only seen a few times in those six weeks*. The Homicide Squad had been unable to trace any previous acquaintance between Mrs Jowett and Kitty Jocelyn. They had never even seen each other until Kitty and her stepmother reached New York a few weeks ago.

"And then a new idea came to me. It was not necessary to trace any previous acquaintance between Kitty and her murderer in order to establish a motive for the murder, for Kitty was not a private citizen. Thanks to Rhoda and the De Luxe Advertising Agency she was a public character, and therefore she could make enemies in her *public capacity*, whom she had never seen or known *personally*.

"I tried to reduce the problem to Schoenfeld's formula: Kitty was the stimulus — the murder was the reaction. Who would react to that stimulus with murder?

"Pretty obvious when you put it that way, isn't it? No one profited financially by Kitty's death. She was described by

Ann as generous, easy-going, indulgent to others as to herself. In all our delving into her history, we found only one thing she had ever done that could endanger the welfare of others — her dishonest endorsement of a patent medicine containing a drug as dangerous as thermol. Kitty's murderer must be someone who had suffered through that endorsement. In that case, the murderer might instinctively try to conceal the motive by denying all knowledge of the endorsement. Mrs Jowett was the one suspect who had done that.

"Only someone who was immature, mentally or actually, would be taken in by the Sveltis advertisements. In Mrs Jowett's office, there was a photograph of a noticeably plump girl about fifteen — her daughter Jane, who had died last May, the same month that Kitty's Sveltis endorsement appeared in the magazines. It had not occurred to any of us before that there might be a connection between Jane Jowett and Kitty, for Jane died long before Kitty reached this country and met Mrs Jowett.

"I owe a great deal to Foyle for the shrewd observations he made during his first visit to Mrs Jowett's office. He noticed the smelling-salts phial that could be used so easily to carry poison. He noticed the occasional slight twitching of her eyelid which suggested that her nerves and mind were not in an entirely healthy state. He described her as *motherly* — the psychological type most likely to avenge a wrong against the immature.

"Because we live in a society based largely on the funda-mental male emotions, greed and lust, we are apt to think of murder as something that occurs only when one of these two emotions is thwarted. But in the female there was, originally, a third emotion, equally impulsive, and so fundamental that it was the basis of many primitive social organisations. This maternal instinct is atrophied in many civilised women. But even today you occasionally find women like Mrs Jowett, who are mothers first and everything else afterward. When you do, outraged maternal love is just as likely to lead to hate, revenge and murder as thwarted lust or greed. The primitive mother, avenging her young, is none the less sadic, because she is unselfish.

"And Mrs Jowett was primitive. Had she been more complex, she would have been more aware of the social and legal implications of Jane's death, and that might have made her personal feeling less morbid. But she had no mind for abstractions. Kitty Jocelyn was a concrete, human object for hatred, which Mrs Jowett's mind could grasp. Revenge replaced her daughter as her object in life. You recall how she said, 'Janey was all I had'? That had a lot to do with the murder. Most nervous breakdowns occur when people put all their eggs in one basket, and something happens to the basket.

"I think this unhappy case demonstrates the value of psychology in criminal investigation. A blunder is the one form of clue a criminal can neither remove, conceal nor destroy — the one clue that is entirely beyond his conscious control. In Mrs Jowett's case, her slip of the pen was the only direct indication of her guilt we had. There were no material clues against her. And it was only by reducing the problem to Schoenfeld's formula that I was able to isolate her motive from the mass of other facts in the case."

After Archer had gone, Basil sat alone before the fire so long that Juniper became worried.

"Anything I can do for you at all, Doctor Willing, sir?" he ventured at last.

Basil roused himself.

"Yes — never let me hear the word Sveltis again! And turn on the radio — see if you can get that Stravinsky concert."

There was a howl of static, and then came a clear, resonant voice:

"...you have just been listening to Stravinsky's 'Fire Bird' through the courtesy of Sveltis, the reducing method of the sophisticate. Science says..."

THE MAN IN THE MOONLIGHT

A DR BASIL WILLING MYSTERY

HELEN MCCLOY

1

EXPLOSION

The day Dr Konradi was murdered dawned clear and windy — a fragrant spring day with a cool breeze.

Patrick Foyle sat on the campus of Yorkville University, looking at a sheaf of printed bulletins the Dean had given him.

Assistant Professor Julian Salt — primitive cultures of Mexico…

Professor Albert Feng Lo — concepts of abnormality…

Professor Raymond Prickett — conditioned response and remote association…

Foyle's pipe was drawing evenly. The lawn at his feet sloped down to the East River where the water reflected the innocent blue of the sky. It was hard to realise that this was as much a part of New York as Police Headquarters and General Sessions. Here, if anywhere, his boy would hear no talk of crooks or graft or murder. Then Foyle noticed the piece of paper.

A bit of rubbish would not have drawn his attention in a public park. But here, where not a single peanut shell or paper bag disturbed the neatness of gravel path and privet hedge, a stray bit of paper could not escape notice. It floated before the wind like a kite, twisting, rising and falling, until it came to rest on the grass. He rose, but the wind snatched the paper away. Clenching his pipe stem between his teeth he charged after it and this time the wind let it lie. He returned to his bench and smoothed the paper on his knee. It was a carbon copy of a typewritten note. It began abruptly without date, address or salutation and ended in the middle of a sentence:

I take pleasure in informing you that you have been chosen as murderer for Group No. 1. Please follow these instructions with as great exactness as possible.

You will enter Southerland Hall from the east entrance just as the library clock is striking the hour of eight (8:00) in the evening of May 4 (Saturday). You must be out of the building by eight forty-five (8:45). This, however, will give you ample time for the murder.

You must be as quiet as possible and be careful not to show a light as you might attract the attention of the night watchman. If you are not out of the building by eight forty-five (8:45) you will find yourself in a very peculiar and unpleasant situation.

Once inside Southerland Hall, you will proceed directly to the laboratory, where...

"You've found it!"

Foyle looked up. A man was standing on the path — a man

without hat or overcoat. His face was the saddest Foyle had ever seen.

"I've lost some papers." He spoke with a faintly foreign intonation. "I saw you run after that paper in the wind. I thought — perhaps—"

"What sort of papers have you lost?"

"Notes on chemical experiments. I doubt if you'd understand them. They're in German and technical."

"Well, I don't understand this." Foyle grinned as he held out the paper he had found. "Do you?"

The man crossed the grass to the bench with a quick, resolute step. His age seemed between 35 and 40. Yet the hand that took the paper trembled slightly and Foyle noticed a few white hairs vivid against the dark head in the sunlight His grave, aquiline profile would have graced a coin.

"Just a gag," said Foyle. "But it gave me a turn. College boys sure do have queer ideas of what's funny."

The man lifted unsmiling eyes. "How do you know it is just a — gag?"

"What else could it be? If anything like that were meant seriously, it would be in code. Besides—a real killer never uses the word *murder.* Political murderers call it *direct action* or *liquidation.* Husbands and wives call it *avenging honour* or *defending the sanctity of the home.* Even gangsters don't murder you—they rub you out or bump you off. Whether a murderer is speaking French or German or Choctaw, he steers clear of plain words like *kill* or *murder*."

"You seem familiar with murder and murderers."

"I'm a police officer." Foyle displayed his gold badge. "Assistant Chief Inspector commanding the Detective Division. I came here to see the Dean about sending my eldest boy to Yorkville. I never had a chance to go to college myself, but I want him to go. My name's Foyle — Patrick Foyle."

"And mine is Franz Konradi."

The name meant nothing to Foyle.

"As a police officer you believe this letter could not have been written by one of your American gangsters?"

Foyle looked at him suspiciously, but there was no hint of humour in those somber eyes. "I don't know just where you come from, but I guess you haven't been over here very long. Gangsters don't say please. And they don't threaten people with 'very peculiar and unpleasant situations'. Neither do they make carbon copies of their correspondence."

Konradi stood twisting the letter in long fingers.

"What's it got to do with you?" asked Foyle.

"I believe my laboratory is the only one in Southerland Hall — I know I am the only chemist with rooms in that building. And this is Saturday, May 4."

"Then it looks like somebody's ribbing you."

"Ribbing?"

"Playing a joke on you."

"But my colleagues aren't given to joking, and I doubt if any student would enter my laboratory uninvited. I'm a research professor in biological chemistry. Everyone knows I'm engaged in experiments that can't be interrupted."

Foyle permitted himself another grin. "I don't know about Europe, but over here our students go for gags in a big way. And nobody's safe — not even research professors in biological chemistry. Maybe this is part of a fancy initiation into some fraternity."

"I only hope you're right." Konradi dismissed the subject with a fatalistic shrug. "I suppose I've reached that unenviable state of mind where every molehill seems a mountain and every pin dropping sounds like an explosion—" The sonorous note of a bell cut him short. He started violently. "Only the library clock. You see—" He held out a hand that was still shaking. "I've lost my nerve. Courage is a curious thing, isn't it? Sometimes I think it is only the active form of fear. There's no chemical difference between fear and rage. The only difference is in conduct—" He drew fingertips across his forehead as if brushing aside a veil. "I think I have been working too hard. I must take a rest — a long rest — soon." His eyes were on the river and he seemed to have forgotten Foyle.

"If I were you, I'd give this Southerland Hall a wide berth at eight o'clock."

Konradi's eyes came back to Foyle. "I shall. But one thing puzzles me. How do they expect to get in? The laboratory doors are always locked when I'm not there and the windows are made of unbreakable glass."

"Has anyone a key besides you?"

"The Dean and the janitor. And my secretary."

"Well, I don't suppose the Dean or the janitor are in this. What about your secretary?"

"Gisela?" Konradi frowned like a man pricked with sudden, unwelcome doubt. "It's impossible. She would never —" He left the sentence unfinished.

Foyle studied him curiously. "If this has you really worried, why don't you see the Dean? Isn't he in charge of discipline?"

"I don't believe I'll trouble Dr Lysaght about it." Konradi handed the letter back to Foyle. "One must not be what you call, in English, a spoil-sport."

He smiled for the first time and even his smile was sad. Then he said something so startling that Foyle was at a loss for a reply.

"If anything should happen this evening, I want you to remember one thing: I am just finishing important research and nothing would induce me to commit suicide while it is still pending. Please understand that, Herr Inspector, and remember it. No matter what happens — no matter what seems to happen — I shall not commit suicide." He bowed with a hint of alien formality and turned away.

Speechless, Foyle watched the tall figure with its resolute stride decrease among the lengthening shadows. The sun was setting behind the trees. Suddenly, the wind seemed chill and unfriendly. In spite of his overcoat, the Inspector shivered as he rose and walked toward the library. Konradi had left so much unsaid. It was only natural he did not confide in a chance acquaintance. But why wouldn't he confide in the Dean?

Foyle met no one on the campus. The gravel path led him into a big, cobblestoned quadrangle bounded by the campus and three buildings. On his left stood the great, grey library parallel with the East River. Opposite him, to the South, was a chapel. To the West, facing the library, stood a three-storied brick building, windows regimented as those of a jail. The only sounds that disturbed the academic peace were the cooing of pigeons and the splashing of a fountain in the centre of the quadrangle.

The Inspector compared his watch with the library clock and saw that the clock was one minute faster. Carefully he set his watch at 5:29 to coincide exactly with the clock. He had no plan of action yet. He still believed the letter was a sophomoric hoax. But it sounded like a rather morbid hoax and he had a vague feeling that something ought to be done about it. He started to walk across the quadrangle to a path that led south-west, between the chapel and the brick building. As he drew near the building, he noticed an inscription engraved on the stone above the main entrance:

1924.

SOUTHERLAND HALL.

Erected by Malcolm Southerland, AB.

Of the Class of 1915

and Trustee of Yorkville University.

Foyle studied the east entrance of Southerland Hall with interest. There was plenty of space around the building planted with trees and shrubs. To the Inspector trees and shrubs meant only one thing — cover. He saw at once that the "murderer for Group No. 1" would have all the cover he needed to approach Southerland Hall unobserved.

The Inspector frowned. And just then the academic peace was shattered by a pistol shot.

WANT TO DISCOVER MORE UNCROWNED QUEENS OF CRIME?

SIGN UP TO OUR CRIME CLASSICS NEWSLETTER TO DISCOVER NEW GOLDEN AGE CRIME, RECEIVE EXCLUSIVE CONTENT, AND NEVER-BEFORE PUBLISHED SHORT STORIES, ALL FOR FREE.

FROM THE BELOVED GREATS OF THE GOLDEN AGE TO THE FORGOTTEN GEMS, BEST-KEPT-SECRETS, AND BRAND NEW DISCOVERIES, WE'RE DEVOTED TO CLASSIC CRIME.

IF YOU SIGN UP TODAY, YOU'LL GET:

1. A FREE NOVEL FROM OUR CLASSIC CRIME COLLECTION;

2. EXCLUSIVE INSIGHTS INTO CLASSIC NOVELS AND THEIR AUTHORS; AND,

3. THE CHANCE TO GET COPIES IN ADVANCE OF PUBLICATION.

INTERESTED?

IT TAKES LESS THAN A MINUTE TO SIGN UP, JUST HEAD TO

WWW.CRIMECLASSICS.CO.UK

AND YOUR EBOOK WILL BE SENT TO YOU.

facebook.com/crimeclassics
twitter.com/crimeclassics

Printed in Great Britain
by Amazon